For Samuel

1.

The Journey Begins

She was running through the night, clutching the small, precious bundle under her cloak tightly to her chest. It was deathly quiet, the only audible sound coming from the flickering streetlamps as they hummed and struggled into life. Her breath caught in her throat, a ball of burning exhaustion rising in her chest. She had been running for what felt like hours, but there was no time to stop and rest. As she sprinted down the street, she caught glimpses of the houses left desolate and empty, abandoned by their owners in fits of panic and hysteria. Cars were parked diagonally across driveways, their doors flung open, awaiting owners that would never return. Dustbins had been overturned and rubbish littered the street as far as the eye could see. Front doors had been left ajar, revealing eerily lit hallways. She wondered how much longer it would be until the power went out altogether, plunging Earth into a permanent darkness.

She turned the corner and continued to flee down another deserted road. The smell of the salt and seawater filling her nostrils and telling her that she was getting closer. She reached a metal sign cemented into the ground, twisted and warped from the heat of a passing solar flare. The top had come askew, but she could still make out the white lettering against the faded green background informing her that Pentewan train station was half a mile to the left.

Before she moved off, she peered into her cloak to check that her journey so far had not disturbed her cargo. Satisfied that all was well, she began to walk, continuing down another derelict street, the flickering lights taunting her as she went. She closed her eyes to block out her surroundings. For just one moment, she imagined that she was walking down the street on a perfectly ordinary evening, perhaps going to meet friends or returning home after a hard day's work. She felt the echo of excitement rise inside of her as the sound of faint laughter filled her head, conjured somewhere from the depths of her memories from a time when normality still existed. The Wars on Earth, as they were collectively referred to, had broken out when she was barely a teenager and she struggled to remember a time when conflict and strife hadn't dominated the day-to-day life of every citizen on Earth. The poverty and lack of resources that had ensued after the numerous wars had resulted in the rise of gangs and looters, causing the fight for survival to move from the battlefield and onto the streets. Once the peace of a mundane life had gone, nothing had ever been the same again.

Her thoughts had clouded her vision, but her legs had taken her to the right location. She arrived at the decrepit train station, flinching slightly at its ghostly appearance in the dark. She pulled a battered pocket watch from her cloak, a prized relic from the old days that she had found on her travels, and clicked it open to read the time, her cold breath illuminated in the clock's glowing face. It was 11:40 p.m., which meant her train was due any second. Terrified she might have missed it, she began scanning the inky black tracks desperately, relief spreading through her body as two headlights pinpricked the horizon.

The silver metallic train pulled up and halted to a silent stop. Two of its doors opened smoothly, splitting in the middle and coming away so that they blended with the side of the carriage. Without hesitating, she stepped aboard, moving quietly through the dimly lit compartments. She didn't need a ticket. There was no driver, no conductors and no ticket inspectors. They had all gone. The magnetic system that ran the trains had been left on, with nobody bothering to switch them off. The trains continued to run, picking up no one and taking them to nowhere. Occasionally, though, they had come in useful, allowing her to move about the country undetected as she had made her vital journey.

The seats were laid back in their reclining position, ready to take tired commuters into the night. A single coffee cup sat upright on one of the cold, white tables that connected one pair of seats to the other. She wondered how long it had been sat there for and under what circumstances it had been abandoned. The faint smell of sweat lingered in the air, almost completely masked by the steely odour of metal that emanated from the train's walls. At the head of the carriage was an interactive screen, blinking slightly from years of damage and neglect. She walked over to it and activated it with a touch of her finger and was greeted by a clinical female voice as the screen sprung to life.

"Welcome to the I-Train," the voice said. "The pioneering way to travel brought to you exclusively by The Interactive-Tech Company."

She selected the main menu, bringing up a display that featured information on the journey. A small icon of a train moved along a virtual winding road, heading towards Charlestown, Cornwall which was marked by a large, red circle. Elsie pressed on the screen and the estimated time of arrival appeared before her, letting her know that she had only fifteen minutes before she would reach her destination.

She swallowed, the fear of failure creeping into her mind like an unwanted pest. She was yet to come up with a proper plan of action to take when she arrived at her journey's end, and she had so little time to prepare. She was about to sit down and begin detailing a plot with all the information she had gathered so far, when a noise from the next carriage along startled her, causing her to stagger backwards.

She paused for a moment, unsure whether she should run and hide, but instinct told her not to be afraid. Boldly, she pressed her hand to the small, sensor by the side of the door that divided the compartments, causing it to slide open. As she stepped across the carriage's threshold, she was greeted by a blonde-haired woman, sitting on a rear-facing seat, a tartan push-trolley sat between her legs. She was leaning forward on its handle, smiling coyly up at her new visitor. A middle-aged man sat hunched on the floor opposite her, his legs drawn up to his chest and his arms wrapped protectively around his body. He was so thin that he was almost skeletal. His sunken eyes stared fixated on the floor and his mouth hung open, forming whispered words that only he could understand.

"Hello, love," the woman said cheerfully. "Come and take a seat."

Elsie hesitated, glancing over at the man with slight alarm. The woman followed her gaze.

"Oh, don't worry about him, he's harmless," she smiled.

Warily, Elsie moved through the carriage and sat on one of the forward-facing seats, swinging her body around carefully so that she could see the other woman.

"The name's Grace," the woman grinned toothlessly. She didn't look particularly old, but her face was haggard, prematurely aged by hardship and sorrow.

"Elsie," she replied. She wasn't sure why, but she trusted Grace. It was clear that she had suffered great stress and loss and that somehow gave them a common ground to stand upon.

"I didn't expect to see anyone on these trains," Grace said after a moment. Her accent was hard and callous. Wherever she had grown up had left a lasting impression on her inflexion.

"Neither did I," Elsie replied.

"We're going to see them off, Bernard and me," Grace continued, gesturing to the man. He did not seem to recognise the sound of his own name and continued gawking, wide-eyed at the floor.

"Them?" Elsie asked.

"You know who I'm talking about," Grace hissed. "Those who are dearly departing on the Mayfly. I reckon we ought to give them a great send off. Let them know how sorely they'll be missed. Bunch of fools!"

She spat on the floor and wiped her mouth with the back of her hand. There was a fury resonating from her eyes that Elsie had never seen in another human being.

"They think they've got it all planned out," Grace ranted. "Leaving us less important people behind to rot like pieces of rubbish while they fly off to start their new world. Well, they're on a fool's mission anyway. Mark my words they are. There is more to this than any of those stuck-up fools can begin to get their tiny minds around."

Her eyes flashed with a passion that Elsie could only interpret as excitement.

"Are you talking about the conspiracy theories?" Elsie asked, beginning to feel she was trapped on the train with a madwoman.

"You've heard them too?" Grace said, her voice ragged with enthusiasm.

"Yes, I have," Elsie replied flatly, her heart twinging with pain as she recalled the fate of the last person she had known to believe in the theories.

5

The bundle beneath Elsie's cloak began to wriggle, causing the fabric to rearrange itself suspiciously.

"What have you got there?" Grace asked, her beady eyes detecting the movement.

"It's nothing," Elsie said quickly, stealing a glance through the cloak's neck hole.

"Are you sure about that?" Grace pressed her as a soft cooing noise emitted from beneath the swathes of cloth.

Elsie said nothing, she knew her secret was out but had no desire to discuss the matter. The true magnitude of what she would lose if she failed to make it aboard The Mayfly was too terrible for her to acknowledge out loud. Grace seemed to understand this, continuing to speak without receiving a response.

"My husband left me, you know," she informed Elsie. "We were married fifteen years. He had another son by his first wife. It caused a lot of problems between us. I can't have children, you see, and I resented the boy for existing."

Elsie nodded, unsure how best to respond to such a personal revelation.

"Anyway, his boy's mum died. She was killed by looters in one of the Cities. Everything changed after that. My husband and I had both agreed we would stay on Earth come the day of The Split, whatever that meant. He believed in the theories too, you see. Had real evidence for them as well. But when he took his boy in, he changed his mind. Suddenly he was applying for The Mayfly, saying he had to give his son a chance of living. I told him I wasn't going, no matter what, but he left anyway. Have you any idea how bad that feels? Being left to suffer and die by the one person who's supposed to love and protect you?" she asked. The question was rhetorical, but it brought a fresh wave of pain to the surface of Elsie's mind.

"I do actually," she said. Grace regarded her shrewdly, a moment of silent understanding passing between them.

"Well then," she nodded. "You know why I have to go and see them leave for myself. It's not just humans on that ship, you know. I've heard whispers"

Elsie nodded but said no more on the subject. She was well aware of the conspiracy theory Grace was referring to and didn't think it wise to voice her harsh opinions on the matter. The only thing which surprised her was how wide-spread the theory seemed to have become. Stupidly, she had assumed she was among the only few people to have heard it.

"What happened to him?" Elsie changed the subject, regarding Bernard with concern.

"Him? His family abandoned him. His parents have been dead a long while, mind, as most of ours have. He had a sister, though, but she married some rich bloke, got her and her kids a place on board and left him here to rot. Apparently, there was "no room" for him. Truth is I think she was ashamed. He doesn't have any skills, you see, or money so he's of "no use" to The Mayfly or the continuation of our species," Grace explained with disgust.

"That's terrible..." Elsie said after a moment. Grace nodded curtly. Whatever pity she had had for Bernard's seemed to have been doused by the overpowering anger she felt towards all those leaving after The Split.

"What about you then?" Grace asked brazenly. "You got any nearest and dearest? Other than the obvious," she nodded at Elsie's cloak.

The question hit Elsie like a knife to the throat. She felt her chest closing in on itself in a futile attempt to cushion the pain to her heart that the words had caused her. She closed her eyes and bore the agony, letting it peak to an unbearable torment before it subsided, allowing her to breathe once again.

"All dead," she said thickly, hoping that would be enough to deter Grace from pressing her any further.

"They been gone a long time?"

"Years," Elsie lied.

Her parents were long dead it was true, but it wasn't the discussion of their absence that was causing her to silently crumble into dust. She could not even think of her more recent loss, for fear the pain would rip through her body and destroy her completely.

Grace seemed to accept this response and the conversation drifted into a comfortable silence. Elsie allowed herself to be lulled into pleasant numbness, concentrating on the whirring sound of the train's mechanism as it pulled them forward into the night. Every so often, she stole a fleeting glance at Bernard, who hadn't moved or changed his posture the entire time she had been in the carriage. She wondered what would happen to him and Grace after The Split, fighting the panicked thought that she might still be on Earth to find out.

The time fell away like raindrops sliding off soft skin and soon enough the robotic, female voice was announcing that they had almost reached Charlestown. Grace rose to her feet immediately, heaving a dazed Bernard into a slumped standing position beside her.

"Well, "she said, regarding Elsie with a look of comradery. "Good luck to you, love. We're heading up the hills to get a good view of them leaving. If you need to, you can find us up there."

Elsie attempted a smile, causing Grace's previously hardened expression to be abducted by unconcealed pity. She raised two fingers to her head in a strange sort of salute and then turned to face the steel doors of the train, which was now slowing to a standstill. With one final lurch, they became stationary, the doors sliding open in one swift movement. Without looking back, Grace disembarked with surprising elegance, dragging Bernard limply behind her. They disappeared into the night. Suddenly, everything was quiet.

Mustering all the courage she could find, Elsie stepped onto the platform. Immediately, she was hit by two powerful sensations. The first was the sharp, crisp air that engulfed her body the moment the train doors shut behind her. It was a deeper degree of cold than she had felt earlier in the evening, and she clutched her arms around her travelling cloak protectively, drawing in as much heat as she could from her body. The second was the bittersweet sting of nostalgia as she took in the familiar appearance of Charlestown, the place that had made her heart leap with joy as a child.

She could still picture it now. Her mother curled up on the corner armchair in their holiday cottage, engrossed in a novel on her I-Reader, her father popping in and out from cooking in the kitchen to sing silly songs and take requests. Elsie would be sat on the window ledge, her bare feet swinging freely as she relished the relief of the cool evening air after a startlingly hot summers day. Her parents would put the 3D television on for her to keep her entertained while they went about their various tasks, but she sat with her back to it, ignoring its persistent noise as she stared out across the moon-bathed hills, that rose and fell all the way to the silent black sea beyond.

Shaking these thoughts from her mind, she made her way to the green, perforated steps that would lead her out of the train station and ascended, quickly reaching the street above. The shops and houses that flanked the road had once been bustling with tourists and cheerful residents but were now haunted by echoes of voices and laughter. She walked past the Tall Ships sat bobbing gently in the bay, their decaying masts rising gloomily out of the mist. She rounded the final corner that would lead her to the beach and stopped still, her feet finding balance on the pebbled shore. She had arrived.

2.

The Mayfly

Elsie had heard many stories about the Mayfly, but nothing could have prepared her for seeing it in the flesh. The spacecraft was gargantuan, its metal frame stretching higher than the eye could see. It rested delicately upon the water, the sheer mass of it covering the entirety of the ocean. It's dark titanium sides ran down the coastline, attached to the shore by open walkways that were manned by intimidating guards. People were still queuing across the beach, waiting anxiously to board in the remaining minutes before take-off.

Elsie gulped and began to move towards the spacecraft with leaden legs. Somehow, she had to get past the guards and onto the Mayfly without being exposed. She had never received formal permission from the Government to board. All the Mayfly's passengers were required to either have a special skill that could be used to rebuild civilisation or be rich enough to be allowed to board from status, although the latter was kept secret from the general public. The applications had been rigorous and had taken up to six months to be processed. It had been an agonising wait and she had waited every day with baited breath, wondering if she would be delivered a message of safety or of doom. Despite all her hard work studying at College, her request to board the ship had been denied with no explanation. All she had to cling onto now was hope. She had found the location of the Mayfly by following whispers on the streets and the tales of fellow travellers, but there was no way to guarantee that she would successfully make it aboard.

She reached the cobbled beach and made her way towards the nearest queue, which had dwindled into a number of thirty people or so. She slipped inconspicuously to the back of the line behind a middle-aged married couple, who were chattering among themselves about what lay beyond the giant metal doors in front of them.

"I heard the Mayfly has its own water park and multiplex cinema," the man told his wife. "Apparently, all the luxury apartments have their own coffee machines too!"

"Honestly, Jared you shouldn't listen to ridiculous gossip. How on Earth would they be able to make coffee in Space?" she replied with a roll of her eyes.

"It's true, I'm telling you!" the man named Jared insisted. "Colin from next door said his brother is part of the team who make all the food and drink on board. They use some sort of cloning procedure to replicate organic food. All they need is one coffee bean from Earth and they can use it to make thousands of pots of coffee."

"Well, I certainly hope you're right. I'm not sure I could handle many early mornings with you without a cup of coffee," his wife scathed. Elsie knew immediately that they must be from one of the gated wealthier communities which had guards protecting them and the best pick of resources delivered to their door for an exceptionally high fee. To still be worrying about something as insignificant as coffee after all the devastation that had ravaged Earth for the past decade was unthinkable to Elsie.

The line moved forwards and the woman in front drew her damask cloak around herself. She itched ahead with her husband, the moonlight illuminating the taught tweed patches on his overcoat. Elsie followed them closely, trying to stay silent so as not to draw any attention to herself. The woman began looking around wistfully, her arms folded against the wind. She had pulled her scarf over her mouth to keep out the cold, distorting her voice so that her husband could no longer hear her.

"All the coffee in the world won't make it Earth though," she muttered, glancing at the Mayfly with disdain.

Elsie stood on her tiptoes, vying to get a glimpse past the gruff guards who were blocking the entrance to the Mayfly. Elsie counted ten of them, checking the prospective passengers thoroughly before they allowed them to enter. Soon it would be her turn. She felt sick. She was sure her legs would disappear at any moment and she would collapse loudly onto the floor. She tried to distract herself, looking up towards the beautiful velvet sky with hundreds of stars visible across its dark canopy. They twinkled majestically, their shiny light winking at her from across the galaxy. This would be the last time she ever saw the Earth's sky, regardless of whether she was successful in her mission or not. No matter her own fate, she was determined that she would save her son, whatever it took.

He had been sound asleep for the entire journey, the motion of her movement lulling him further into the sweet ignorance of his dreams. She peered down to look at his peaceful face. He was only a few months old and had no idea of the suffering and torment that had passed in his short life. It was her dream that he would never know the pain she had felt. Even if she was not allowed on board, she would plead with the guards to take her innocent son. There was no way she was going to let him die on the disease-ridden Earth.

She closed her eyes and thought of Austin. If she was going to die tonight, that meant she would see him soon. She imagined him greeting her and the two of them sharing a joke. She terribly missed the way he used to laugh, his head tipped back, his eyes closed in hysteria as a loud and infectious noise burst from within him. She was pleased by her ability to so accurately conjure him in her mind, even after spending months trying to erase his image from her brain. Despite his final act of betrayal, she found that thinking of him still brought her great comfort, particularly in what she was beginning to feel certain would be the final moments of her life.

Reluctantly, she opened her eyes to re-join reality and found that the woman in front had been staring at her most curiously. She gave her best apologetic smile, hoping that she wouldn't fear her insane and alert the guards. She was just about to turn to her husband and say something when a stern voice from ahead distracted her.

"Next!" it called. They were at the front of the line. As soon as one of the guards finished with their passengers, Elsie would be next. She desperately scoured the reaches of her mind for something clever to say when questioned but found she could think of nothing. All too soon, she was called ahead.

"Ma'am" a guard to her left called, motioning her forwards. She reached the Mayfly's entrance and stood perfectly still, awaiting his next instruction with a sense of dread.

"Present your fingers please Ma'am," he told her, holding up a DNA scanner. Elsie sized him up. He was tall and stocky. The lines around his eyes and mouth placed him in around his mid-forties. He had scars on the back of his hands and across his face from years spent in service. One of his eyes was discoloured from a blunt trauma and he had no emotion in his face whatsoever. His body language was indifferent, his gaze unseeing. He was a man who was simply doing his job. Elsie could tell that there was no way begging was going to work on him.

"Your fingers, please Ma'am," he prompted her. Unsure what to do, she pulled her arms out of her cloak, careful not to disturb her son. She delicately placed her hands on the screen of his scanner. A whirring noise and a blue light indicated that the reading of her fingerprints was taking place. After a few seconds, the screen flashed red with a large thick "X" in the centre.

"Access denied," a woman's voice informed them. Elsie tried to keep her expression neutral, fearing that a show of any emotion would give her away.

"Ma'am, can you confirm that you have received permission to board this spacecraft from the Government of the United Kingdom?" he demanded.

"Er... I... yes," Elsie stammered, not knowing what else to say. The guard's eyes narrowed suspiciously and then began roaming over her, looking for a clue or a sign of danger. He faltered upon the bundle beneath her cloak and froze, his whole stance changing from nonchalant to alert in a matter of seconds. He reached into his back pocket and pulled out his weapon, pointing it directly at her.

"Put your hands in the air," he said, his voice shaking.

"No! It's not what you think! Look!" she motioned to undo her cloak and reveal the sleeping baby underneath, but this only caused the guard to begin shouting even louder.

"Do not put your hands under the cloak!" he yelled. "Keep your hands where I can see them."

Several of the other guards turned to see what was going on, running over and abandoning their posts as they rushed to join the confrontation. The last handful of passengers waiting to board on the beach gasped and screamed in horror.

"It's not a weapon!" Elsie pleaded, but it was no use. None of the guards could hear her over their frenzied shouting. The man who had first discovered her was talking into his Personal Device that was strapped tight around his wrist.

"Do I have permission to shoot, Sir?" she heard him say.

She tried to scream, but the sound caught in her throat before it could escape. Her vision began to blur, the world around her whirling faster and faster. It was happening. The guard was going to shoot her dead. She took a deep breath to steady herself, wondering with desperation if there was any way to protect her son from the bullets that would surely hit her at any moment.

"Hold on," a voice said from the other end of the Personal Device. The voice sounded eerily familiar, but Elsie couldn't make it out over all the commotion.

"Stand down, stand down," the guard informed the others. They stopped yelling and lowered their weapons. Elsie remained frozen, petrified that even a slight movement would give them the incentive to shoot. A black silhouette appeared in the long corridor that led to inside the Mayfly. The guards stood statue still, their backs to the approaching figure and their faces fixed in a new expression of calm.

Suddenly, a man stepped out of the doorway and Elsie blinked. There was a moment of confusion followed by a crippling sense of relief. She knew this man. She knew him very well.

"Alfie," she whispered, her voice hoarse. Alfie smiled, his unmistakeable features coming into focus.

"It's 'Captain Alfred Sommers' now," he grinned.

She took in his uniform; the white high-neck jumper made from a smooth airy material, the sleek black trousers that seemed to fit perfectly, the golden badge depicting two planets with a dotted line between them. Her mouth hung open. Alfie noticed her expression and began to laugh. She flinched, momentarily transported back in time by the musical sound.

"Come inside, Elsie. We can talk," he said. His voice enveloped her in a warm blanket of comfort and without having to think for a second, she stepped over the threshold of the Mayfly, watching as he motioned for the guards to return to their posts and continue their duties, forgetting about the entire event.

"Just wait there a second," Alfie smiled. Elsie stood still in the Mayfly's entrance, watching as he conversed with the guard who had discovered her.

"If they show up, don't let them, board, their apartment is no longer vacant," she heard him say. There was some murmuring before the guard nodded and saluted Alfie, rotating back to face out into the night. Alfie returned to her side and indicated for her to begin walking down the long passage. She did so, looking around with hesitation. High walls of sheeted metal rose up around her, spanning over her head to form a strange titanium archway. Yellow lamps had been fixed into the wall at periodic intervals, their dim artificial light leading the way to another door a few yards ahead of them.

"I can't believe you're a Captain now," she said to Alfie as they headed towards it. He looked at her with confusion, perhaps wondering how she could make light conversation after having been seconds from death.

"Yes, I applied for my Captaincy after we left College," he explained.

"Well, congratulations," she praised him.

"Thank you," he replied, his face suddenly twisting into an awkward expression of discomfort. "Sorry I didn't keep in touch Elsie. I meant to, I really did, but I was so preoccupied with all of this..." he gestured to the Mayfly. "Time got away from me."

"We were all busy," Elsie smiled. As she spoke, her baby grizzled from beneath her cloak and began to stir.

"What was that?" Alfie asked.

Elsie pulled the cloak over her head and revealed the sleeping baby underneath, his little head resting daintily on her chest. Alfie craned his neck so that he could look into his face.

"It seems you've earnt a 'congratulations' too," he beamed. "He looks just like you. What's his name?"

15

"William," Elsie replied.

"After your father," Alfie nodded.

"Yes, I thought the world could do with another William James. Although," she paused, her voice faltering with confusion. "I'm not sure if I can even say that anymore- 'the world'. There is no world anymore, is there?"

Alfie grinned.

"There will be," he assured her.

"I assume Austin is the baby's father," he said after a few moments, his tone matter of fact.

"Yes," Elsie answered.

"Where is he?" he asked as casually as he could, keeping his eyes fixed on the door ahead of them.

"He's dead," she said wearily, the extreme emotions she had experienced that day beginning to take their toll. Alfie stood still, immobilised by the news.

"He's dead?" he repeated in shock. Elsie nodded. He began shaking his head back and forth, his eyes darting from side to side as if he were trying to solve an equation that had no answer.

"How did it happen?" he asked, deep confusion spreading across the recesses of his usually composed face.

Elsie gave him a meaningful look and he nodded, piecing the clues together in his mind as he began to understand.

"He didn't let it go, did he? His belief in the 'Great Conspiracy'"

"No, he didn't," Elsie replied.

There was a brief moment of silence, during which Alfie cleared his throat several times, stalling as he determined how best to phrase his next question.

"Do you ever think about...them?" he asked, his tone suddenly fearful. Elsie sucked her breath inwards.

"No," she told him. "I don't. If I did, I'd end up driving myself mad like Austin. Besides, there are bigger things to think about now."

Alfie nodded, folding his arms behind his back and straightening his posture as they came to the end of the passage. A sensor on the left-hand side of the door flashed impatiently, demanding a fingerprint to scan.

"Well Elsie, are you ready?" Alfie asked her. Elsie smiled at him weakly. She lacked the energy to indulge his schoolboy excitement as he prepared to show her his shiny new toy. She longed to find the oblivion of sleep and lose herself in it, exhausted by the emotional toll of her long journey. She was certain that nothing could impress her enough to keep out the sadness that was slowly creeping into her mind, pouring through the floodgates that had been opened by her painful thoughts of Austin. To her shock, she found that she was wrong.

The door opened with a touch from Alfie's finger and the pair of them stepped into the heart of the Mayfly. They found themselves in a gigantic lobby, the size of at least two football pitches. The floor was made from smooth white marble that gleamed and glistened from the reflections of the numerous lights that were fixed overhead. Large, oval, glass elevators were transporting people from the ground to the floors above, moving smoothly at first before suddenly jolting in all directions. The lobby itself was circular, and transparent walkways ran around its outer edge on every floor. Elsie could see passengers hurrying along them, some carrying bags and suitcases, others strolling with their families, pointing with enthusiasm whenever they saw something new. The ground floor was filled with venues designed for the passenger's entertainment, with coffee shops, clothing boutiques and toy stores making up just some of the available outlets. Her eye was drawn immediately to the familiar 'I-Tech' logo hanging above one of the shop windows, every gadget and device imaginable laid out on display. A gigantic wafer-thin screen hung from wires in the centre of the floor, presently displaying the fifteen-minute countdown to The Split.

"It's so big," Elsie mused, her bleary eyes struggling to comprehend the wealth of new sights in front of her.

"Come this way," Alfie urged, leading her towards the nearest lift. The lights seemed to become a hue brighter as she stepped somewhat dubiously into the oval pod. Alfie tapped on the glass and an interactive screen appeared, his fingers moving across it at such a speed that she could not discern what he was typing.

"I'm taking you to your apartment now," he informed her.

"I have an apartment?" she replied with confusion.

"Yes, you'll be on the top floor with me," he confirmed, pressing a final button that caused the lift to begin vibrating wildly. In a flash, they were flying up towards the ceiling, with Elsie certain she had left her stomach behind on the ground floor. Their speed increased as they shot past the different levels of living accommodation, the blue carpeted corridors blurring into one gigantic sea of cotton. Elsie closed her eyes and turned away, the sight beginning to make her dizzy. By the time they had reached the top floor, they had reached such a speed that she was convinced they would break through the ceiling, launching into Space independently from the Mayfly.

Mercifully, the lift slowed to a smooth stop and they disembarked into a small but extravagant atrium. A large chandelier hung from the ceiling, casting dancing shadows across the floor, which was paved with marble in hues of swirling gold and bronze. Five sets of wide double doors stood at precise intervals around the walls, each marked with a number. The doorknobs were made of crystal, and silver-plated archways twisted around the doorframes. Alfie led Elsie to number 'three', delicately taking her hand and touching her finger to the sensor pad beside it.

"You'll be able to gain entry yourself now," he explained. She nodded, her head swimming as she attempted to take it all in. Alfie's mahogany eyes and dark eyebrows blurred into his brown hair when she tried to focus on his face, leaving her to wonder how much longer she could stay awake without collapsing.

She followed him into her apartment, a vast space that was as lavishly decorated as the atrium would suggest. Plush rugs spilled across the laminate flooring, so soft she could almost feel their tenderness through her worn and beaten boots. Large mounted paintings of vivid landscapes from Earth hung across the wall, providing a comforting reminder of home. A shiny electric fireplace was attached to the wall at the end of an elongated black glass table, complete with matching chairs. A series of white sofas and chaises were arranged in the living room around a quartz coffee table that had a variety of brand new tablets laid out on its surface, never having yet been touched.

"This is it," Alfie announced. "There are also three bedrooms, two bathrooms and a spacious kitchen."

"Oh..." Elsie replied. "That's good."

"I expect you'll be wanting to get some rest now," he noted and she nodded readily, allowing him to lead her semi-conscious body into the master bedroom.

Once inside, Alfie strode over to the large wardrobe and produced a pair of red, silk pyjamas from its depths. He laid them on the bed and then turned his back to her, tapping on a small rectangular screen that was fixed into the wall. Elsie undid her travelling cloak and removed it, along with her boots. She carefully detached William from her body and placed him gently on the bed, his sling falling to the floor with a delicate thud. Hastily, she pulled off her mud-covered trousers and fraying jumper and put the fresh pyjamas on in their place. Her whole body sighed with relief as she found herself physically comfortable for the first time since she could remember. She sat down on the bed, ready to fall asleep at any moment.

From across the room, there came a whirring noise. Alfie's head snapped to the direction of a hatch carved into the furthest wall. It was protected by a curved, metal door which opened upon Alfie's touch, revealing the contents within. Elsie gasped with surprise. Sitting inside was a beautiful cream cot, complete with a holographic mobile depicting whirling planets and zooming spaceships. In one swift motion, Alfie heaved the cot into position next to Elsie's bed.

"You can order anything you want from there," he said, pointing to the rectangular screen. "The people downstairs will send it up."

Elsie wasn't sure what any of this meant. She watched somewhat distantly as Alfie picked William up and placed him into the cot, pulling a soft blue blanket up to his shoulders and tucking him in.

"Thank you," Elsie murmured, falling backwards and allowing a feathery pillow to catch her head. "For everything."

"You don't have to thank me," Alfie replied, putting the warm duvet over her aching body. "So long as you're aboard my ship you'll never have to worry about a thing. You're safe now."

There was a moment's pause as he stared into the distance.

"You should remember that I said that," he advised her mysteriously, turning on his heel and walking from the room, his arms folded behind his back.

Elsie lay in the dark for a moment, letting the silence swallow her up. She looked over at William's peaceful face, his mouth hanging open as he slept deeply. She had done it. She had saved him. She was victorious in her quest, yet the strangest feeling of emptiness engulfed her as the Mayfly's engines burst into life, shaking the room from floor to ceiling. Unable to cling on any longer, she succumbed to the lull of sleep, knowing that by the time she awoke, they would be deep in Space. Life on Earth was over.

3.

Thirteen Years Later

Will opened his eyes, blinking as they adjusted to the light in his bedroom. Reluctantly, he kicked off his duvet and sat up, swinging himself out of bed. Feeling groggy, he walked across the room to his wardrobe, his bare feet padding across the dark blue carpet. He opened the doors and picked out a maroon jumper and pair of sleek black trousers to wear. Even though he was thirteen years old, his mother still chose his clothes for him. She had them specially made by an upmarket designer who lived alongside them on Floor One. He shrugged out of his pyjamas, the light grey material crumpling into a pile at his feet. Once he was dressed, he folded his nightclothes carefully and put them in pride of place in his top drawer. They were adorned with images of his favourite Rocket Racer, Pablo Pianthus and his famous Solo Rocket XR2. Last year, he had broken the record for the fastest ever journey undertaken in a one-man rocket. When Will grew up he wanted to be just like him, though he hadn't told anyone about this particular dream. He was certain that his friends would make fun of him and that his mother would panic at the thought of him catapulting through space at top speed in a small metal rocket. She wasn't the biggest fan of flying, mostly due to the fact that Will's father had died in some sort of spacecraft explosion before he was born. He had never been told the full story, but he knew enough to be sure that his mother wouldn't be cheering him on should he choose racing as his career.

 After he had finished getting ready, Will headed over to the computer screen fitted securely into the wall above his desk. He sat down and turned on the display, which told him the date – 1st of September 2113. A large dialogue box popped up, flashing to announce a message of some sort.

"Good morning Will, this is a reminder to inform you that you will be departing for The Space Academy today at 11.11 A.M"," the robotic voice notified him.

Will swiped the notice off the screen. As if he could have forgotten! He suspected that Marie, his private tutor, had logged the event into his computer's diary. He brought up another screen and checked his inbox. A small, speech bubble icon informed him that he had one new message from Spencer Hullington, his friend who lived across the hall. He opened the message and began to read:

"Hello Will,

Just letting you know that my father has pulled some strings and managed to arrange for our rooms to be on the same floor at the Academy, just like here! He designed a lot of the school's architecture and they owe him a few favours. Anyway, I'll see you later on the Shuttle. It leaves at 11.11 exactly so don't be late! I'll try to save you a seat.

From Spencer.

P.S Have you packed yet? I think I'm going to ask Anita, our maid, to do mine. She's so much better at folding than I am!"

Will frowned as he finished reading. He supposed that he should be excited that he and Spencer would be living near each other at the Academy, but instead he felt a thud of disappointment. He had looked forward to making a fresh start and experiencing something different, finally free from the confines of his life on Floor One.

Spencer's message had reminded him about packing. He had promised his mum that he would finish it before he went to bed the night before and yet he hadn't managed to pack a single thing. He had spent the evening playing his favourite virtual reality game "Earth Wars" instead and had been so absorbed in it that he had completely lost track of time. He had been in the middle of killing the last evil General, jumping about his room with his virtual sword and fighting the holograms that were spawning around him, when he had suddenly noticed the time and realised it was far too late for him to be awake. He had shut the game down and scrambled into bed, shutting his eyes and willing himself to sleep before he was caught still awake in the small hours of the morning.

Rummaging under his bed, he found the brand-new suitcase his mum had got him from the lobby the week before and pulled it out, yanking his clothes from their hangers and throwing them inside in a haphazard manner. He wasn't sure how many outfits he would need, and so decided to pack his entire collection. He left his Pablo Pianthus pyjamas in their drawer, selecting a few pairs of plainer nightwear that he felt were less likely to embarrass him.

He scanned his room carefully for anything else he would need. His Personal Device that would allow him to send and receive messages was already attached to his wrist after he had fallen asleep wearing it. Other than that, he didn't have many possessions that he treasured, save for a photograph of himself and his mother that had been taken when he was a baby. He was sat on her lap, wearing a pair of green dungarees over a stripy T-shirt, beaming at the camera with very little teeth. He picked up the frame and wrapped it in his dressing gown, placing it in his suitcase with the rest of his things.

When he had finished packing, he pulled the zip on the case to ensure it was secure and positioned it in the middle of his room, making sure it would be immediately noticeable should his mum come in to check on him. He stepped out of his bedroom, the doors sliding apart automatically, and walked down the hallway into the dining area. His mother, Elsie, was sitting at the long glass table, drinking a cup of hot coffee whilst reading her day's schedule from the tablet in her hand. When Will entered the room, she looked up and smiled.

"Good morning, darling," she said, motioning to the chair beside her. "Come and sit down".

Will went and sat where she had gestured and began delving into the breakfast spread that the family's assistant, Derek, had laid out for them. Derek insisted on being referred to as an 'assistant' and not a 'maid', 'butler' or 'cleaner', or else he refused to do any work. Will could hear him in the background as he ate, cleaning the bathroom and muttering curses under his breath. He stifled a laugh as he heard something heavy drop and smash, causing a string of obscenities to pour from Derek's mouth, forcing Will to take a long swig of orange juice to stop him from choking with amusement.

"Well, today's the day," Elsie said, leaning on her hand and looking at him wistfully. She was smiling, but her voice was choked with emotion. In all his life, Will had never seen his mother cry. However, he had learnt to look for the sadness in her eyes, which often gave her away.

"I know," Will answered, suddenly becoming fascinated with his breakfast muffin.

"How do you feel?" she asked, folding her arms and leaning back, as though he were one of her counselling clients.

"I don't really know," Will answered with a shrug, devouring the rest of his breakfast.

"School was very different back on Earth, you know" Elsie began. Will tried to fix his face into an expression of interest as he prepared himself for another 'Earth' story.

"We didn't learn nearly as many interesting things as they teach at The Academy," she continued. "Only College was really exciting, and people were lucky to be able to get a place there. That's where I met the Captain, you know."

"And Dad," Will said casually. As soon the words had escaped his mouth he regretted them. He scrunched up his face and cringed at his unfortunate mistake. Elsie swallowed and looked away. Composing herself, she turned back and continued chattering brightly.

"I've cleared all of my appointments this morning so I can take you to the Shuttle," she informed him. "We haven't got long until we have to get going."

"Already?" Will asked incredulously. He felt as though he had only just got up. He glanced out of the large windows that hung along the right-hand wall, but it was impossible to tell the time of day by looking through them. Special UV lights had been installed on Floor One to give the impression of sunlight flooding through from outside. However, the illusion could easily be broken by sitting in the same room for a long period of time. The lights were set to a timer, coming on with a sudden burst at eight in the morning and disappearing again abruptly at eight p.m. From what he had been told by old Earth dwellers, this had nothing on the real beauty of a brightening sunrise and faltering sunset.

"Get your coat on," Elsie's voice interrupted his reverie. "We'll be meeting Alfie and Lois soon. Have you packed?"

"Of course I have mum what do you take me for?" he replied. His mum narrowed her eyes but said nothing. She called for Derek and asked him to fetch Will's suitcase from his room. He nodded and repeated the word "certainly" several times before balling up his fists and storming pointedly into Will's bedroom. He returned with the black suitcase, wheeling it to the front doors before stepping away, heading off to continue with the day's chores. Seconds later, there was a loud knock on the door. Will pressed the sensor pad with his finger, opening the door to reveal Alfie and his daughter, Lois, standing out in the atrium. Alfie was stood behind Lois, his large hands fixed on her shoulders as he grinned in a bemused sort of way. Lois stood stony-faced, not seeming to have inherited her father's cheerful nature. Her long, blonde hair was scraped back into a high ponytail, fastened with an over-sized black hair band. She wore a green tartan dress with a black shawl, bright white tights and a pair of brown, clunky shoes. Will thought she looked like one of the frightening china dolls available to purchase in the toy store. She was clasping a large, pink travelling bag between her hands and had three more suitcases on a golden luggage rack behind them, currently being manned by one of their many staff.

"Hello Elsie, hello Will," Alfie greeted them each with a nod of his head. "Are we all ready to go then?"

Lois frowned as though even standing in the doorway was causing her a huge inconvenience.

"Yes, we're all ready here," Elsie beamed.

"Great!" Alfie grinned. "Lois is really excited, aren't you Lois?"

Lois could not have looked less excited if she was being chased by a ten-legged alien. She continued to scowl furiously into the distance, refusing to look any of them in the eye. An involuntary laugh burst out of Will before he could stifle it, causing Elsie, Alfie and Lois to stare at him strangely.

"Sorry. I just... remembered something funny," he stammered in a feeble attempt to cover himself.

With Will's suitcase added to the luggage rack, the group set off through the atrium, their footsteps echoing across the walls as they walked. They reached the lift and climbed in, Elsie tapping the screen on the glass to key in their destination. There was a sudden lurch to the left, causing them all to lose their balance as they began whizzing away from Floor One. They

25

whooshed up and down and side to side, hurtling in all different directions until finally the lift slowed and turned a corner, it's mechanisms clicking as it shuddered to a halt.

They stepped out, blinking as their eyes adjusted to the sudden stillness of their surroundings. Will didn't recognise this part of the Mayfly. The carpet was a worn beige and the walls were painted in a dull shade of grey. There were several heavy-looking brown doors running down the hallway, which appeared to open manually with a handle instead of by the touch of a sensor pad. A small sign stuck to the wall informed them that "Loading Deck E" was to the left, a helpful arrow pointing them in the right direction. Alfie took the lead, guiding them to a set of thick steel doors. He turned around to face the rest of the group.

"Well this is it," he announced. "Are you two ready?"

William and Lois exchanged a nervous glance, the first time they had properly interacted on their journey so far.

Will nodded, a sudden surge of nerves passing through him as Alfie opened the doors. The group stepped forward and found themselves on a large loading platform, usually used for the purpose of transporting goods between the Mayfly and other spaceships. That morning, however, it was bustling with hundreds of people. Mothers and fathers were saying goodbye to their children, brothers and sisters were chattering with excitement and friends separated by the long school holiday were gleefully calling out and waving fervently when they recognised each other. The biggest transporter ship that Will had ever seen was sitting stationary on tracks that ran across the shiny white floor. The ship sat calmly, unmoved by the gathering hordes of Space Academy students and their families. There were five doors along its side, which, as Will watched, opened to reveal comfortable blue leather seating inside the ship's belly. Crowds of students began moving towards the doors, hugging their parents and siblings goodbye and then hustling forwards. Will and Lois looked at Alfie and Elsie, unsure what they should do next, only to discover their own dumbfounded expressions reflected on the adult's faces. Their uncertainty was addressed a few minutes later when the sound of a strong, female voice carried across the platform.

"All new students this way!" the voice called.

The four of them began following in the direction of the voice, bustling their way through the crowd, Alfie's member of staff trailing behind them, the wheels of the luggage rack squeaking on the cold, hard floor. They edged their way past a family of mousy-brown haired children. The mother had her hands on the youngest boy's face and was talking to him in a soft voice, her eyes full of tears. An older boy and girl were stood to the side, their arms folded around their chests as they rolled their eyes and huffed in the direction of their mother. There was a younger girl too, clutching her mother's hand. The little girl was looking around apprehensively, craning her neck to see into the faces of everyone who was passing by. When Will's group drew level with the family, the girl's eyes widened and she let out a gasp, tugging on her mother's coat and pointing at them with her mouth open.

"Mummy, mummy it's the Captain! Look! It's the Captain!" she shouted. Her mother turned and stared at Alfie, as did the rest of the family.

They all stood perfectly still, gawking as though they had never seen another human being before. As they stood in their strange, fascinated unison, Will couldn't help but notice the tatty and worn state of their clothing. The mother's canary yellow coat was fraying at the edges and the younger boy, who looked to be about the same age as Will, was wearing trousers that were slightly too big for him, their hem dragging across the floor. The older girl and boy's clothes looked as if they had been hand stitched together by somebody who wasn't very skilled and the youngest girls flowery dress and navy coat were clearly hand-me-downs, their once richer colours faded with time and use. Will knew these sorts of clothes were not produced by the designers on Floor One and he had never seen a family dressed in such a dishevelled manner before. He pulled at his own jumper self-consciously, suddenly embarrassed by the rich quality of its material.

"They must be from a very low floor" Lois whispered to no one in particular, as if this hadn't already been clear. The family stood out vividly against the sea of smooth fabrics and dark colours that swarmed the platform, making it hard not to notice them. Alfie smiled diplomatically in their direction and then continued steering Lois through the crowd of people. However, it soon became evident that the little girl's shouts had attracted the attention of more than just her family. A ripple had started to spread across the platform and a tide of faces turned to watch as they passed.

Lois' cheeks flushed a dark shade of magenta as she tried desperately not to meet the eyes of their onlookers. Will saw her face visibly flood with relief as they caught sight of their old tutor group from Floor One. She moved with haste, settling herself in the midst of the other girls, while Will went to stand quietly between Spencer and their friend Alasdair. The tutor group was stood amongst a crowd of about ninety other students their age, every single pair of eyes fixed on a young woman who was stood at the head of the gathering.

The woman's arms were folded behind her back as she waited somewhat impatiently, scanning the crowd for anyone new approaching the group. Her dyed-blonde hair was scraped back tightly against her head and her lips were fixed in a permanent pursed position. Will turned to follow her gaze, which was currently patrolling over the perimeter of the platform, and wondered how much longer it would be until everybody else arrived. Whilst looking for other students, he was pleased to see his mother and Alfie standing close behind them in a small congregation with the other parents, relieved he hadn't missed his chance to say goodbye.

After a few more minutes, the severe woman began to count heads, whispering to herself as she did so. When she finished, she clapped her hands together and immediately commanded the attention of everyone around her.

"Hello," she boomed, more as an announcement than as a greeting. She flashed a brilliant white smile in the direction of the parents, seeming to direct her speech over the student's heads and straight to them.

"My name is Miss Fortem. I am a teacher at the Space Academy and it will be part of my job this year to look after all of the first years and make sure your transition to life at the Academy is smooth," she explained with a carefully inflected tone of voice.

"As you can see, we are standing next to a large transporter ship, aptly named the 'Shuttle' which will be taking us to the Academy shortly. For many of you, this will more than likely be your first ever journey through outer-space and you may be feeling quite anxious about the experience. Rest assured that the Shuttle has been tested by both the Academy and officials aboard the Mayfly over one hundred times and is among one of the safest built spacecrafts we have. Despite knowing this, the first time flying can still be nerve-wracking and so I urge any of you who are feeling scared once we are aboard to approach me without hesitation and I will do all I can to ensure the rest of your journey is more comfortable."

She smiled her dazzling smile, her eyes still fixed on the parents as she stressed her point. Will started to wonder if Miss Fortem was always on the platform to give such an encouraging welcome, or whether the school had simply gotten wind that The Captain's daughter would be starting that year.

"Right then," Miss Fortem clapped her hands together causing several members of the crowd to jump. "Without further ado, I must ask you to board the Shuttle," she gestured to the giant spacecraft next to her. "We will be leaving at 11.11 am precisely! First-years must board through the first door on the left. I ask parents and those helping to take any luggage to the stewards, who you will find outside the back compartment of the Shuttle."

At these words, the parents poured upon their children and began their emotional goodbyes as butlers and staff began to hurry towards the rear of the Shuttle. Will found Elsie, who was standing in a clearing of people and smiling proudly at him from a distance. He walked over and she crouched down to tidy him up, readjusting his coat and smoothing his hair, which he immediately ruffled again. Elsie smiled and cupped her hands around his face.

"Well," she said. "I suppose this is goodbye."

"Don't worry Mum, it's not that long until the school holidays." Will smiled.

"I'm sure you will have a fantastic time," Elsie said, fighting hard to keep her sadness at bay, "but I will miss you."

"I'll miss you too mum," he replied. "At least you'll have Derek to keep you company."

Elsie laughed. It was a lovely sound and Will wished he had heard it more often in his childhood. The two of them embraced briefly and then pulled apart, Elsie blinking back tears as she released him.

"Make sure you call! " she ordered him, though her voice was light and weary.

"Of course I will, all the time! You can't get rid of me that easily," Will grinned. He would miss home, it was true, but the excitement of starting a new adventure at the Space Academy was luring him. He could be anyone he wanted to be there. He no longer had to be 'Will from Floor One'. He had always felt a powerful conviction that there was much more to life than he had known and he was filled with a burning curiosity for all the things he was yet to discover and all the people he was yet to meet.

He took a deep breath and closed his eyes, forcing his feet forward and into the Shuttle. The voices of the other first years filled his ears and the smell of new fabric shrouded his nostrils as he entered the large transporter ship. He allowed himself a moment's pause before he opened his eyes again and began the next chapter of his life. His entire transition from a boy into a man would occur at the Academy and he struggled to comprehend the significance of the moment.

"Erm, excuse me?"

A voice snapped him out of his reverie, forcing his eyes open as he whipped his head around to see a tall, lanky boy with dark hair standing behind him, clutching a rucksack with a bemused look on his face.

"Did you know you were just standing there with your eyes shut?" he smirked. "You're holding the whole queue up!"

Will tried with all his might to stop the inevitable flush of red that was making its way up through his neck to his cheeks. He looked over the boy's shoulder to see a line of students, peering around one and other to see what was holding up the line.

"What were you doing?" the boy pressed him. "Were you having a seizure or something? Should I go and get a medic?"

A few of the boys behind him began to snicker. They were all staring at him, trying to work out if something was genuinely wrong or if he was just incredibly strange.

Will's mouth moved soundlessly as he tried to think of something to say that would save him from eternal social damnation. Those who were already seated around him had stopped their conversations to see what was going on. Whatever he said next would determine their first impressions of him, and yet he could not come up with a single reasonable explanation as to why he had been stood completely still in the middle of the Shuttle with his eyes closed.

"Leave him alone Rudy, he's probably just nervous," said a girl's voice from within the queue. Will was both simultaneously grateful for her intervention and morbidly embarrassed that he had to be rescued by a stranger. He turned and began making his way towards the rows of seats decorated with navy blue upholstery that filled the first compartment, wishing that the metal bottom of the Shuttle would give way and let him fall through the platform and into deep Space. He was mortified when he noticed that the seats were designed for two people, realising with a sudden fit of panic that nobody was going to want to sit next to him and he would have to face the humiliation of riding the entire journey on his own.

He slumped into the nearest chair and pretended to be very interested in looking out the window, hoping he would blend into the furniture and disappear.

"Mind if I sit here?" a voice said.

Will jumped and looked up to see a girl standing over him. She flicked her long, chestnut hair from her shoulders and smiled at him, her arms folded nonchalantly as she awaited his response. He recognised the voice as belonging to the person who had saved him from Rudy's mockery.

"Y-yes of course," Will stammered, caught off guard. The girl sat down beside him and swung her handheld luggage onto the floor, resting it safely between her knees. For the first time in his life, Will became acutely aware of his limbs and wasn't sure where to place them. He was certain that even an accidental brush of his arm against hers would cause his head to explode in a fire of embarrassment and so positioned himself awkwardly against the wall. He didn't have much time to worry about how to seat himself however, for no sooner had the girl sat down than Rudy had begun to call out from the back of the compartment where he and a group of his friends were sitting.

"Emily what are you doing?!" he scathed."I know there's obviously something wrong with that boy but you don't have to feel sorry for him. Come and sit with us!"

Emily continued staring forwards as though Rudy had never spoken, her deep blue eyes flashing with contempt.

"Just ignore him," she told Will. "He's always like that."

"Wow!" Rudy continued, ensuring that he was in earshot of everyone around him, "it must be true love! Good job your mum's a nurse Emily, I think that one is going to need all the help he can get."

Rudy's gaggle of followers burst into exaggerated, raucous laughter, though Will didn't find the insult was particularly clever or funny. He looked around to see if any of his peers from Floor One would jump to his defence, but they were all doing an extremely convincing job of pretending not to recognise him. In fact, Lois seemed to find him completely invisible when he attempted to catch her eye. She looked around wildly, terrified that somebody would have seen her with Will on the platform and would expose her for knowing him.

"We used to be tutored together, Rudy and I" Emily explained calmly, as though this situation was a regular occurrence for her. "He always seemed to think that we were friends. I don't know why, I never liked him. I was hoping that going to school would mean I could get away from him and make a fresh start."

"I can relate to that," Will replied, throwing a cursory glance towards Spencer, Alasdair and the rest of the tutor group.

A wave of silence suddenly fell across the compartment. Will looked around in confusion, unsure what was going on. It took him a few seconds to notice the boy from the ragged looking family he had seen earlier, frozen in the doorway of the Shuttle, aware that every face inside was turned towards him. He was holding on to his patchy bag so tightly that his knuckles were turning white. Sitting down on the very front seat, which was vacant, he turned his back on all his spectators and positioned himself as motionless as a statue. Before a single word could be uttered, Miss Fortem appeared, her presence alone stifling any taunts or nasty remarks that might have been aimed his way. Will saw his shoulders sag with relief as Miss Fortem began to speak, distracting everybody's attention towards her.

"Okay first years," she began, "the Shuttle is about to take off at any moment. Please make sure you have arranged yourselves as two to a seat. There are protective seat belts located to the left of each person, however they will be not needed unless we experience any difficulties-"

Will swallowed hard. He wasn't entirely sure what 'difficulties' they might encounter flying through Space and nor was he in any hurry to find out.

"If they are required, you will see a flashing red light in the compartment at which point you must immediately take your seat belt and clip it across your waist, securing it firmly in the slot on the right-hand side. I must ask that you do not move around whilst the Shuttle is in motion, unless absolutely necessary. "

Will remembered her soothing words in front of the parents about approaching her on the journey if anybody felt scared and was suddenly convinced that anyone seeking her help would find more peril going to her than they would ever encounter in outer-space.

"The journey takes roughly fifteen minutes," she continued. "When we arrive at the Academy, we will enter into the Gathering Hall where you will attend your first assembly. You will be addressed by the Headmaster who you are to refer to as 'Admiral Allance'. After that, you will be assigned into three classes and further instructions will be given to you. Does everybody understand?"

There were a few nods and noises of compliance.

"Good then. Without further ado, I must ask that we prepare for take-off."

Miss Fortem sat down at the front next to the ragged boy. He turned his body sideways, shrinking into the window and resting his face against the glass as he stared blankly at the back wall of the platform.

At that moment, everybody in the compartment began leaning backwards and forwards, stretching their bodies as high as they could manage to see onto the platform as they attempted to get one last glimpse of their families before they launched. Will caught sight of his mother moving through the crowd, pushing her way right to the front so that she was almost touching the Shuttle. She blew kisses to him with both hands and waved furiously. Will grinned and waved back, bemused to see his mother so expressive.

 The engines beneath them whirred into life, shaking the entire ship with the force of their activation. They lifted into the air, Will's mother and the other parents pushed backwards by a sudden surge of energy that pulsated out from under them as they took off. They hovered towards the ceiling, floating higher and higher until the people below began to resemble toys in a dollhouse. Will kept his eyes on his mother, even as she became minuscule, fixated upon her figure until the metal roof of the platform snapped shut and they found themselves in an enclosed capsule. As one roof closed, a second one above their heads opened, providing their exit into Space. They ascended through it, sitting suspended for a moment as they hung still in the infinite black sky. Will felt Emily stiffen beside him as they waited in the silence, full of bewilderment and fear. The moment lasted only a few seconds before there was a sudden jolt, flinging them forwards as the Shuttle began hurtling through the air.

"This is it!" Emily said.

"This is it," Will repeated, taking a deep breath.

4.

The Space Academy

Emily peered out the window, straining her neck to see past Will who had pressed his face upon the glass in awe. There was something wonderful and yet equally terrifying about being in the depths of Space as they travelled to the school, the stars blurring into a silvery haze as the speed of the Shuttle increased. Emily felt a deep sense of discomfort as she gazed at the Universe around her, realising how small and insignificant she was in comparison to its sheer size. Suddenly, Will turned to her with a concerned expression on his face, breaking the silence and rescuing her from her thoughts.

"What do you think it's like at the school?" he asked her, his eyes wide and eager.

"My brother's in third-year and he's told me a few things. You get to study real-life aliens and you get to fly your own rockets through Space," she replied, making a conscious effort to keep her tone cool and indifferent in order to impress him.

"Wow" he said after a moment. "Are you sure he isn't winding you up?"

"He does enjoy winding me up," she acknowledged. "But no, I don't think he is this time. He knows how excited I am about starting at the Academy. It's the only way I get to escape from our dad. He and I don't get on."

The words ran off her tongue before she could stop them and she flushed crimson with embarrassment, internally berating herself for having shared such personal information with someone she hardly knew. She braced herself for the awkward, stuttered reply she was customary to receiving after bringing up her terse relationship with her father.

"That's a shame," Will said with sincerity. "But at least you have a dad. Mine died before I was born."

"I'm sorry to hear that," she told him, surprised by how truly sad she felt at the thought of him suffering such a loss. He smiled with gratitude and the two of them exchanged a moment of understanding, each one entrusting the other with what they had revealed.

"What do you think you'd like to be then?" Will asked her. "When we get to Novum. I mean that's the whole point of the school, isn't it? Train us up and make us useful!"

Emily laughed but was momentarily thrown by the question. No one had ever asked her this before. There had been so much focus and emphasis on her getting into The Space Academy and not embarrassing the family by falling short of her brother's achievements, that no one had ever considered what she would decide to be once she had completed her training.

"I don't know," Emily mused. "I like technology. I think I want to be something to do with that. My dad wouldn't like it though. He doesn't think subjects like that are suitable for girls."

Will raised his eyebrows.

"Well, I suppose you'll have to prove him wrong then, won't you?" he grinned.

"Yes," Emily agreed. "I suppose I will."

As the journey continued, their conversation flowed thoughtlessly and with ease. Emily couldn't help finding herself hoping that their friendship would continue once they had disembarked from the Shuttle and arrived at the school.

After a while, an excited wave of voices went up in the seats around them. Emily and Will returned their attention to the window to discover what had caused the ruckus and were quick to lay eyes on the culprit. Looming out of the darkness just in front of them was The Space Academy. The school itself was encased in a huge transparent dome that was floating graciously in mid-air. Through its surface, a grand building could be seen, set in the centre of the grounds and rising to the height of at least a hundred feet or more. A colossal, white tower lurched out of the floor to the left of the school, reaching almost to the top of the protective dome. A smattering of buildings filled the rest of the campus, most notable among them a silver observatory, glittering as it caught the light from the stars above it.

"Wow" Emily breathed as they drew closer to the school, circling around the edge of the dome until they reached a round, metal door in its casing- just big enough for the Shuttle to fit through. It sprung open as they approached and revealed a hidden room designed for spacecrafts to land in, providing just enough room for them to begin their descent. The door sealed shut immediately behind them as they juddered into landing and oxygen was pumped noisily through a ventilation system. Despite this, Emily felt as though all the air had disappeared from around her and her head swam with anticipation as the engines cut, immersing the first-year students into a sudden, sharp silence.

Miss Fortem leapt straight into action, jumping out of her chair and twisting around to face everybody in the same, swift movement.

"Right boys and girls," she said. "We are about to get off the Shuttle, but before we do, it's important that we listen and all understand exactly what needs to happen."

She pursed her lips and tilted her head down, widening her eyes to emphasise the importance of the point she was making. She waited until she had personally ensured that every individual student was listening.

"First of all, I need everyone to check that they have all their belongings. Most of you will have bags stowed in the luggage compartment as well. That luggage will be taken for you and unloaded into your new rooms."

A hum of excited whispers sounded at the mention of "new rooms". Miss Fortem cleared her throat loudly.

"Secondly," she continued, "I want you to have a look at the person sitting next to you."

Emily and Will glanced at each other for a second before looking back at Miss Fortem.

"This person is going to be your partner on our walk up to the school. Unfortunately, we have had incidences in the past where pupils have got over excited about the Academy and wandered off, only to be found somewhere in the grounds hours later. As you may have noticed, our school campus is very big, so it is extremely important that you do not make any detours. You are each responsible for ensuring that your partner stays with you for the entire walk. Are we all clear?"

There was a mild murmur of understanding.

"Yes, Miss Fortem," she demanded.

"Yes, Miss Fortem," the compartment repeated.

"Okay, we are now going to get off the Shuttle, so please stand up with your partners."

There was a flurry of movement as everyone scuffled to their feet, hauling rucksacks and holdalls off the floor and out of the overhead bins. Emily bent down to grab her bag from the floor, catching sight of Miss Fortem gently putting her hand on the arm of the scruffy looking boy as she stood up.

"You can walk with me," she told him. He nodded dejectedly without making eye contact. Miss Fortem scanned her thumb against the touch pad on the door and it opened with a puff of air. The scruffy boy by her side, she began to lead all the passengers out of the Shuttle in their pairs. Emily and Will waited patiently for a chance to leave their seats and join in the queue. At least a dozen students had passed them on the way out, when Rudy drew up alongside them.

"Are you two love birds going to stay here forever?" he taunted, his eyes full of malice.

"Give it a rest, Rudy," Emily sighed, folding her arms.

"Please," he said sarcastically. "Go in front of me. I would hate to be the one responsible for delaying the beautiful journey you two are about to embark on."

Glowering at him, Emily took the place he had gestured to, dragging Will by the arm and causing Rudy to snort loudly. Together, they filtered down the middle of the compartment, listening to the gasps of the people ahead of them as they made their way outside. They reached the door, a wave of cool air washing over their faces, providing pleasant relief from the warmth of standing too close to so many bodies in a confined space. Disembarking the Shuttle, they exited the room they had landed in and headed into the school grounds, finding themselves at the foot of the Ivory

Tower. So impressive was its size, that it had to have its own shuttle ship waiting at the base, ready to fly students to the classrooms high above.

"This building is where Alien Studies is taught," Miss Fortem explained when the last of the first years had joined in the gathering. "The height of the tower provides extra security should any of the aliens that are held there try to escape."

"Still think my brother was winding me up?" Emily smirked at Will, whose eyes had widened in bewilderment.

"Okay, I take it back," he conceded.

Feeling satisfied, Emily tore her eyes away from the tower and began to scan the rest of the grounds, trying to take it all in. Even though it was technically daytime, there was no sunlight- fake or otherwise- to be found here. The grounds were mainly lit by lampposts, placed strategically alongside the interconnecting pathways that wove their way around the school.

Miss Fortem led them all to the front entrance, which proved to be two colossal navy doors fitted into the front of a small dome that was attached to the main school building. They were without a doubt the biggest doors that Emily had ever seen. She glanced to the side and saw the same look of amazement reflected in Will's face.

"What do you think that means?" he asked her, pointing to a golden sphere that was fixed above the doors, a small, model rocket positioned in mid-flight next to it.

"It's the school's logo," Emily explained, pleased to have superior knowledge to him on the subject. "I've seen it on the school uniform. I think the planet in the middle is meant to be Novum and the rocket represents the Mayfly."

"You seem to know a lot about this already," Will replied. "I'll have to stick around with you,"

Emily felt a wave of happiness spreading across her body and tried hard to stifle it in case he could see how much his words had pleased her.

"Welcome to The Space Academy, " Miss Fortem smiled, interrupting their conversation as she addressed them all. "These are the main doors as you can most probably see. Above them is a 3-D representation of our school logo. The sphere signifies the planet Novum, and the rocket, of course, stands for our journey towards it. You will become very familiar with this image during your time here."

"Well done," Will whispered to Emily. She smiled with pride and glanced up at the logo again, the figure of Novum looming over her head and casting her face into shadow.

"Now, we are about to enter the school," Miss Fortem informed them. "Once we are inside I will take you straight into the Gathering Hall. You may sit beside whoever you want, as long as you sit in the first row."

Before anybody had a chance to process this, Miss Fortem turned on her heel and began knocking on the front doors with efficiency. They swung open on her command, moving backwards at the same speed as though being pulled by synchronised strings. Following Miss Fortem, who had promptly made her way inside, the children passed through a set of security scanners and found themselves in the school's Reception Hall.

The floor was made entirely of white tile, polished to such a dazzling hue that the students could see their reflections shimmering across the surface. In the centre of the hall was a bronze statue of a man, at least three times of the size of any real human being, standing regally on a large platform, a tiny planet balancing in his outstretched palm. His pupil-less eyes stared forwards, seeing into a future that nobody else could view. Behind the statue, flanking each side of the hall, were two glass lifts in the shape of bullets. The walls were decorated in banners of navy and gold and were covered in framed photographs that documented the Academy's proudest achievements thus far- including a victory against the Rocket Racing team for Weltraumschule, the German version of the school. A trophy case stood proudly on the left-hand side of the room, drawing immediate attention to itself upon entry. From where she stood, Emily was able to read the inscription for a prize given to the Academic Decathlon team who had won the competition in 2110, an accompanying video replaying the moment of victory from a small screen inside the case. To the right of this was a large collage containing photographs of all the members of staff at the school, each one beaming out from behind the frame. Overhead, a great, glass roof revealed a magnificently clear view of the stars above, a holographic projection of the current solar system they were travelling through spinning in mid-air underneath it.

To the left of the Reception Hall was a door marked "Gathering Hall" in important gold lettering, with a second marked "Dining Hall" on the right. The smell of piping hot food began to waft from the latter, causing Emily's stomach to growl as she suddenly realised how long it had been since breakfast. To her disappointment, Miss Fortem ushered the children towards the Gathering Hall and away from the delicious odour of the lunch she so yearned for.

They entered a large, rectangular room, congregating at the front under Miss Fortem's instruction. Emily craned her neck to look at the seating behind them, which rose up in staggered levels to the back of the hall, giving her an impression of the large number of students at the school. Directly in front of them was a huge stage set in front of a glass wall, which boasted an impressive view of the school grounds. Whilst gazing through it, Emily noticed an artificial lake she hadn't yet seen, its surface glinting and glistening in the starlight. She was just imagining how it would feel to take a dip in its cool, clear waters, when a booming voice shook her from her thoughts.

"Good afternoon new students!".

Emily turned to see a tall and broad looking man striding across the stage, his arms outstretched in welcome. He wore a deep blue suit that seemed to accentuate the silvery-grey hue of his hair and eyes. His thick, bushy eyebrows were drawn together and his slanted mouth set in what resembled a permanent frown, despite the fact he was trying his utmost to attempt a smile. His footsteps crashed across the smooth stage, reverberating all around the room as though a stampede of wild aliens were heading towards them.

"Miss Fortem," he grunted as he addressed the gaggle of students. "You have brought us a fine, young bunch of children yet again. How lovely."

He regarded them all with a strained look of delight.

"My name is Admiral Allance," he nodded curtly, his hands folded neatly behind his back. "Welcome to The Space Academy."

5.

Alderin Class

Standing shoulder to shoulder amongst the crowd of anxious first-years, Will waited with baited breath for the Admiral to speak, certain that he had never laid eyes on a man who could command so much attention simply by being present. His mannerisms and general stature gave the distinct impression that he was someone to be taken seriously, and Will made a mental note to himself never to fall into the Admiral's bad books if he could help it.

"Now as you may be aware," Allance continued, "I am your Headmaster here at the school.

There was a brief silence as he allowed for this information to sink in. Will wondered if he expected some sort of applause or congratulations for the announcement.

"It is with great warmth that I welcome you all here. It's our pleasure to receive such bright and wonderful students every year, all finely selected from the most suitable of backgrounds."

He paused to stare at the ragged boy, who looked as though he wanted to jump through the glass wall and run away as fast as he could.

"I will now ask you to take your seats," Allance requested, not taking his eyes off the boy. "In your first year, you must always sit in the front row. Our start of year assembly will be commencing shortly, in which further information will be given to you about the school. Please, be seated."

Obediently, the first years trumped over to the midnight blue seats, shuffling around on the soft, spongey material as they got into a comfortable position. Will tried very hard to keep his expression neutral as Emily came to sit beside him and stared forwards with determination so as not reveal his pleasure. His efforts proved to be in vain, however, when Rudy wolf-whistled from further down the row as soon as Emily's body made contact with the chair.

Once everyone had settled, the older students began pouring into the Gathering Hall from opposite sides, flowing smoothly into the rows behind Will and the other first years. All the students were wearing the same uniform; a navy jumper emblazoned with a yellow emblem of the school logo and a pair of plain black trousers. Will drew his legs under his chair sharply as the fifth years passed him, making their way to their seats without giving the first-years a single cursory glance. He felt very small compared to some of them and his mind was abruptly filled with worrying visions of being trampled to death during the panicked rush between classes.

"Hey sis," came a cheerful voice from behind them. Will and Emily both turned to see an older boy with messy, brown hair grinning jubilantly at the pair of them. His cheeks were rosy with happiness and his familiar blue eyes glinted with mischief. He had a smattering of freckles across his nose which protruded slightly against his otherwise delicate features. Will recognised him immediately as Emily's older brother, the resemblance between them unmistakeable.

"Hello Charlie," she beamed at him. "This is my friend Will."

She pointed towards Will, who grinned, pleased to have been introduced as a friend.

"Nice to meet you, Will," Charlie said with genuine enthusiasm. "You two better brace yourselves. The first day here is a bit mind blowing."

"Will thought you were winding me up about the aliens." Emily laughed, then added uncertainly, "it was all true, what you told me, wasn't it?"

"Yeah," Charlie replied ecstatically, "and there's so much more than I can even explain. Just you wait!"

He rubbed his hands together with glee, unable to control himself. Will was distracted by a procession of stern looking teachers entering the hall, but was soon forced to turn his attention back to Admiral Allance, who had raised his hand in the air pointedly. Slowly, the students began to copy his action and the excited racket of chatter died down from a buzz into a hum before falling silent.

"Welcome, welcome all!" the Admiral bellowed. "I do hope you have all enjoyed your holidays and are now fully prepared to put your thinking caps on and study hard for another year."

Every word he spoke was enunciated with expert care, his voice travelling around the hall with ease. He walked across the stage as he spoke, looking students directly in the eye to capture their attention, his overwhelming presence spreading to every corner of the room.

"Now, tradition dictates I must begin the welcome Assembly by addressing our wonderful new first-years. Let me start by saying that we hope you will be very happy and well looked after here. The Academy strives to provide each and every student with the best academic experience we can muster, but in order for you to properly thrive, I must explain a few things about our school that will help you to understand both what our aims are and what we have achieved thus far.

"This will be the thirteenth year that The Space Academy has been up and running and we hope that it will be our best and most successful year to date. Our school was built at the same time as the Mayfly and was sent into Space a few days after The Split, latching on to the Mayfly's gravitational field and orbiting from a safe distance. I won't bore you too much with the physics though, as I must say I don't really understand it myself!"

He laughed a booming laugh. There were a few titters of courtesy from across the Hall.

"What will we find when we reach Novum?" the Admiral asked rhetorically. Some of the students looked at each other in confusion, unsure whether they were expected to raise their hands and answer.

"We cannot answer that question," the Admiral clarified, "because nobody knows. What we do know, however, is that we will need to rebuild a civilisation from scratch. Here at the school, we intend to give you the skills you will need to help us rebirth humanity from the ashes. Of course, we also wish to share our knowledge with you about the many exciting things we discovered during our last years on Earth. From the most mind-blowing technologies to the in-depth study of aliens, we provide a curriculum that is as thrilling as it is comprehensive.

"We offer many exciting extra-curricular activities here as well. Although we do not study literature, we have a large selection of downloadable I-Books in our library. We also have a virtual reality club, a camping club - which takes place in the Resources Biodome- an Earth Appreciation Society and a Rocket Racing team that students can try out for once they have their personal licence."

William's whole body reverberated with excitement as he pictured himself as the next Pablo Pianthus, telling interviewers with delight that his successful career began when he joined the Rocket Racing team at The Space Academy.

"Now onto the boring part," Admiral Allance continued. "Of course, it goes without saying that there are rules here. These rules have been put into place not for our benefit, but for your protection. Therefore, I must ask that you listen carefully and heed what I am about to tell you. Firstly, no student must ever leave the school grounds without a chaperone. I must remind you of this, older students, for as you may recall we have had some rather grizzly incidents involving rocket hijacking,"

"Two boys stole rockets and flew to the nearest moon," Charlie whispered, sticking his head between Emily and Will. "They caught some weird Space sickness and turned purple. They've been in the Medic Ward on the Mayfly ever since."

"Secondly- "Admiral Allance boomed. "Students must not leave their bedrooms after curfew. The reason for this being that our Alien Studies teacher, Mr. Krecher," he gestured to a shabby, stout man who was dressed head to toe in tweed, "takes some of the creatures out of the Alienary at night for exercise and hunting purposes. Though I can assure you that none of these aliens hunt students, it would be very unwise and foolish to cross paths with them during their one daily glimpse of freedom."

"The third and final most important rule is that no student enters the Resources Biodome without a teacher unless they are part of an authorised event. This rule has been created due to a very nasty situation in which a student entered the Biodome without proper guidance and has been lost in one of its unlimited settings ever since. "

"There's all these different settings," Charlie explained in a hushed voice. "Rainforest, desert, tundra, etc, etc. There's literally millions. They keep shuffling through them, hoping they'll find him in one of the terrains, but no luck so far."

"That's awful," William whispered back.

"Yeah," Charlie agreed. "I mean there'll be enough food and stuff for him to survive but could you imagine the boredom? There's no technology in there. It'd be just him and … nature." He shuddered.

"Now that the serious part is out of the way, I am pleased that to announce that it is finally time for the long-awaited "back to school" lunch," Admiral Allance projected.

A few of the older students cheered.

"Yes, yes," he continued. "Our cooks have gone out of their way to once again produce a delicious meal to welcome you all back. I believe the menu is traditional shepherd's pie with sticky toffee pudding for desert."

An excited chorus of "yes!" echoed around the hall.

"I must add that there will, of course, be vegetarian and vegan options for those that need them, although whether they will be as spectacular I personally could not say."

"Typical," Emily rolled her eyes. "I'm a vegetarian. We always get left out."

"That said, I will not delay you from your taste-bud Heaven any longer," Admiral Allance proclaimed. "First-years if you would like to stand up and make your way towards the Dining Hall," he gestured towards the door.

Will leapt to his feet with avid enthusiasm and followed the trail of first-years out of the Gathering Hall and back into the Reception Hall. They bounded past the eye-less statue with haste, the prospect of food bringing a new spring to their step as they rushed to sample the much-anticipated meal.

They entered the Dining Hall, which was laid out like any normal canteen, with gleaming, silver picnic tables lined up in rows across the wide space. There was a serving station that spanned the length of the entire front wall, manned by shiny, white robots that whirred into life upon their entry and began rapidly producing plates full of sumptuous food from shutters behind them. When Will and Emily reached the station, the robots provided them with two steaming hot plates of shepherd's pie and vegetables, the delightful aroma of the food causing Will's stomach to gargle as he suddenly realised how hungry he was.

"Please, enjoy your meal," the robots said in unison.

"Hmm," Emily said under her breath. "How do I get it to give me the vegetarian option?"

"I don't know," Will shrugged."Try speaking to it?"

"EXCUSE ME!" he yelled at the robot. "SHE'S A VEGETARIAN!"

Emily burst into a fit of laughter.

"You don't have to shout at it Will, it can understand you," she said with amusement.

"Is there a problem, Miss?" one of the robots asked her, regarding her with empty, grey eyes.

"I'd like the vegetarian meal please," Emily replied.

The robot removed the plate of shepherd's pie, putting it back in the shutter. There was a click, and the robot swiftly produced a plate of cheese pasta.

"Thank you," Emily said graciously.

"You are welcome, Miss. Please, enjoy your meal," the robot replied.

"You won't have to ask them to change it every time, will you?" Will asked her, glancing with concern at the build-up in the queue they had caused with their interruption to the serving.

"No," she answered confidently. "They would have scanned my image and committed it to memory. They'll recognise me now and will remember."

Will blinked.

"How do you know that?" he asked her in awe.

"It's very basic technology," she assured him, though Will was not convinced.

Together, they carried their meals towards one of the drinks machines at the end of the service station.

"Right then technical whizz," Will teased Emily,"how does this one work?"

She regarded the machine for a minute, rubbing her fingers under her chin as she considered its appearance.

"It's just a touch screen," she shrugged, tapping on it and producing two ice-cold glasses of apple juice. They placed the drinks on their lunch trays and made their way over to the nearest free table, sitting down and tucking into their food ravenously. A few minutes into their meals, a pair of older students approached them, carrying a box full of peculiar looking devices that Will had never seen before.

"Welcome fellow students!" exclaimed the boy on the right, waving his hands in the air in an exaggerated fashion. Emily jumped, spilling some of her juice into her lap.

"My name is Ant," he announced, "and this is Sam."

He gestured to the boy next to him who was carrying the heavy box, balancing it on his knee and struggling not to show the strain of carrying its weight.

"We are two of your school Prefects and we are here to deliver you your SPs," Ant continued, pausing to await their reaction. They stared back at him blankly.

"It stands for Student Planners," Sam explained, heaving the box onto the table and puffing through red cheeks. "They were going to name it the "Space Academy Device" but abbreviating the name to "SAD" created far too many jokes about the students in the Technology Club who created it."

Sam and Ant exchanged a brief smirk, causing Will to strongly suspect that they were responsible for the origin of said jokes.

"Here you are," said Ant, pressing a device firmly into Will's hands while Sam passed one to Emily. Will looked at the oblong object with curiosity. It was a similar size to his Personal Device but felt much heavier to hold, its thick, silver casing making it look far older than the technology he was used to on the Mayfly. At the centre of its face sat a rectangular black screen that was currently blank and empty. Will turned it over in his hands, in search of an 'on' button.

"To turn it on just press your finger into the middle of the screen," Ant instructed him, noticing his confusion. He did as he was he told and the screen blinked and flickered into life, an hour glass icon appearing as it attempted to load its functions.

"This reminds me of the computers I've seen in the Museum on the Mayfly," Emily laughed.

"Oh, give it a chance!" Ant replied with mock indignation. "The Tech Club spent almost an entire school year working on them, you know."

"As if they'd let anyone forget," Sam rolled his eyes.

A moment later, a holographic projection sprung out of the screen, suspending the image of a piece of paper in front of them, the image so realistic that Will was sure he could reach out and touch it.

"Wow," Emily said, poking her fingers through the hologram.

"Not bad, is it?" said Ant.

"I didn't expect that," Emily admitted.

"The image you're seeing in front of you is your timetable. It'll give you all the information you need about your lessons as well as tell you which class you're in. Anything you need to know about the school will be on this device. Keep it with you at all times," Sam instructed them.

"Anyway, we better be going, we've got to hand these out to all the newbies," said Ant. "Good luck with your first week."

With that the pair of them headed off, leaving Emily and Will to inspect their timetables in peace. Will read the top of the piece of the paper carefully.

"It says I'm in a class called 'Alderin,'" he told Emily, stumbling over the pronunciation of the word.

"I'm in that class too!" Emily replied. The two of them beamed at each other for a moment, unable to supress their happiness, then looked away quickly.

Will scanned down the page to follow the timetable. He located Monday and let out a loud groan as he read the name of the day's first lesson.

"We have Arithmetic first thing on a Monday," he informed Emily begrudgingly. "I didn't think we'd have to study Maths here! I hated it when I was tutored."

"I quite like Maths," Emily admitted. "We probably have to study it because its the same no matter what planet you're on. It's like the Universal language."

"Well, you can help me with the homework then," Will replied with deflation, miffed that such a mundane subject had made it into the Space Academy's famed curriculum.

He continued reading his timetable in hopes of finding more exciting subjects to learn. After Arithmetic was break, followed by Civilisations followed by Technology and then lunch. Will's heart leapt when he read the section for Monday afternoon, which was filled up by double Rocket Control lessons. He could hardly believe his luck that his first day at the Academy would involve rockets and he began wolfing the remainder of his food down at record pace. He was just in the middle of wondering whether they'd be allowed to fly in their first lesson, when a shrill voice interrupted his pleasant thoughts.

"Alderin," the voice squawked across the hall. "Alderin first-years here please."

By now, the second and third years had begun to filter their way into the Dining Hall, making it hard to locate the whereabouts of the speaker. Thankfully, Emily noticed the familiar faces of some of their peers that were weaving their way through the crowds of older students. The pair of them followed onto the trail and found the small gathering of their new classmates congregating nervously around a female Prefect.

She was a stern looking girl, her tight bob groomed to absolute perfection without a single hair daring to fall even slightly out of place. Her strong jaw was set into a firm and unwavering stance of severity and her face projected an expression of deep contempt upon seeing the first-years gathered around her. Will noticed that she was wearing a light blue fitted jacket with a golden "P" embroidered on the left breast. He supposed that the "P" stood for "Prefect" but a quick scan around the hall confirmed that she was the only one wearing it. He wondered in a moment of genuine depression if she had gone to the trouble of fashioning it for herself just so she could appear more important. He watched her adjust the jacket sleeves so that they were at the exact same length on either arm and felt as though his question had been answered.

"My name is May Parsons and I am the Head Prefect here at the Space Academy," the girl announced.

"No-such-thing," coughed Ant as he walked past her to exit the Dining Hall. There was a murmur of giggles amongst the group which were soon silenced by May's cold stare.

"I am here to escort you to your first lesson since it appears that none of you can be trusted to find your way around without making pests of yourselves," she sneered. Will felt a shudder of dislike pulsate around the entire class.

"Follow me," she demanded, swivelling on her heel and sticking her nose into the air as she sauntered towards the exit. Will and Emily raised an eyebrow at one and other and then proceeded to follow the throng of students that would become their class for the rest of the year. As he scanned the faces around him, Will was ashamed to feel a surge of relief that Spencer and the other boys from his old tutor group were not present. Though they had never wronged him in any way, he looked forward to being able to have his own ideas and interests without their snide comments and scathing opinions to put him down. He did, however, notice Lois amongst the group, looking remarkably out of place without her Floor One counterparts.

They walked across the Reception Hall, careful not to obstruct the smattering of older students that were beginning to mingle around the school, some of them heading to the Dining Hall and others making their way jovially to their first lessons, heading towards shortcuts they had memorised long ago. Will caught snippets of their conversations as they lined up to use one of the lifts, casually eavesdropping with the aim to find out more about the Academy.

"I heard Mr. Krecher nearly got sacked last year for letting a Runhorn loose in his class! My brother was there and he said half the students nearly got impaled," he heard one boy ecstatically tell his friend.

"No way," his friend replied, waving his hand dismissively. "Allance didn't even sack Ms. Dido for leaving the Resources Biodome unlocked the night Riley Fitch got lost. He'd never get rid of Krecher."

"You reckon they'll ever find Riley?" Will heard the boy ask before the pair moved out of earshot.

51

When the lift arrived, Alderin class piled in, finding it to be deceptively spacious. They rode to the top floor where they disembarked, following May down a long corridor. TV screens mounted the steels walls on either side, displaying the school's internal temperature, the current time and a countdown to when the first lessons were due to begin. At the end of the corridor was an interactive map of the grounds that was several metres long. It displayed every building in satellite view, featuring multicoloured dotted lines that demonstrated the quickest way to get from one to another. A group of students were stood in a cluster around the far end of the map, pressing on the image of what Will assumed was the Resources Biodome and enlarging it to reveal a series of notices relating to the subject.

"Awesome!" a boy said upon reading the information. "Resources Club starts again on Friday."

He began typing with speed into his Student Planner, which informed him in an electronic voice that a reminder had been set. Will was eager to search for details on Rocket Racing try-outs but May had become impatient with the younger student's fascination with the school map.

"Yes, yes, it's all very interesting," she snapped. "But we can't stand here all day. I have classes to get to as well you know."

May turned on her heels and the first-years followed her into the next corridor, which featured gigantic hangings of inspirational quotes printed onto great blue plaques. The words passed in a blur as Will walked beneath them, but he managed to discern one memorable phrase along the way.

"A journey of a thousand miles begins with a single step".

Eventually, they reached their destination, with May coming to such an abrupt halt that several of Will's classmates bumped into each other with the shock.

"For those of you who's reading ability exceeds that of a five-year-old's, you will see that we are at the Launch Bay," May sniffed, gesturing impatiently to the tall lettering that labelled the door she was stood in front of. "This is where all your Rocket Control lessons will take place. Never enter the Launch Bay without proper authorisation and never attempt to fly any rocket outside of class without holding the proper licencing. Now, as terribly sad as it is, I must leave you and get to my own lesson. Mr. Zeppler will be out shortly to collect you."

She made to leave and then turned back, adding as an afterthought;

"Try not to make too much of a nuisance of yourselves."

The moment that she was out of sight, the entire class erupted into a buzz of excited conversation, unable to contain themselves with the anticipation of their first official lesson at the Academy. Will, however, was too agitated to speak to anyone, ignoring even Emily who was forced to talk instead to a pair of giggling girls in light of his new-found mutism. He rubbed his fingers together repetitively as he twitched with impatience, watching the door so intently that his vision began to blur.

Just when he was beginning to feel that he may burst if he had to wait for another moment, a clicking noise from beyond the door commanded silence over the babbling students and they turned in unison towards the source of the noise. The doors swung open, revealing a young-looking man with long auburn hair that swung down to his waist. He smiled coyly, his hands casually placed on his hips as he took in the awed face of the class that stood before him.

"Well then," he grinned. "Who's ready to fly some rockets?"

6.

The Ragged Boy

Finley was going to be late. He ran down the corridors, his breath coming out in wheezes as he willed his legs to carry him faster. He cursed himself for allowing this to happen. He had been desperate for his first day to go well- and that meant attracting as little attention as possible. So far, it hadn't gone to plan. It seemed the more he tried to blend in, the more people seemed to notice him. At lunch, he had tried his hardest to ignore all the whispers that were buzzing around his ears like angry flies. He had been confused by the robots at the serving station and was rather alarmed when one of them started speaking to him in a loud, monotone voice. It had taken him every ounce of restraint he had to stop from jumping backwards in shock and embarrassing himself irreparably. Once he had taken his meal, he had found that he was unable to use the fancy drinks machine, which was much more up-to-date than anything he was used to at home. The idea of asking another student for help and revealing himself to be even more of an alien than they already thought him was unthinkable, and so he had loitered about as inconspicuously as possible until he had gathered how it worked.

 By the time he had sat down to eat, most of the other first-years had finished their meals and were beginning to head out of the Dining Hall. He shovelled his food into his mouth, burning his tongue as he tried desperately not to be left behind. He might have caught up in time, had he not been further delayed by a pair of Prefects, who came to his table to give him a device they called a "Student Planner". They did their best to keep their attitude friendly and their tone light, but Finley could still feel their eyes burning with curiosity as they scrutinised him between sentences, wondering, just like everybody else, what the boy from Floor Seven was doing here.

It took him several minutes to locate his timetable on the somewhat mesmerising Student Planner, which informed him that he was in 'Alderin' class. He looked up to discover that the Dining Hall had filled up with older students and was unable to see anybody he recognised from the Shuttle. Panic rose in his throat as he leapt to his feet, crashing into the table and searching the hall for a familiar face. Eventually, he gave up, realising he had no choice but to ask the two Prefects for help.

"Excuse me," he called as he approached them. "My timetable says I have Rocket Control next, but I don't know where I'm supposed to go."

"No problem mate," replied the taller, dark-haired boy. "I can download you a map onto your Student Planner if you want?"

He flashed his best helpful smile, but Finley couldn't help but notice how taken aback he was at having heard him speak. He wouldn't have been surprised if most of the students at the Academy had grown up thinking that people from the lower floors spoke a different language, or could only communicate through the medium of interpretive dance.

"Don't worry about downloading anything," Finley said urgently, desperate to get to his first class on time. "Could you just give me directions?"

The Prefect looked at him strangely then shrugged.

"Okay, are you sure you'll remember?" he asked.

Finley nodded. When he was a small boy, his father had been forced to take him to work while his mother was doing her shifts as a maid on Floor One. His dad worked as a maintenance man and had taught Finley to memorise the directions back out of the service tunnels in case they ever got separated. The tunnels ran like a labyrinth beneath the main body of the Mayfly and without knowing how to get around, it would be possible to become lost for days - or even weeks. Finley felt confident that a few simple directions around the school would be much easier to follow.

The Prefect gave him his instructions and he set off, repeating the Prefect's words silently in his head. He rode the lift up to the correct floor and then departed at a brisk run, turning the heads of students and teachers alike as he passed. He had been here less than two hours and he had already failed at his goal of blending in. He could only hope his lateness wouldn't be a mark against him academically - for he was certain his education was all he had now - his hopes of making any friends at the Academy firmly squashed.

He must have been a faster runner than he realised, for he rounded the corner and reached the arched door labelled "Launch Bay" just as the last members of his class had disappeared inside it. Taking a few seconds to catch his breath, he smoothed his trousers down and tucked his shirt in to hide its fraying edges. Once he felt he had made his appearance as satisfactory as it could be, he mustered all of his courage, stood up as straight and tall as his body would allow, and walked into the class.

For one brief and magical moment, Finley forgot himself completely as he took in the room around him with awe. He had entered into a giant hangar, filled from corner to corner with spacecrafts of every shape, size and design imaginable. The entire back wall was covered by a large window of re-enforced glass that perfectly showcased the millions of stars that surrounded them in deep Space.

He sidled up to the back of his class, who had congregated around the long-haired teacher. He was stood next to a small, two-seater rocket which only reached the height of his waist. Despite its size, it boasted an incredible appearance. Its body was dazzling white and sleek, its wings painted in a deep crimson and set at a perfectly perpendicular angle. Across the dashboard, just behind the steering wheel, was an intricate control panel, designed to regulate hundreds of different functions. Finley had never been interested in rockets, but even he had to admit that this one was something to admire. Directly behind it was the entrance to a large tunnel that fed through the floor and, judging by the numerous amount of "caution" signs that were plastered all over it, out into Space beyond.

"Good afternoon," the teacher spoke, his voice light and cheery. "My name is Mr. Zeppler, and as you may have guessed, I teach Rocket Control here at the Space Academy. Who can tell me why they think it might be important for the students here to learn how to fly rockets?"

There was a moment's silence and some shuffling before a few hesitant hands reached into the air.

"Yes," Mr. Zeppler nodded towards a tall, gangly boy at the front.

"Because it's awesome?" he suggested. The class erupted into a giggle.

"That may be so," Mr. Zeppler smiled, "but being able to fly rockets can have many uses. Does anyone else have an idea?"

Before he could help himself, Finley raised his hand.

"Yes, you at the back there," said Mr. Zeppler, gesturing in his direction.

Finley cleared his throat nervously as he felt every single pair of eyes in the room burn into his person.

"Well we might need to use them when we reach Novum," he explained. "In case we have transport things or… travel to other planets…" he trailed off, dropping his gaze to the floor as his classmates continued to watch him.

"Correct!" exclaimed Mr. Zeppler with great enthusiasm. "When we reach Novum, it will be essential that we are able to use rockets to help us build our new civilisation by either transporting goods or using them for exploration. What is your name young man?"

"Finley."

"Well Finley, would you like to come and join me at the front of the class? I'll be needing a volunteer."

Mr. Zeppler had posed the offer to him as a question, but Finley knew he really had no choice. The class parted in the middle and he headed towards the front, feeling as though he were on death row aboard the Mayfly, marching towards his execution. Once he had reached Mr. Zeppler, he turned to face his audience. He was relieved and more than a little surprised to see that most of the thirty-odd faces looking his way were wearing expressions of blank intrigue. Only two of the class members seemed to be sneering at him in disgust. One was a ginger-haired boy with pale, amber eyes and a crooked smile. The other was a girl with dark hair and sallow skin, her black eyes outlined with dark circles that gave her a rather unhealthy appearance. They stood side by side, united in their telepathic hatred for him. He tried not to be intimidated, but there was something about them that made him extremely uncomfortable.

"Okay," Mr. Zeppler smiled. "Since you gave such a good answer Finley, you now have the privilege of being the first in the class to sit inside one of our rockets."

There was an audible "oh!" of disappointment as Finley's classmates failed to conceal their jealousy.

"Don't worry," Mr. Zeppler assured them, "a few more of you will be getting a chance throughout the lesson. Now! Finley if you could please do the honour of stepping inside the rocket to my left."

Finley did as he was told. He stood on the footstall that had been placed beside the rocket and clambered inside its open-topped body. The chair was leather and rigid, designed with expertise to provide maximum comfort for the driver and dyed to match the precise shade of red that covered the rocket's wings. The moment his body touched the seat, a thick steel bar descended over his head and secured him tightly into position. He looked down at the control panel in front of him. It featured more buttons, knobs and confusing looking levers than Finley had ever seen in his life, including on the complicated systems his dad had used while performing maintenance on the Mayfly. He was completely bewildered and hoped he wouldn't have to do anything other than sit in the rocket and not touch anything.

"Okay," Mr. Zeppler addressed the rest of the class. "As keen as I'm sure you all are to experience flying a rocket, for obvious reasons in our lesson today we will mainly be focusing on safety and procedures. Some of you may have noticed a metal bar coming down across Finley's seat. This function is motion activated, so will automatically occur whenever anyone enters the rocket. However, there are also seatbelts that must be applied manually to secure the driver. Once all this has been put in place, there's still something very important we have to do before we can fly. Who can tell me why I shouldn't just send Finley into Space right now?"

There was a long silence and Finley wondered whether anyone was going to answer or if they were all in favour of him being blasted off into Space and never seen again.

"He can't go into Space like that. He'd die," a boy answered at last.

"And why is that?" Mr. Zeppler pressed him.

"Well the rocket is open-topped and he hasn't got any gear on," the boy replied. "He wouldn't be able to breathe."

"Correct!" Mr. Zeppler exclaimed. "What is your name, son?"

"Will," the boy answered.

Finley craned his neck to get a glimpse of him and recognised him immediately as the boy he had seen walking with the Captain on the platform earlier that morning.

"Excellent Will, you can be my next volunteer," Mr. Zeppler beamed. He hurried off towards a second small rocket with blue tipped wings and began typing on its control pad at an impressive speed. A moment later, it hummed into life and began moving at a meticulously slow pace across metal tracks on the floor until it stopped a short distance behind Finley's rocket.

"Okay Will, if you wait there..." Mr Zeppler said, pointing beside the rocket. Will followed his instructions with haste, scrambling to stand beside the spacecraft.

"Will will kindly be demonstrating what protective gear every rocket user must wear on any journey into Space," Mr. Zeppler explained, heading towards a concealed door in the wall of the hangar, his waist-length hair floating about his back as he moved. He pressed a button and the disguised door slid back to reveal several spacesuits hanging from a battered iron rail.

"In this cupboard, you'll find spare suits in various sizes, but it usually customary for students to purchase one for their lessons. It would be a good idea if you could contact your parents at home and have them send you what you need," Mr. Zeppler informed them as he pulled a small suit from the rack.

Finley swallowed hard. He wondered if his parents would be able to get him a suit with their current credit status. He pondered whether he'd be able to return to the Launch Bay and steal one without being discovered, or else face the humiliation of having to borrow gear every lesson. He sat uncomfortably in the driver's chair, listening rather than watching, as Will tried on the spacesuit and clambered into the rocket behind him, which Mr. Zeppler informed the class was named a "PR-11" and was the best model for beginners to fly in. He was just in the middle of fixing the complicated seatbelt system around Will, when a cold voice interrupted his teaching, causing Finley to startle.

"How do you actually make the rockets go?" the voice asked. Finley knew immediately that it belonged to the sallow-faced girl who had unnerved him earlier with her loathsome looks.

"Well, I suppose I could demonstrate," Mr. Zeppler answered, eagerly proceeding to press a series of buttons on the control pad in Will's rocket.

It happened in a flash. Mr. Zeppler finished his display and went back to teaching the lesson. In a second, the sallow girl was next to him, a strange smirk on her face and a deep look of malice in her eyes. She reached inside his rocket, her fingers moving seamlessly across the controls as she looked at Finley with contempt. He was completely frozen, paralysed by shock and fear. There was a second's pause. He twisted his body round sharply, his ribs jamming into the metal bar with the force of the movement. Panic engulfed him as he called out for help. Time seemed to be distorted, passing with an unnatural slowness. His class appeared in a tableau, their looks of confusion turning to horror as they realised what was about to happen.

With one final sneer, the girl pressed the last button that triggered the rocket to activate. He heard the screams of the class, saw Mr. Zeppler reel backwards in alarm and watched the Launch Bay disappear before his eyes as he hurtled down the metal tunnel and out towards Space. Without a helmet on, he would certainly suffocate. Strangely, a vivid memory flashed into his mind of when, as a small child, his parents had saved up all their credits for the month and taken him and his siblings to the Water Park on the Mayfly. Riding the biggest slide there, he had clasped the rubber ring as tightly as he could in his tiny hands, exhilaration and fear filling his entire body as he slid down the impossibly large flume. As he hurtled down the tunnel and towards Space, he felt a similar sensation of adrenaline and terror pulse through his veins. He prayed silently to no one in particular, hoping his suffering would be over quickly as the exit grew larger in his vision. He closed his eyes and braced himself for the end.

Several things happened at once. A loud cry pierced the tunnel, echoing horribly across the walls and bouncing back towards the entrance. Finley didn't know whether it had come from him or someone else. He felt a tight, painful sensation across his neck and shoulders as though he were being grabbed from behind. A second later, he was flying through the air, independent of the rocket. He hit the hard floor of the tunnel, a wave of pain shooting down his back and head. At almost the exact same moment, there was the sound of what he could only assume was the exit opening and a deafening roar filled his ears as he was sucked towards the vacuum of Space. A second later, the noise subsided and everything was still.

He opened his eyes slowly and saw the roof of the tunnel above him. The pain in his neck twinged and he realised there was something lodged uncomfortably beneath him. He propped himself on his elbows and looked around. The object that had been stuck underneath him groaned and began to stir and Finley realised with a jolt that it was a person. He looked down to see Will in a full spacesuit, complete with helmet, lying spread-eagled on the floor. He had followed him into the tunnel and saved his life.

"Are you okay, mate?" Will asked dazedly.

"Er... yeah... thank you..." Finley replied, unsure what else to say. He blinked as he tried to comprehend what had just happened.

Their stunned silence was interrupted by voices calling out from the other end of the tunnel.

"Will! Finley! Are you alright?" Mr. Zeppler shouted with concern.

"We're okay! We're down here!" Will called back.

"Oh, thank the Universe," Mr. Zeppler exclaimed with relief. "Stay there! I'll come and get you!"

Finley lay back down on the floor next to Will, overwhelmed by both relief and exhaustion now that the adrenaline had stopped pumping through his veins. Will groaned loudly, not attempting to move, let alone get up.

"How did you save me?" Finley asked him after a minute, staring up at the metal ceiling that encased them.

"I followed you in as soon as that creepy girl sent you down. Mr. Zeppler tried to stop me but he wasn't quick enough. Once I caught up with you, I kind of jumped out of my rocket and pulled you out of yours, then both the rockets flew out from underneath us and we hit the floor. I don't know how I actually managed to pull that off," he laughed in disbelief, "It's lucky you weren't going very fast. Still, I couldn't just do nothing could I?"

Finley didn't answer. He had no idea how to express his gratitude appropriately.

"I can't believe that girl did that to you!" Will continued, unperturbed by Finley's silence "Was she trying to kill you? It's insane!"

Their conversation was abruptly ended by the sound of an approaching engine. Mr. Zeppler rode towards them on a larger rocket, floating slowly and with perfect control. Finley glanced towards the door at the end of the tunnel, afraid it would spring open again and pull him out into Space without a suit.

"Don't worry," said Mr. Zeppler through his helmet. "I've disabled it. Get in."

He extended a hand towards the boys and the two of them clambered into the backseat of the rocket. Mr. Zeppler carefully turned around in the small space and drove them safely back into the classroom.

Everybody applauded as they disembarked. Finley smiled awkwardly while Will took an exaggerated bow and laughed. Notably not applauding was the ginger-haired friend of the sallow girl, who herself had disappeared from the class completely. Almost immediately after their feet had touched the floor, a girl with long, dark hair rushed over to Will, demanding to know whether he was okay. He nodded and she gave him a hug, which caused him to go redder than a beetroot.

"I'm fine Emily," Will re-assured her.

Once she was satisfied that he was, in fact, all in one piece, she approached Finley and squeezed him in a tight embrace.

"I'm glad you're alright too," she told him sincerely. "What that girl did is terrible! She's been taken away now. Hopefully, she won't ever come back!"

Finley nodded profusely, still tongue-tied. It was only the second time someone at the Academy had spoken to him out of choice and he seemed to have become inexplicably mute as a result.

Mr. Zeppler regained his control of the class and wrapped the lesson up by tying the horrible incident into his earlier point about safety, continuing to preach about the importance of taking rocket use seriously and never engaging in any flying activity without the proper experience to do so. At the end of the lesson, he sent everyone down to the Dining Hall where they would be informed what to do next. As the students began to file out, chattering chaotically about what they had witnessed, Mr. Zeppler called Will and Finley back in to speak them, Emily waiting by the door.

"You'll probably be sent to speak to Admiral Allance," he told them, running his hands through his hair. "Nothing like this has ever happened before. I mean the school has had accidents, but nothing on that scale. I'm not even entirely sure that it was an accident"

He rubbed his eyes, suddenly looking exhausted.

"Anyway, I apologise to you both," he sighed. "I wanted you to have a first lesson you'd remember, but that's not quite what I had in mind."

"It's okay, Mr. Zeppler, it isn't your fault," Will re-assured him.

"I shouldn't have been so keen to show off how to start up the rockets," he frowned, returning his hands to his hips and standing jauntily. "Just for future reference though boys, if that ever were to happen again, there is an "emergency seal" button which will contain about fifteen minutes of oxygen inside the rocket. I'll cover it properly next lesson – just in case."

"Is this likely to happen again?" Finley asked him dubiously.

"Of course not! In all my years of teaching I've never witnessed something as appalling as that," Mr. Zeppler shook his head. "Anyway, you boys better get going, nothing more to do around here but clean up the scene of the crime."

He winced at his choice of words.

"Just an expression," he added sheepishly.

Finley smiled to show he hadn't taken offence and followed after Will as he made to exit the Launch Bay.

"I don't know about you," Will said to Emily as he strolled over to where she was waiting for him, "but I could really do with a good cup of tea after that."

"Agreed," Emily laughed and the pair began to walk off together. Just before they left the room, Will stopped and turned back.

"Are you coming, Finley?" he asked.

Finley glanced at Emily who smiled with encouragement.

"Yeah, I'd love to," he replied, catching up to walk in step beside them, a huge grin spreading uncontrollably across his face.

7.

Room 211

It was safe to say that Emily's first day at the Academy had been eventful. As she slid into the bed in her new room for the very first time, she let her mind drift into a sleepy state, her weary body grateful for the luxury of rest. The bed was extremely comfortable, more so than her one at home, and she burrowed into its warm depths. The inexplicably comforting smell of fresh laundry rose around her as she swathed herself in the thick duvet adorned with stars, feeling as though she were wrapping herself up in the night sky itself. She soothed her aching feet against the soft cotton of the bedsheet and resisted the strong urge she felt to drift into a sound sleep, clinging onto consciousness so that she could revisit the afternoon's events in her head.

After the drama of their first Rocket Control lesson, Emily and Will headed down to the Dining Hall with Finley to have hot drinks and discuss what had happened in detail. Upon their arrival, however, it became clear that Will had become some sort of mini-celebrity after the event and a mob of students both from Alderin class and the other two classes in their year group, Armstrong and Grissom, had descended upon them with a flurry of questions. Will had thoroughly enjoyed recounting the tale and those present at the gathering of his new fan club had listened with delight as he explained how he had flown down the tunnel at maximum speed and leapt fearlessly from his rocket, pulling Finley to safety seconds before they hurtled into Space. It seemed like everyone in first year was ecstatic over Will's heroics - everyone that is, except Rudy who skulked about in the background. Will's tutor group from Floor One, who he pointed out as they sat haughtily at their own table, also refused to acknowledge the hum of excitement around them. Even the Captain's daughter, who Will had been seen with on the platform, didn't come over to congratulate him or ask if he was okay.

Emily had rolled her eyes as some of the older students started to drift over, catching wind of the story and shaking Will's hand as they shared their admiration for what he had done. Some of them clapped a bemused Finley on the back as they walked past, but none of them stopped to say much to him, perhaps uncertain of what was appropriate given the situation.

"How is it fair that I'm the one who nearly died but Will's the one getting all the glory?" Finley laughed as yet another student they didn't know came over to congratulate Will.

"He's getting all the glory because he's milking it for all it's worth!" Emily replied.

"I am not!" Will insisted, before flashing them both a grin.

The three of them enjoyed hot chocolates with whipped cream, mixed to perfection by the drinks machine. They chatted happily amongst each other, the seriousness of what could have come to pass overshadowed by the extraordinary way things had turned out. Halfway through their conversation, their Student Planners beeped to inform them that first-years would now have some free time before dinner to explore the school and do as they please. Not wanting to pass up the opportunity, the three of them leapt to their feet and headed off into the Academy.

They rushed through the Reception Hall, passing the statue of the no-eyed man as they did so, and headed to the first floor via the lift. They traipsed around the identical looking corridors, not managing to discover anything of interest unless bathrooms, teacher's offices and classrooms could be considered interesting. They were just about to give up when they overheard a group of students discussing their intention to visit the library and decided to follow them. They kept a safe, calculated distance, walking just far enough behind so that they weren't noticed by the gang they were stalking. Discussing how crowded the lifts were at the start of term, the older students opted to take the stairs, with Emily, Will and Finley close on their tail. After clambering up five staircases, Emily was ready to turn to the boys and demand through ragged breath that they find the nearest lift immediately when a set of double doors labelled "Library" appeared just ahead of them.

"The pot of gold at the end of the rainbow!" Will huffed, his face rosy and glistening with sweat.

"The what?" Emily asked, glancing over at Finley who looked back at her with an equally befuddled expression.

"It's just something my mum says. I think it's some old Earth expression," he explained.

"I like it," said Emily, despite having no idea what the saying meant. "To the pot of gold!" She cringed slightly at her own overenthusiasm but Will smiled at her with gratitude.

When they entered the library, their hike to reach it was immediately made worthwhile. Of all the things Emily had seen at the school that day, this was by far the most impressive. Standing strikingly tall, at least twenty rows of silver shelf-units spanned the length of the room in pairs, their tops touching the high ceiling. Each individual unit featured thousands of cubby holes cradling small sticks of downloadable book files. Robotic machines were whizzing around the shelves, retrieving the sticks that were unreachable to the human hand and bringing them down to the ground. In the centre of the room were several round, white tables where groups of dedicated students were already beginning to gather to start their work for the year.

The librarian's desk was situated on the right-hand side of the room and was currently being manned by an older boy with dishevelled brown hair and thick, black glasses. Upon seeing the three of them standing motionless, he strode over, kindly asking if he could be of any assistance.

"This place is huge," Will informed him, as though he wasn't aware. The librarian laughed.

"Yes, we do have the biggest collection of titles anywhere since The Split," he informed them.

"It's amazing," Emily replied and he smiled brightly as though she had paid him a personal compliment.

"I'm Martyn by the way," he said, offering Emily his hand to shake. She took it and blushed, noticing both Will and Finley staring at her from the corner of her eye.

"I'm Emily," she told him.

Will cleared his throat loudly.

"And this is Will and Finley," she added.

"Good to meet you," Martyn nodded.

"What are those things?" Finley asked, pointing towards the data sticks.

"They're the sticks you use to download books," Martyn replied, confused by the question. "They're called I-Books? Have you not heard of them?"

"Oh, we don't have I-Books at home," Finley explained. "We still use I-Readers."

Emily glanced at Will who looked back at her with the same expression of surprise. Her family had donated all their I-Readers to charity several years ago when they had been made obsolete by the flurry of new technology that was constantly being developed on the Mayfly.

"Yes, well the I-Books are a new invention, created, of course, by the Interactive-Tech company. It's taken them long enough to develop. The technology of books and reading has always taken a backseat to the production of new gadgets," Martyn sighed, momentarily lost in anguish.

"Allow me to explain how the library works," he said, snapping back to reality. He walked them to the nearest storage unit and demonstrated how to browse through all the different titles it offered by using a touch screen fixed into its side. Once a title had been selected, it was retrieved by one of the robots and passed carefully to its new temporary owner.

"The I-Books can be used with any device, you simply point and click the button in the middle and the data will be transferred across. It works with Student Planners, tablets, any T.V screen or even laptops," Martyn informed them with passion.

"Laptops?" Will repeated with confusion. "Does anyone still use them?"

"They have proven to be quite popular here at the Academy. Students seem to find something satisfying in typing on a real keyboard. It's quite therapeutic, actually" Martyn replied, adjusting the buttons on the light brown blazer he had donned over his school uniform.

"Retro," Will nodded. "You'll feel right at home then Finley!"

Their conversation with Martyn was cut short by a loud, beeping sound that Will and Finley discovered was coming from their Student Planners.

"Uh-oh," said Will after checking the screen.

"What is it?" Emily asked, attempting to peer over his shoulder.

"A video message from Miss Fortem," Will swallowed, pressing play.

"William James, please report to the Admiral's office immediately," Miss Fortem said in the recording, her facial expression and tone of voice giving no indication as to what the nature of the meeting would be.

Finley played his message to find that he had received the same summons. The two boys exchanged a look of mutual fear and panic.

"Do you think we're in trouble?" Finley asked Will, his eyes wide with worry.

"You can't be. You didn't do anything wrong," Emily assured him.

"Well, I did nearly fly a rocket into Space without a licence and without permission from a teacher," Will pointed out.

"You were saving Finley if you hadn't have done that who knows what would have happened," Emily argued.

"We don't even know where the Admiral's office is," Finley fretted.

"I was just about to finish my shift here so I can show you if you like," Martyn offered. The two boys accepted and headed out of the Library alongside their new guide. Emily stood still for a moment after they left. It was the first time since she'd entered the Academy that she had been alone and she was unsure what to do with herself. After a moment of deliberating, she decided to make her way back down to the Dining Hall, hoping that the boys would soon return there after their meeting. To ensure she didn't get lost, she adopted the tactic of climbing down every staircase she came across until eventually she reached a lift and was able to descend into the Reception Hall.

Veering right, she was surprised to find the Dining Hall packed to almost full capacity with a hungry pack of students already swarming on the serving station. She scanned the tables, seeking out any first-years she recognised. To her relief, she caught sight of Cara and Matina, the two girls she had spoken to briefly before Rocket Control. They were sitting with a boy she hadn't met yet, but she made her way over anyway, sitting down confidently and hoping they wouldn't object to her intrusion. She needn't have worried, however, as the three of them seemed all too keen to discuss the details of Finley's earlier ordeal

"Alasdair doesn't believe us about what happened," Cara told Emily with indignation after she had seated herself midway through their discussion of the event.

"Weren't you there?" Emily asked him.

"I'm not in Alderin class," he told her with a hint of disgust. "I'm in Gagarin with all of the other Floor One pupils."

"Except Will and the Captain's daughter," Emily reminded him. "They're in Alderin class too."

"Yes well, Lois is very displeased with her class placement. As for Will, he seems to have forgotten where he comes from entirely," Alasdair replied. Emily raised her eyebrows.

"Tell Alasdair what happened," Cara encouraged her.

Emily paused for a moment, choosing her words carefully.

"A horrible girl in our class took a disliking to Finley for no reason whatsoever and decided to try and launch him into Space without any oxygen. If Will hadn't have gone after him, he could have died," she explained.

"Will was so brave," said Matina dreamily, resting her face in her hands and staring towards the ceiling. For a moment, Emily felt extremely resentful of her pretty features, noting with envy her big, round doe-eyes, her jet-black hair and small, pink mouth. She quickly dismissed the thought from her mind and turned her attention back to Alasdair, who unfortunately had decided to speak again.

"You've got to feel sorry for Finley," he sighed, though Emily was unable to detect any real sympathy in his voice. "It was such a mistake for him to come here. You know his mother is one of our family maids? It's just embarrassing. Cruel to let him into the Academy if you ask me."

"Except I don't think anybody did ask you, did they, Alasdair?" Emily shot back at him, unable to control the fire that was building inside her with his every word.

"I can see my opinions aren't welcome here," he said coolly. "Perhaps I should find somebody from Gagarin to sit with."

Emily said nothing, her glare informing him of how strongly she agreed with the idea of him leaving. Affronted, he got to his feet, his chair scraping noisily against the floor. With a scathing look in Emily's direction, he turned on his heels and sauntered off to find the rest of the Floor One.

"Sorry about him," said Cara, once he was out of earshot. "We didn't know who he was, he just started talking to us."

"It's okay," said Emily. "It isn't your fault. He was obviously just being nosey about Finley."

"What's he like anyway?" Cara asked. "Finley, I mean?"

"He's just a normal boy," Emily replied, confused by the question. She couldn't understand why there was so much intrigue surrounding Finley's enrolment at the school. After all, he had passed the entrance exams, the same as everybody else. There was no rule that said that only children from the higher floors could attend The Space Academy. In her mind, he had more of a right to be there than pupils like Alasdair and his smug friends, whose parents had no doubt used their influence and credits to get their children a place at the school.

Cara and Matina seemed to sense Emily's reluctance to discuss the topic any further and changed the subject to what had they learnt so far at the Academy. Following that, they launched into an in-depth conversation about how handsome they found Mr. Zeppler. They were just in the middle of arguing over whether "Cara Zeppler" or "Matina Zeppler" sounded better, when Will and Finley came to join them at the table, full of energy and exuberance.

"How did it go?" Emily asked them the moment they arrived. Finley glanced towards the other two girls at the table, hesitant to answer in their company.

"It's okay," Emily re-assured him. "This is Cara and Matina. They're nice."

The girls looked at her with gratitude and leaned in, readily waiting to hear the private conversation they were being let in on.

"It went well," Finley grinned. "The girl has been expelled. Her name was Josie Jones. Apparently, she kept insisting that it was only a prank and that she just wanted to scare me, but Allance said there could be no excuses and sent her home."

"Yeah," Will chimed in, impatient to tell his part of the story. "I got told off for flying a rocket without a licence but I was also commended for my bravery." He puffed his chest out with pride.

"The only bad thing is that the school had to tell our parents," Finley frowned.

"My mum's going to be beside herself," Will sighed.

"I've already spoken to my mum and dad," Finley said. "They wanted me to come home but I said no. I'm not going to let anything spoil my chance to be here."

"So that's it then? It's all over?" Emily asked with relief.

"It's all over," Will confirmed.

"We were offered follow up care with Miss Fortem in case the event had traumatised us but we turned it down," Finley added.

"I'd be more traumatised spending one-on-one time with her than I would being blasted into Space!" Will exclaimed. "She's terrifying!".

Cara and Matina burst into high-pitched, exaggerated laughter at his joke. At this, Emily stood up sharply and ushered the boys over to the serving station, insisting that she was suddenly ravenous. The three of them collected their dinners from the helpful robots and moved around the hall until they found an empty table to sit at so they could speak in private. They ate with enthusiasm, returning to collect second helpings and stuffing themselves until they were sleepy and satisfied. Their conversation was light and full of laughter, with all of them basking in the knowledge that the day's drama was over and they could now continue their academic lives as normal students, united in their conviction that nothing bad would ever happen to them again for the entirety of the five years they would spend at the Academy.

After they had finished their meals, the first-years were gathered together in the Reception Hall by Miss Fortem where it was announced that their belongings had been sorted through and that they could now be shown to their new rooms. The excitement was uncontainable and the students spent the whole march across the school grounds buzzing with anticipation. They were led to a mini-complex of buildings, each one varying in size and shape but all of them coated in the same light grey material. Miss Fortem stopped outside the closest of the small cluster and touched the sensor pad beside the door to allow the first-years and their Prefect escorts inside.

They entered a small foyer, carpeted in the same shade of navy blue as the material used for the school jumpers. The room was dimly lit by rectangular lights that buzzed and flickered with the effort of staying on. Four tall plants in wide terracotta vases flanked the corners of the foyer, wilting with neglect and lack of UV light. The walls were decorated with paintings of cats, birds and enough other species of animals from Earth to make up an entire menagerie. An old, wooden desk stood in the corner, its surfaces worn and stained with age. Behind the desk stood a dowdy woman, her grey hair pulled into a scraggy bun, strands of hair escaping around her face and tangling around her thick horn-rimmed glasses. She was wearing a long, blue dress embellished with the images of yellow flowers, their green stalks weaving and intertwining to form a swirling pattern across the fabric that was somewhat harsh upon the eyes. Upon their entrance, she shuffled towards them, the slight stoop of her posture dwarfing her in contrast to Miss Fortem.

"Boys and girls, allow me to introduce Ms. Everly," Miss Fortem began. "She is in charge of running your rooms and making sure that our service bots keep them clean and tidy. She also patrols the corridors at night to make sure that nobody is out of bed past the ten o'clock curfew. If you need Ms. Everly's assistance during school hours, you will find her in the foyer which she decorated herself- "

There was a silent moment of understanding among the first-years as they compared Ms. Everly to the decor.

"She'll be here for most of the day so if you have any questions feel free to ask her," Miss Fortem continued.

"I have a question," called Rudy from the back of the group.

"Yes, what is it?" snapped Miss Fortem.

"Did Ms. Everly design all of our rooms too?" he asked, attempting the question to sound innocent, though its true meaning was thinly veiled.

"Oh no, dear," laughed Ms. Everly. "All the student's rooms were designed by a proper architect. Something Hullington I think his name was."

"Spencer's dad," Will said under his breath with disdain. Emily was wholly relieved that their bedrooms would not be following the decorative theme of the foyer and wondered if Ms. Everly needed stronger glasses so that she could see the proper outcome of her work.

"Thank you, Rudy, for that interesting yet highly unnecessary question," said Miss. Fortem, turning her attention back to the task at hand.

"Now," she continued, "as you may have seen, behind me there are three lifts which can be used by students at any time of the day. Of course, I will remind you again that nobody should be out of bed after curfew, which is ten p.m sharp. If there is an emergency after this hour you must use your Student Planner's to contact a member of staff. In the event of a fire, you will hear an alarm ring out, after which you may use the lift if necessary," Miss Fortem explained.

"'If necessary'," muttered Will in disbelief.

"There are three floors of rooms above us. We are currently on the ground floor. I will now ask Ms. Everly to send your room numbers through to your Student Planners. Once you have received these, one of our Prefects will show you the way," Miss Fortem concluded.

Ms. Everly moved back to her desk at a painfully slow pace. Emily was desperate to find out where her room would be and, more importantly, who she would become neighbours with. When she reached the desk, she produced a battered tablet from its depths and began squinting at its screen, stabbing it extremely hard with one finger before retracting it again, as though she were afraid the tablet would bite her. Several agonising minutes passed before the message was sent, the foyer erupting in the sound of beeping as everybody scrambled to check their planners. Emily huddled next to Will and Finley, eager to find out how close to each other they would be.

"I'm in 311!" announced Will as the number appeared on his screen.

"211," Emily replied. "We're not on the same floor."

"No but you're right underneath me," Will grinned.

"No late-night dance parties then please," Emily teased.

"Only on a Tuesday," Will retorted.

Finley cleared his throat.

"What room are you in, Finley?" Will asked him, glossing over the fact that he and Emily had momentarily forgotten his existence.

"101," he responded.

"Oh, I hoped we'd all be near each other," Emily sighed.

"Don't worry, I'm used to being on a low floor," Finley said with a weak smile.

Emily frowned, but she had no chance to console him before Miss Fortem began ordering them to be taken to their rooms. They were divided into three groups, one for each floor, and called over to their designated Prefect. Emily was pleased to see that her group was being led by Sam and not by the loathsome May who had taken them to their Rocket Control class. Her relief was cut short, however, by the sight of Rudy strutting over to join them, surrounded by his entourage of faceless cronies. When he noticed her, attempting to shrink into the back of the huddle, he strode over and placed his arm tightly around her shoulders.

"Hey, Em," he smirked. "Take it you're on the second floor too?"

"Unfortunately, yes," Emily replied through gritted teeth, removing his arm from around her.

"It'll be just like old times," he laughed, nudging her a little bit too hard with his elbow.

She groaned, unable to think of anything worse than having to endure Rudy's presence on a daily basis. She silently cursed her own bad luck that she had been the only girl from her tutor group to get into the Academy, meaning that Rudy and his insufferable gang of followers were the only familiar faces she had from home. Desperate to escape, she weaved her way to the front of the group, cramming herself amongst the more eager students who were all staring at Sam, awaiting his instructions.

He led them to the lift in the middle of the foyer and they followed him in, comfortably able to fit inside the spacious interior. The ride to the second floor was smooth and swift, lasting only a matter of seconds. Once they had come to a standstill, Sam escorted them out into the corridor, decorated in a fashionable silver tile that was buffed and polished to perfection, as though it had never had a spot of dirt on it. Thick, blue doors lined each side of the walls, each displaying a number in the school's favoured gold labelling. With a helpful point in the right direction from Sam, Emily made her way towards her room, which was at the very end of the corridor.

After a brief walk, she came face to face with her door, the number "211" emblazoned across the middle. She pushed gently and the door swung back on its hinges, having been left unlocked for her access. She took a deep breath and stepped over the threshold, taking in the sight of what would become her home for the next year.

A Queen-sized bed stood to the left of the door, tucked up snugly in the corner and dressed in fresh bedding that had never been slept in. Against the back wall stood a triple-fronted, black wardrobe with a matching dresser beside it. There was also a desk complete with a large touch screen on a stand, a set of shelves for storage and a comfortable looking sofa. A mini drinks machine stood between two chutes that fed into the wall marked "laundry" and "rubbish". A small, white door led into her en-suite bathroom, which featured an I-Bath, shower, toilet, washbasin and a round mirror. She walked across the room and gazed at the view of the school grounds that could be seen through her window, pausing to watch the artificial lake as the starlight from the sky above twinkled upon its surface like a million dancing fairies.

Facing back into the room, she decided to call Will on her Personal Device to see what his bedroom on the top floor was like. He gave her a virtual tour and she saw that it was much larger than hers with significantly more furnishings. His room was light and airy, with all of his décor painted in matching shades of white and beige to give the space a perception of brightness.

"It's almost twice the size of mine!" Emily complained.

"That'll be Spencer's dad's doing," Will said, rolling his eyes. "Can't resist making the higher floors better than the lower."

The two of them continued to chat while they unpacked the belongings that had been left for them at the end of their beds. Half-way through the conversation, they remembered Finley and added him to a group call, getting a tour of his own much smaller room. Will spent the remainder of the call informing them of which gadgets he was going to ask his mum to send from home- including his virtual reality headset, his television screens and a snack vendor. There was some speculation about their new subjects, particularly about which one would be the most exciting. Emily was outnumbered two-to-one on her notion that it would be Technology while Will and Finley both voted for Alien Studies.

 After a while, they all became tired, the events of the first day taking their toll. They said goodnight and Emily got ready for bed, sliding into the warm covers where she now lay. After re-living the past twelve hours in her mind, she finally felt ready for sleep and rolled over to burrowed into her pillow. As she drifted into unconsciousness, she found herself wondering with a feverish delight what the future had in store for her and her new friends, hardly able to contain the anticipation of discovering what new excitement her second day at the Academy would hold.

8.

The Study of Aliens

Kurt Krecher awoke at six a.m. sharp on the morning of his first day back at work and rose straight from his bed to make a cup of strong, black coffee. Still wearing the threadbare dressing gown his wife had bought him for Christmas many years ago, he went and sat at his desk and proceeded to open his laptop – an old souvenir he had kept from Earth. As was customary, he downloaded the files of information Admiral Allance had sent him regarding their new students that year and -though he suspected he was the only teacher to do so- read through the details carefully so he could get to know his new class. Scrolling down the list of names and birth dates, it struck him that this was the first class to ever attend The Academy that had never set foot on Earth. It gave him a strange feeling to comprehend the thought that so many of them had been born on the Mayfly and had never known any other life outside its unyielding, titanium walls.

As he continued to scroll, he was surprised to find one of the pupils was listed as being from Floor Seven. He had heard rumours that a boy from the lower floors was being admitted to The Academy, but had never believed it could be true. He had always advocated for the school to open its doors to all the children on the Mayfly that were of the right age to attend, but Admiral Allance had vehemently rejected the idea on several occasions. He wondered what, or indeed who, had convinced him to allow this new student in, suspecting a hefty increase in budget from the Governors may have changed the Admiral's mind. A note in the boy's file informed him that there had already been an incident with another pupil in his first Rocket Control lesson, in which he had narrowly escaped being launched into Space without any oxygen. A hard lump of disgust formed in his throat that turned the taste of his coffee sour. It troubled him that the rife inequality between the social classes had followed them from Earth onto the Mayfly and would no doubt be transferred to Novum. They had been promised a better world before The Split, but the more time went on, the less Kurt was able to believe in such a dream. No doubt the same suffering that had occurred in the last days of Earth would follow humanity wherever it went. There was no escaping it in his opinion. In all his years of studying and teaching, he had never come across an alien race that was able to inflict as much cruelty onto their own kind as human beings were. Sighing, he made a note of the poor boy's name - "Finley Campbell"- and committed it to memory. If he couldn't fight for social justice on a wider scale, he would certainly ensure it was practised in his own classroom.

He took another deep swig of his coffee and continued to read about the new year group through bleary, bloodshot eyes. His heart fluttered in a funny sort of way when the image of a strangely familiar face appeared on his screen. The picture was of a boy from Alderin class, the name "William James" attached to his file. It took him a moment to place him, his brain desperately searching through the memories of the thousands of students he had taught over the years. As soon as he remembered, he wondered with a slight twang of panic how he ever could have forgotten. The boy was the son of two of the most memorable people he had ever met and his inability to immediately recognise him served as further proof to himself that his mind was softening with age.

He got up and strode over to the window, looking out pensively as he finished his warm drink. For a moment, he had forgotten where he was, expecting to see the Sunrise bathing the horizon in its glorious shades of red, orange and pink. He imagined he could see rolling green hills, running into each other as they peaked and brayed, creating a sea of brown and green in the distance. He pictured wispy clouds and tall trees and houses with thatched rooves with black birds flying overhead. He hoped with all his heart that he might see such views again one day, but for now there was only the infinite black of Space.

As he dressed himself in his patched brown suit and silk waistcoat, his mind began to wander. Thinking about William James' parents had triggered an involuntary trip down memory lane and he became immersed in a powerful recollection of the past.

The time in which he had first encountered William's mother, Elsie, and his father, Austin, had been a dire time on Earth. The population was at its lowest ebb, having fallen to around twenty percent of what it had originally been, and the conflict for Earth's limited resources had been rife and violent as ever. Kurt was a professor at one of only a hundred existing colleges around the country and by a stroke of luck, had managed to find himself a haven. The college was situated in North Wales and was aptly named College Snowdonia after its magnificent view of the Welsh mountains. The Split had not long been announced and as a result, everyone with the slightest bit of intelligence was desperately trying to improve their skills and make themselves worthy enough to gain passage on the Mayfly. Due to the sudden boom of enthusiasm in education, the Government had taken it upon themselves to ensure every college still running received enough food, water and power to sustain itself, with security installed to protect the various campuses.

The small city where College Snowdonia was based had been almost completely deserted and so the teaching staff and students had had their pick of the empty houses. Kurt and his wife had discovered an old farmhouse in the city's surrounding countryside and had spent all their free time renovating it until they had created themselves a beautiful, rustic home. They herded animals from the fields around them and were able to live off the land, being successful enough in their farming to donate some of their produce to the other local residents. It had been an oasis of peace in a desert of atrocities. Over time, everybody associated with the College came together to form a tight-knit community and as the days and nights rolled on, it was almost possible to forget that the Earth was slowly dying around them.

He hadn't known William's parents well at first, for his mother had studied Psychology and his father Navigation. However, he often saw them about the stone corridors of the college building, looking like love's young dream, their awkward friend Alfie bumbling after them, always in their shadow. No one ever would have guessed that he would become Captain of the Mayfly, beating out the other thousands of hopeful Navigation students across the country. Kurt had strongly suspected that his mother's influential position in society had a lot more to do with him getting the job than his skills, though he had been careful not to voice this to anyone.

It wasn't until their final year that Kurt had come into contact with the three, when they had unexpectedly signed up to do a module in Alien Studies. They all claimed to have been struck by a sudden interest in the topic, but Kurt was always suspicious of their true motives. The real reason for their joining his class, however, had been far stranger and more twisted than he could ever have imagined. To even think of it now made the hairs on the back of his neck stand on end and gave him the distinct feeling that he was being watched.

Shuddering, Kurt shook the memory from his mind and left his apartment, walking briskly across the school grounds. The cool air filtered around the enclosed bubble of the school, causing him to shiver and hug his jacket tighter about his person. When he reached the main school building, he stepped quickly through the entrance, glancing up at the oppressively large representation of Novum as he did so. Every time he passed under it, he was afraid it would somehow come unattached and fall, crushing him as if he were nothing but a mere ant. On this occasion, however, he had managed to survive, and so he headed into the Dining Hall, intending to reward himself with a second cup of coffee.

He grunted at the robot at the serving station to give him his usual and sat down at the nearest table, chewing unenthusiastically on a limp piece of toast. They had tried their hardest to replicate Earth's food at The Academy, but the results of their labour could simply not compare to the taste of his wife's freshly baked bread, warm from the agar. Still, he had no choice but to make do.

The hall was quiet, with only a few members of the teaching staff milling about as they prepared to start their day. Kurt responded to their obligatory greetings with mumbled "mornings" as they passed him to gather in a gaggle on the other side of the room. He tried to block out the noise of their chatter as he read over his lesson plans on the tablet he kept in his inner jacket pocket.

Once he had filled himself sufficiently with food, he got up and left the hall, his hands shaking from the amount of caffeine he had already consumed that morning. He walked back out of the main entrance and turned left, walking down the asphalt path that led to the Ivory Tower where his lessons took place.

He reached the tower's base and climbed into the open-topped shuttle rocket that was stationed beside it. The tower had no stairs and was designed to prevent the alien subjects kept inside it from escaping.

Therefore, the only way for Kurt to access his office and classroom was by flight. He had always hated flying, finding the whole experience entirely unnatural and he clung tightly to the metal bar around his waist as the rocket took off.

The driver, Jeff, was a friendly man with a relentlessly positive attitude, despite the fact he spent his days ferrying Kurt and his students back and forth on the same monotonous journey. He was of a similar age to Kurt, his hair grey and thinning and his hands wrinkled and battered from a lifetime of hard work. For that reason, Kurt felt a strange sort of affinity with him and was willing to indulge his inane conversation, which usually centred around his grandchildren back on the Mayfly and how proud of them he was for no obvious reason.

When the brief ride was over, Jeff parked on the small landing pad on the tower's side and Kurt disembarked, thanking him courteously for his service. He walked inside, dropped his things off on his desk and headed straight for the large Alienary located next to his classroom.

The vast storage room was the home to dozens of different species, all kept in enclosures that varied in size and design to suit their individual needs. There were cages covered in red dust, with burning lights fixed overhead to represent the scorching planes of far-off desert planets. Others were packed with foliage, filled with soaring trees and wild bushes, thick brown grass growing up from the soil-covered floor and tangling to form a dense hideaway for the aliens within. There were high tanks, filled to the brim with the swirling multicoloured waters from different worlds, underwater rock formations providing shelter for their inhabitants. Overhead, there were giant, swinging cages, attached firmly to the ceiling, their winged occupants waiting impatiently to be allowed out onto the grounds to fly. It was Kurt's favourite place in existence, and he spent his free period that morning doing his usual rounds, ensuring that the alien creatures were comfortable, well-fed and clean.

He had grown increasingly fond of his captives over the years, caring wholeheartedly for the beings, who's intelligence matched only that of the animals that had roamed Earth, making them oblivious to their imprisoned state. He wandered through the cages, greeting each beast he met with affection. He petted the ten-legged Timor as though it were a domesticated dog, dodging its snapping jaws with expert precision. He crooned at the feral Runhorn, soothing its angry disposition with a helping of raw meat he'd had delivered from the kitchen. None of the species in the Alienary caused him the slightest bit of an unease or fear. In fact, over the years, they had become his only trusted companions, providing him with relief from his otherwise lonely existence.

Noticing the time, Kurt began hurrying to collect the resources he would need for his first lesson. Rushing back to his classroom, he placed an unhatched, yellow egg on each desk, eagerly anticipating the arrival of his students. A moment later, the sound of faltering engines and the cheerful hum of chatter outside the door announced it was time for his class to begin. He stood up straight, placing his arms by his side and nodding at the students as they entered and looked around his classroom with bewilderment, gasping with delight when they noticed the eggs. Kurt had become so used to the room that he had forgotten how spectacular it was to behold for the first time. The semi-circular walls were covered with small, paned windows that fitted together like an intricate jigsaw, enabling for an exceptional view of the school below. Sick of the constant darkness, Kurt had requested UV lights be installed outside the building to give the impression of sunlight flooding in. Watching the dust particles dancing in the light reminded him of Earth and provided him with great comfort, inspiring him to start his lesson with a positive attitude in mind.

"Good morning everyone," he greeted the class. There was a faint reply of "good morning" as the last of the students scrambled to find their seats. Once a small disruption between a brown-haired girl and a tall, smug-looking boy had been settled, Kurt continued.

"My name is Mr. Krecher," he announced, pressing a small button on the control hidden in his hand, causing his name to appear on the interactive board on the back wall.

"As you may have noticed, there is an egg on each of your desks, does anybody know which species of alien they belong to?" he asked, pacing up and down at the front of the class. His question was met with a resounding silence.

"No? Very well, I shall tell you. What you see before you are the unhatched eggs of a Beakin," he pressed the button again so that an image of the small creature appeared on the board. There was a chorus of "ahh" from the students as they looked upon its small yellow spotted body, its large, round eyes and its shiny, beaked mouth.

"Yes, they are rather charming creatures," he continued. "They make excellent pets which is fortunate for you, as your task for the term will be to care for one in the pairs you are now sat in."

The brown-haired girl from the earlier scuffle shot her hand up in the air with extreme force.

"Yes, er – "

"Emily," she prompted him.

"Go on," he said.

"Do we have to work in these pairs? Can we not change?" she asked, her green eyes full of desperation. Kurt glanced at the boy sat beside her, the confidence draining from his face as everyone in the class stared in their direction.

"I'm afraid it's bad news Emily. The partner you are with today will remain your partner for the rest of the term" Kurt answered. "Teaching the whole year group together can be difficult, so the less discrepancies there are over partners, the easier it will be for me to remember all of your names."

Emily looked nauseated.

"It's not all doom and gloom," he re-assured her. "Perhaps you will all learn something about each other."

He cast his eyes over the rest of the pairs sat around the room, noticing that the boy from Floor Seven was partnered with William James. Looking at William would almost certainly have sent his mind catapulting into the past again if it wasn't for the eyes of the other eighty-nine students in the room staring at him expectantly.

"Underneath your desks you will find a drawer with a tablet device inside," Kurt continued. "You will use this tablet to send me weekly videos, images and reports on your progress. I will also be checking the health and happiness of your Beakin during our classes where will continue to learn about their origins, history and development."

"Now, the first things you must do as new carers is hatch your egg. Like most creatures, Beakin eggs require light and heat to hatch, however, their affectionate nature means they also need a demonstration of love to come out of their shells. Desk lights can be collected from the front of class to take care of the former necessity, I shall leave the 'love' part for you to interpret. There will be extra credit for the first pair to hatch their egg during the lesson," Krecher explained.

There was a small commotion as the class got to their feet to retrieve their lamps. Kurt meandered around the room, which had erupted in a loud discussion of the task, and watched with interest as his pupils showcased their different approaches to expressing love. Some were stroking their eggs, while others hugged them to their chests, inspecting their shells carefully for any cracks on the surface. One boy had taken to kissing his egg with such force and enthusiasm that Kurt couldn't help but feel sorry for any future romantic partner he might have. Unsurprisingly, none of them were successful in hatching their Beakin.

When he approached William and Finley, he hung back, intrigued by the snippets of their conversation he could overhear.

"Do you think it's scared?" William asked Finley, contemplating their egg with concern.

"What do you mean?" asked Finley.

"Well I reckon if I'd been sat inside an egg all my life and suddenly some strangers were trying to get me to come out I'd be quite scared," William replied.

"Yeah they probably are frightened. I mean, they don't even know that there's anything outside the egg. How do they know they're not destroying their only home for no reason?" Finley reflected.

"Shall we try and comfort it?" William suggested.

"I'm not sure how," said Finley, chewing his lip in deep thought. There was a moment of silence between the two boys before Finley spoke again.

"Well... there is something, but it's probably stupid," he said, looking at the ground with embarrassment.

"What is it?" William encouraged him.

"It's something my mum used to say to me when I was little. You know, when I had nightmares and stuff," Finley continued.

"Try it," said William.

"Are you sure?" Finley asked.

"Yeah, go on, it might work."

Finley picked up the egg and brought it close to his face, glancing around quickly to check that nobody was watching him. Kurt averted his eyes and pretended to be extremely interested in something he could see out the window so as not to put him off. When Finley was sure no one was listening, he spoke to the egg in a gentle voice that Kurt could only just hear over the chatter.

"Don't be scared" he told it. "As long as you are loved, you are safe."

He put the egg down swiftly, as though dropping something red hot and placed his arms behind his back as he cheeks flushed scarlet. His discomfort only lasted a few seconds however, for almost as soon as the egg had touched the surface of the desk, it began to tremble and shake, splitting open to reveal the infant Beakin inside.

"Excellent work boys," Kurt exclaimed, rushing over to congratulate them. "You completed the task in record time!"

"How did they do it?" an irritated boy asked from across the room.

"The Beakin's have telepathic abilities," Kurt explained, "They are able to read people's genuine intentions, regardless of what they might say out loud. This particular egg knew that Will and Finley had its best interests at heart. It felt loved enough to hatch."

"Well done mate," William told Finley, patting him on the back. "It was all you."

There was a loud scoffing noise from the desk beside them, as the tall, smug looking boy beside Emily let out a cruel laugh.

"Is something the matter?" Kurt asked him.

"How could Finley know anything about love?" he laughed. "I'm surprised his parents didn't try and sell him off so they could buy a loaf of bread that week."

There were a few titters from around the classroom.

85

"Why don't you shut your mouth, Rudy?" William shot back at him, stepping towards him in a fit of fury.

"Why don't you make me?" Rudy challenged him.

Before Kurt could react, William was upon him, shoving him hard into the desk behind him and causing several students to jump back in shock, clutching their eggs to their chests to stop them breaking. The boys began to fight, throwing punches at each other blindly and falling about the classroom.

"Enough!" Kurt boomed, using the full volume of his voice. The whole room fell deathly quiet and the two boys ceased their brawl immediately.

"How dare you disrupt my lesson! Fighting on school grounds is completely unacceptable" he scolded them, "You will both see me after class."

The boys looked down at their feet in shame and made their way sheepishly back to their desks, avoiding the gaze of the other pupils around them.

"Idiot," Emily whispered to Rudy upon his return. Kurt pretended not to hear.

The rest of the lesson passed smoothly, though the atmosphere in the room was somewhat tense. Kurt advised the rest of the year groups on how to hatch their eggs and sent them away with instructions relating to the Beakin's care. He provided them each with a suitable carry-cage and enough packets of food to last until next lesson and then dismissed them, sending them out to Jeff as they chatted about their first lesson, gripping their Beakin's cages with delight.

William and Rudy stayed behind, scuffing their feet on the floor and refusing to look at each other as they awaited their punishment. Kurt sighed and rubbed the bridge of his nose. Discipline was the least favourite part of his job, but he knew it had to be done.

"Rudy, I'll speak to you first," he announced, leading him through a door to the right of his classroom and into his office. The room was furnished entirely with antique pieces from Earth and the smell of old, musty wood filled their nostrils as soon as they walked in. His desk and coffee table were cluttered with papers and his bookcases were filled with assorted junk that he had failed to organise at the end of the last school year. His eyes darted instinctively to the corner, where a floor-length mirror was hidden by a white sheet draped over its twisted, metal top.

He sat on his favourite patchy blue armchair, a cloud of dust arising from its fabric as he sagged into the cushion, and gestured for Rudy to sit on the pale red chair opposite. He perched on the edge, shifting uncomfortably in the cushions so that the chair's heavy, golden feet creaked noisily with the effort of holding his weight.

Kurt launched into an obligatory lecture, reprimanding him for making offensive comments and exhibiting violent behaviour in a classroom environment. He went through all the necessary points, emphasising the importance of proper conduct at school and threatening to involve Admiral Allance if another incident of this nature should occur. After Rudy had apologised, Kurt nodded his acceptance and dismissed him, instructing him to send William in after him and then wait for Jeff so he could be taken back to the ground.

Moments later, William walked in, sitting down in the red armchair without having to be asked. Kurt paused for a moment, deciding to change tact for their conversation.

"Now William- "

"It's Will," he interrupted.

"Will," Kurt continued. "I understand that you were defending your friend in this situation, which is admirable, but you must realise that the way you behaved is not appropriate for the classroom. There are better ways to deal with people like Rudy than having to resort to violence."

"I understand," said Will. "Sorry Mr. Krecher."

Kurt regarded him for a moment. He had expected Will to have his mother's disposition, knowing he was raised by her alone, but he could see now that he much more of his father in him than Kurt had thought possible. He sat back in his chair and exhaled, softening his tone as much as his gruff voice would allow.

"When we left Earth, we were told that inequality would become a thing of the past. Now you and I both know that isn't the case, but that doesn't have to continue. Your generation have the power to change things before we reach Novum. If you wish to help Finley, then you need to make others see that he is no different from the rest of us, despite where he comes from. Attacking anyone who insults him will only draw more attention to him and cause problems in the long-term. The boy needs a friend, not a bodyguard. That is my advice to you."

Will nodded, a muscle twitching in his jaw as he digested Kurt's words. Not wishing to punish him too much for a display of loyalty, Kurt decided to draw the conversation to a close.

"Now of course you must be aware that if you are caught fighting again in my class I will have to inform the Admiral. Unfortunately, I also have no choice but to withhold your extra credit for completing today's egg task" he told him.

"That's okay," said Will sincerely. "You should give my credit to Finley. He's the one who worked out how to hatch it."

Kurt nodded and dismissed him, his thoughts already on the upcoming lunch hour and which creatures he would visit in his Alienary. Will excused himself and stood up, making his way towards the door. Just before he reached for the handle, he stopped and froze, rendered immobile by something he could see in front of him on the wall. He turned his head back slightly, as though he were going to speak, but then seemed to think better of it, walking through the door and slamming it behind him.

Kurt stood up and walked over to where he had stood, searching for a clue as to what he may have seen. When he noticed the offending picture on the wall, his body became momentarily numb. How could he have been so stupid to forget what he had hanging there? He gazed at the smiling faces of Will's parents staring innocently out from behind the frame, trying to ignore the whispers that had started buzzing in his ears, reminding him of secrets he had long hoped to forget.

9.

The Quest For Answers

Will's first few weeks at the Academy had passed in a flash, and before he knew it he was enjoying the seven-day break given to the students half-way through the term. He had spent the first days of his holidays holed up in his room with Finley and Emily playing games on his virtual reality machine, the three of them only emerging into the real world for meal times and to walk their Beakins. On the fourth day, Finley had started to panic about all the homework they'd been set and had made them go to the Library to start on some of their written assignments. Emily had insisted they begin with their Technology essay, since it was her favourite subject and had rolled her eyes profusely when Will and Finley complained of not understanding the title.

"'The advancement of technology is a danger to the survival and overall welfare of human beings'," Will read for a second time from his Student Planner. "Do you agree with this statement? Give reasons for your answer."

"I'm still not sure what exactly that means," Finley frowned.

"Me neither," Will huffed.

"Come on," sighed Emily. "You must be aware of the dangers of technology, surely?"

The boys looked at each other and shrugged. Trying to conjure an answer, Will cast his mind back over the Technology lessons they'd attended so far that term. Held in the Tech Lab, the class provided the students with access to an array of different gadgets and machines with hundreds of different functions. From robotics to teleportation systems, there was nothing about the lessons that hadn't completely fascinated them, including their teacher, Mr. Mayheim, aptly nicknamed "Mr. Mayhem" by the students. As ditzy as he was intelligent, Mr. Mayhem was an older gentleman who was so rarely seen without his white lab coat on, that legend at the school was he never took it off, even when he slept or showered. He was deeply enthusiastic about his subject, so much so that his teaching style often involved him embarking on passionate rants about various devices, during which Will was unsure whether he even was aware of the presence of his students. On his desk, he kept two large spheres containing trapped electrical energy that sparked and swirled in various shades of blue and yellow. Nobody knew exactly what the spheres were for, but a boy in Will's class, Scott Holmes, was adamant that they were the responsible for Mr. Mayhem's long, white hair being constantly stuck on end.

"I'm telling you," he had whispered to Will in class one day, "why do you think no one's allowed to touch them?"

Mulling the essay title over again in his mind, Will concluded that the only real danger he had ever encountered in Technology was Mr. Mayhem himself, who had successfully managed to blow up two ancient computer monitors worth thousands of credits and cause a minor fire in the first week alone. Other than that, he had been completely amazed by everything they had studied so far and couldn't see how anything that made life easier could possibly be a danger to humanity.

He voiced this opinion to Emily which proved to be an unwise decision that resulted in a ten-minute lecture about the War on Earth that was caused by artificial intelligence rebelling after their capabilities became too highly developed. Emily finished her essay in less than half an hour and proceeded to help the boys come up with ideas for their own work that were just varied enough from hers to avoid accusations of copying. Once they had finished, they took a break, during which they argued over which piece of homework to tackle next. Finley wanted to do their Combat and Weaponry task, which involved researching, drawing and labelling three weapons of their choice. Emily, who currently had custody of her and Rudy's Beakin, ironically named "Monster" by the latter, wanted to work on their diaries for Alien Studies. Will disagreed with them both, suggesting they write instructions on how to start and move off in a rocket for Mr. Zeppler. Eventually, they agreed to do their Civilisations essay – an exceptionally dull piece on the flaws of the Roman Empire- before moving onto subjects they enjoyed.

"The worst thing about Civilisations," Will reflected after attempting to write his opening sentence six or seven times, "is that it's so boring, but because Miss. Fortem is absolutely terrifying, you can't even zone out and daydream without putting your life at risk."

"At least we don't have Arithmetic homework," Emily pointed out, referring to Will's second most hated subject.

"Or Resources," quipped Finley.

"I like Resources," Emily countered.

"I did at first," said Will, "but how many times can you walk round a forest looking for fruit before it becomes incredibly dull?"

"It would be nice to try some different terrains," Emily admitted.

"Our exam is in the Forest, though," Finley reminded them.

"Oh yeah," Will remembered. "I think it'll be quite fun being left in the forest all day and having to fend for ourselves."

"'Fun' or highly irresponsible of the school?" Emily laughed.

"At least Ms. Dido will be in the biodome with us the whole time," Finley replied. "I can't imagine her letting anything go wrong after Riley Fitch."

"Yes, that's true," Emily concurred. "If there's anything dangerous in there she will definitely scare it off."

Will nodded in silent agreement. Ms. Dido was, without a doubt, the most impressive woman Will had ever seen, her height alone dwarfing anyone that stood beside her. Every inch of her body was defined with taught muscle, her clothes stretching and straining as they struggled to cover her wide frame. Even her hair, which she wore in two tight braids on the side of her head, gave the impression of strength somehow. When Will had described her appearance to his mother during one of their calls, she had told him the polite way of describing her was "Amazonian", but Will had no idea what this meant.

After sitting for several hours amongst a sprawled mass of laptops, tablets and I-Books, Emily, Will and Finley decided enough was enough and headed to the Dining Hall for their evening meal.

They were joined at their table by Cara and Matina, which seemed to set Emily off into a bad mood, though Will couldn't understand why. He had always found the two girls very pleasant. They wolfed down their spaghetti and meatballs, discussing their holiday so far and comparing notes on the homework they'd completed. Emily sighed loudly, watching them chew their dinners in disgust while picking at her own mushroom risotto.

"I don't know how you eat that stuff," said Will, gesturing to her food. "I couldn't live without meat. Especially bacon. It'd kill me off."

"I'm sure you'd survive," replied Emily drily. "Meat isn't good for you."

"Did you know that back on Earth they used to raise animals for slaughter," said Cara darkly. "Food wasn't made in labs like it is now."

"How do you know that?" Will asked.

"Matina and I joined the Earth Appreciation Society. We've actually found out some really interesting things."

As Cara and Matina launched into a gruesome fact-file about Earth, Will glanced up and noticed Kyan Smith, the unsettling former best friend of Josie Jones, staring at him from across the room, where he was sat alone. When they made eye contact, he didn't look away as Will had expected, but continued to watch him menacingly for a few more seconds. The uncomfortable moment was interrupted by Charlie, who walked over to the table and blocked Will's view of Kyan. By the time he had moved from Will's line of sight, Kyan had disappeared.

"Hey little sis," Charlie grinned at Emily, taking a seat opposite her, sending Cara and Matina into a flutter as he sat beside them.

"Hi Charlie," replied Emily. "To what do we owe the pleasure of your company."

"Now, now that's no way to talk to your big brother," Charlie teased. "Especially when he's come over to invite you to a party."

"A party?" Cara repeated with excitement.

"Yeah, in my room. It'll be after curfew, when all the teachers go to bed," Charlie replied.

"Your rooms in the third-year dorms," Emily frowned. "We can't be caught in the grounds after curfew, we'll be in so much trouble."

"That's the beauty of it," Charlie beamed, leaning in and speaking in a hushed voice. "I overheard Miss Fortem talking to Admiral Allance in the library earlier. It turns out that Mr. Mayhem is trying to invent some inter-planetary teleportation device that keeps going wrong. Miss Fortem was telling Allance that all the teachers need to be on guard tonight, because apparently Mayhem blew all the cameras out with a massive power surge! None of them are working! There's no surveillance at all."

He leant back in his chair triumphantly, watching his audience's reaction to the tale with his tongue pressed in his cheek.

"But Charlie..." Emily said after a moment, "if all the teachers are on guard we'll still get caught."

"That's the best part," Charlie responded. "Allance told her that as long as none of the students know about the broken cameras then not to bother. He told her just to keep it hush and then none of them have to go on patrolling duty."

"Seems a bit risky," Will mused, wondering how the headmaster could be so nonchalant about a possible breach in security, especially when Mr. Krecher took his aliens out to roam the grounds at night. Charlie rolled his eyes, a corner-stone trait of the Pannell family.

"Who cares?!" he exclaimed. "The point is, are you coming or not?"

"If it means that much to you," Emily sighed.

"Great, see you there," Charlie beamed.

"Can we come?" Cara and Matina asked.

"Sure, the more the merrier," Charlie shrugged, excusing himself from the table with a wink.

After dinner, Emily retreated to her room to get ready, Cara and Matina following her and giggling as they discussed outfit choices. Will and Finley went to collect their Beakin - named "Beaky" - and took him for a walk around the school grounds, a small, pink leash tied around his neck.

As they strolled around the Resources biodome, listening to the sound of the torrential rain inside its core, Will broke the news to Finley that he wouldn't be attending the party that evening.

"Oh, come on Will, I need you there," Finley pleaded. "The older students still look at me like I'm an alien with three heads."

Will apologised and fobbed him off with a weak excuse about being tired from doing homework and wanting to call his mum.

"Anyway," he reminded Finley, "you don't need me around when you've got Emily to protect you. She's far scarier than I am."

Finley accepted his point and the two of them returned to the dorms where they parted ways, promising to meet for breakfast so Will could be filled in on the details of the night.

Will rode the lift to the third floor and walked briskly to his room, closing the door behind him as the relief of being alone flooded through his body. He took a long shower, the hot water cascading over him and relaxing his mind. His thoughts drifted back to his first Alien Studies lesson, as it always did when he was alone, and the niggling memory of what he had seen when he'd been called into Krecher's office after his fight with Rudy.

Hanging on the wall, there had been a framed photograph. As Will had made to leave, something about it had caught his eye. Standing in the photo with Krecher was Will's mother, her face fuller and brighter with youth but unmistakeable nonetheless. Among the gathering of students they were posing with was a young man, his sandy-blonde hair, tanned skin and height making him stand out sharply against the rest of the group. Will studied the man's features carefully, taking in his blue, shining eyes, strong jaw and pronounced nose. He knew these features well. He saw them every morning when he looked in the bathroom mirror. They were his own. This man was his father. He had always been told that he looked just like his mother, but now as he stared at his father for the very first time, he realised he was more like him than anyone had wanted to admit. He must have only been stood still for a few seconds, but he had sensed Krecher's eyes burning into the back of his head. In a fit of adrenaline, he left, without saying a word to anyone about what he'd seen.

In all the Alien Studies lessons that had followed, Will had stared at Krecher whenever he wasn't looking, as if he might find the answers he was seeking written on his face. If the memory of teaching Will's parents was so precious to Krecher that he kept a framed photograph of them on his wall, then why had he never mentioned knowing them? His mother had never so much as uttered Krecher's name, which made no sense if she knew he was a teacher at The Academy. He had the strong inclination that something was being kept from him and he was determined to find out what.

Occasionally, Krecher had caught Will's eye in class, and each time his face had clouded with what Will could only describe as an expression of guilt. His behaviour had only enflamed Will's curiosity further and he had begun to plot a way to find out the truth.

He knew, by the strength of gut instinct, that the information he sought would be found in Krecher's office. He also knew that Krecher took his aliens out at precisely half past ten every night, having watched him through the window for several weeks. By carefully studying the interactive school map in stolen moments between classes, he had discovered the fastest way to reach the Ivory Tower from the first-year dormitories. The only obstacle that had been standing in his way were the security cameras that were dotted around the grounds. The moment Charlie had announced they were broken, he had made his decision. Tonight was the night he would put his plan into action.

At quarter past ten he got up from his bed, where he had been lying all evening, staring absentmindedly at the patterns in the plastering on his ceiling. He walked purposefully over the wardrobe and, pushing his school uniform to the side, he rifled through the clothes he had brought from home to find the darkest pieces of attire he owned. After successfully locating a black hoody and matching trousers, he dressed and went to the window, waiting for his cue to leave. A few minutes later, the faint pinprick of yellow light appeared in the distance that signalled Mr. Krecher had left the Ivory Tower and was walking through the darkened grounds by torchlight.

Will made for the door and headed down the hallway without hesitating, keeping a sharp pace as he moved. He saw Lois just ahead of him, standing in her bedroom doorway and gossiping with a group of the Floor One girls that were gathered in the corridor. He cursed himself for not preparing for the possibility of bumping into anyone. After all, there were no cameras in the student dorms, with it apparently being considered "unethical" by the school board, and so the only form of security the first-years had to contend with was the achingly slow patrol Ms. Everly conducted each night. Once she had gone, the dorms were available for free roaming, which many of the students regularly took advantage of.

Will ducked into the lift as discreetly as possible and descended to the ground floor. He hurried through the foyer and out the doors without stopping, allowing the thrill of his mission to carry him forwards into the night. Without the lamps on, The Academy was swathed in an almost impenetrable darkness and Will could only see a few feet in front of him. He found his route from memory, using his feet to feel out where the paths bent and twisted as he snaked his way around the back of the campus. Buildings loomed out of the shadows as he passed them, menacing in the gloom. He strained to recognize their exteriors, which were strikingly different in the deep darkness. Hoping to be comforted by a familiar sight, he glanced up at the blanket of stars that hung above him. In the black of night, he could see the glinting edge of the dome that encased the school. Gazing upon it made him feel claustrophobic, as if he were trapped inside one of the novelty snow globes his mother had purchased from the Earth souvenirs shop on the Mayfly.

After what felt like an eternity, he saw the Ivory Tower in the distance, a shiny, white beacon in the black. He raced in its direction, his eagerness to reach it growing with every step. The sound of aliens screeching in the distance informed him that Krecher was still outside and that there was still time. He approached the foot of the tower and stopped short, taking deep breaths as he paused to collect himself. The next stage of his plan would be the most difficult to execute.

With a quick scope of his surroundings to check he was truly alone, Will climbed into Jeff's shuttle and fastened himself into the driver's seat. After much pestering , Jeff had admitted to Will that he programmed the shuttle onto autopilot, so that a simple flick of a switch would activate its flight path. Jeff had made Will promise not to tell anyone, for fear he would become redundant if his lack of purpose was made public. Little did he know, it was more than in Will's best interests to keep the secret to himself. Praying he wouldn't be seen or heard, Will turned the switch on, ducking down to conceal himself from potential onlookers as the rocket made its ascent.

When he reached the docking bay, he exited the ship, making his way into the classroom beyond. He passed through the dark room with haste, the eerie silence filling him with unease, and reached the door to Krecher's office. He was relieved and rather surprised to find it was unlocked and pushed on the handle gently to enter.

The room was cast into shadow, and Will struggled to make sense of his surroundings as his eyes adjusted to the lack of light. He took a step forward and crashed into Mr. Krecher's desk, cursing loudly as his leg painfully caught on the wooden corner. Rubbing the swollen bruise, he tapped his Personal Device on his wristband and selected the torch feature, shining the bright light around the room as he searched for clues.

His first thought was to examine the photograph that had drawn him to the office in the first place. He shone his light on the back wall where the collection of framed pictures hung, trawling over each image slowly until he located the right one. It didn't take long for him to recognise the photo, hanging innocently between Krecher's graduation picture and a snap of a smiling blonde woman. Moving closer, he noticed for the first time that Captain Alfie was also in the photograph, standing between Will's mother and Krecher, his arms folded behind his back and a sombre expression on his face. Will bent down to read the plaque at the base of the frame, wondering if he would recognise any more names.

"Alien Studies class, Snowdonia College 2098," it read, "Taught by K. Krecher (middle). Students: Joel Emmett, Faye Ibrahim, Charlotte Mazur, Austin De Havilland, Elsie James, Alfie Sommers..."

The list continued but Will had stopped reading. He had always known that his mother had given him her surname, but she had never told him what his father's name was, and after a while Will had given up asking questions. Seeing the name etched in fine print before him sent Will's mind into overdrive. For a moment, he was lost in a daydream in which he was William De Havilland, a normal boy from a normal family, and not William James - the boy who grew up without a father.

He tore himself away from the photo and searched the rest of the room, raiding Krecher's drawers that were filled with piles of unorganised papers and heavy, bound journals, covered in dust. At the bottom of the pile was a thick, green notebook that had been secured with a padlock. Will picked it up and turned it over in his hands. It was rough and dog-eared, creases forming over its cover from where it had been opened and closed so many times. Peering down at the thick mass of pages, he saw that some of them had been torn out, leaving a jagged edge where they had once been. A small, white sticker on the sleeve read "September 2097- June 2098". Will knew that his father had died before The Split in 2100, the year Will was born. That meant that Krecher had known his mum and dad just two short years before the tragic event had happened. Something during this time period was significant enough for him to keep a framed photograph of the class and a padlocked journal. Will had a strong feeling that whatever was inside the journal may be linked to his dad's death and began searching for a key.

After hunting for several minutes to no avail, he began to feel defeated. He slumped into Krecher's armchair, contemplating whether to abandon his mission altogether. Suddenly, the most peculiar sight manifested before his eyes. A mirror that was standing in the corner of the room had spontaneously sprouted a handle on its surface; shiny, round and inviting. A voice in Will's head urged him forwards and he reached out and turned it, the mirror swinging backwards to reveal itself as a door.

He dithered for a moment, hesitating between investigating further and leaving the office altogether before he found himself in deep trouble. His mind was made up for him, however, when the sound of approaching footsteps from the classroom outside echoed through the door. He jumped and sprinted forwards, running at full pelt through the mirror-turned-door and into whatever lay beyond.

10.

The Looking Glass

The sensation of cold air smothered Will's face and body as he realised with a jolt that he was outside. He bent over to catch his breath, disorientation causing his head to spin. He looked at the solid concrete beneath his feet in disbelief. Just moments ago, he had been at the top of the Ivory Tower, miles and miles from the ground. There was no way he could have survived a fall from that height. It was impossible and yet, there he was, all in one piece. He turned around, searching wildly for the mirror he had run through, but it had disappeared completely. He staggered backwards as his surroundings came into focus and the understanding of where he was dawned on him.

He was standing upon a street flanked with red-bricked houses, their tiled rooves forming perfect triangles that pointed into the sky. Cars of various make and model sat in driveways that were decorated with flower pots and protected by thick, metal gates. The road was lit up by a combination of yellow street lamps and the pale moon that shone ghost-like over his head. He had paid enough attention in History to know why the scene was so familiar to him. He was on Earth.

The wind blew coolly around his face and he hugged himself tightly to shelter from its sharp bite. There was a crisp freshness to the air that he had never experienced before and he inhaled deeply, his lungs filling gratefully with the clean, unfiltered oxygen. After a few seconds, his head began to steady itself as he sought a reasonable explanation for what had happened. The mirror must be some kind of teleportation device, he concluded, and Mr. Krecher must be making secret trips to Earth without anyone knowing. He was certain the footsteps he had heard before he fled belonged to Krecher and knew it wouldn't take him long to realise his office had had an intruder. He could only pray that he would put two and two together and realise where Will was, rescuing him before he ended up stranded on Earth forever.

He glanced around the street, hoping to find himself alone. The people who had been left on Earth after The Split were referred to as "Forgottens" and Will had heard enough about their volatile and violent nature to know that he would be in danger if he were to encounter anybody in the dark of night. With a sudden stroke of panic, he checked his Personal Device to call for help but found it had gone dead since his arrival. He closed his eyes and conjured the image of his mum's face, trying to comfort himself by imagining when he would next see her.

A noise behind him made him jump and he immediately realised that he was no longer alone on the street. A woman had appeared a few yards in front of him, a thick winter coat and scarf drawn around her body to protect her from the cold. She had her back to him, but Will could see her chestnut brown hair billowing out behind her as she moved. Something about her posture and way of walking told Will that she wasn't a threat, and deciding she would be his best chance for help, he pursued her, calling after her as he ran.

"Hello!" he shouted as he levelled with her. "Excuse me!"

The woman did not stop or even slow her pace. Desperate for her attention, Will ran in front of her, jogging backwards to keep up with her stride. A gust of wind blew her hood back and Will reeled with shock when he saw that the face of this woman was the very same face he had been picturing just a few seconds earlier. It was his mother.

"Mum!" he cried, a mixture of euphoria, confusion and fear convulsing through his body. Much to his displeasure, she still did not stop, speeding past him as if she could not hear him at all.

"Mum!" Will yelled. "It's me!"

She walked faster still, his words having no effect on her whatsoever.

"Mum?" he faltered, beginning to feel that something was wrong.

He ran after her, reaching out to grab her coat, but his hands slipped through the material as if it wasn't there. He tried to grab hold of her arm but all he felt between his fingers was the cold, night air.

"What's happening?" he asked himself out loud. His mother was here but she was a ghost, or a hologram, unable to see, hear or feel his touch. He was utterly terrified and perplexed beyond anything he had ever experienced. Not knowing what else to do, he carried on following her, hoping she would lead him to safety.

They turned a corner and the suburban road they were walking on suddenly began to descend sharply, giving way to a magnificent view. Will paused for a moment, his breath taken by the sight. Glorious mountains rose in the distance, their peaks topped with heavy dustings of white snow that tumbled down the sturdy rock of their faces until it reached the ground. Spanning between the mountains were rolling hills and plummeting valleys, dotted with sheep and a smattering of small cottages. It was a truly beautiful sight to behold.

Will continued to tail his mum down the road, following her as she veered into an alleyway and stormed through it, arriving at a vast body of water that he knew from his lessons was referred to as 'the sea'. She headed towards the water's edge with Will a few paces behind her, stones crunching beneath his feet as he struggled to keep his balance on the strange, new terrain. At the end of the beach, a figure was waiting, his back turned to them as he contemplated the infinite, black surface of the water.

His mother stopped and for a moment everything was still. Will stood quietly, listening to the sound of waves breaking on the shore. He watched as the figure turned and walked towards where Will invisibly stood, his face becoming clearer as he drew closer. It was his father.

"Elsie, I'm so glad you came," he smiled as he reached her, taking her hands in his own. "I was afraid you wouldn't come."

Will listened intently, hardly daring to move.

"Of course I came," Elsie replied. "You disappeared Austin. You promised me you would come home.

"We've got to go, Elsie," Austin said urgently. "We can't trust the Government. We've got to make our own escape from Earth."

"No, Austin," Elsie shook her head. "Please, stop this."

"Is it really so hard to believe Elsie, after all the things we've seen?" Austin pressed her.

She said nothing, her face twisted with despair.

"You're too scared to admit the truth," Austin sighed, shaking his head. "You know that I'm right."

"I thought we had dropped all of this," Elsie said, her eyes beginning to fill with tears. "I thought we'd moved past it. You have to forget about the Great Conspiracy. It's not real."

Austin opened his mouth to protest but Elsie cut him off, raising her voice louder to be heard.

"No one is trying to interfere with the Mayfly. Humans ruined the Earth and this is our only chance to start over. I know it seems too good to be true, but we have to trust that there's a better life out there somewhere. Otherwise, what's the point of all this?"

"I've got something for us," Austin said calmly when she had finished speaking, gesturing down the beach to a large spacecraft parked a few metres away. Will was surprised he hadn't immediately noticed it, its sheer size making it difficult to miss.

"Where did you get that?" Elsie demanded, panic rising in her voice.

"The flying department at the College has very lax security" Austin boasted. "It was easy enough to steal. The ship is big enough to accommodate us for several years. We can find our own new planet to live on. We don't need Novum or the Mayfly. This is the only way."

"Austin, stop this! You sound insane," Elsie pleaded with him. "We need to go home. We need to get away from this place, it's not good for you to be here."

"I can't do that," Austin replied.

"Yes, you can!" Elsie argued. "Come home and apply to the Mayfly with me. It's the only hope the three of us have."

She put her hand on her stomach, drawing Will's attention to her pregnancy. His heart began to pound in his ears as the sickening reality of what he was about to witness dawned on him.

"We can stand here and argue about it all night," Austin said. "But the fact of the matter is, the Mayfly isn't safe. I've been saying it since College and I know I'm right. I'm leaving. And you can either come with me or you can stay here and die with everyone else."

Elsie jerked her head back as if he had slapped her.

"How can you say that?" she whispered, tears escaping down her cheeks. "You would really leave me and your child here to die?"

Austin didn't reply for a moment, watching in contempt as she continued to sob.

"I'm disappointed you didn't believe in me Elsie," he said thickly, his voice shaking with anger. "Now this is what it's come to."

"You can't be serious," she spluttered. "You can't leave us."

"You've given me no choice," he replied coldly.

Elsie sank to her knees, watching as Austin strode with determination down the beach, her sobs growing louder and more uncontrollable with every step he took. Will watched with horror as his father left, not stopping once to look back at his mother or the unborn child he was leaving behind.

He tried to reach out to comfort Elsie but she couldn't feel him. He yelled out in rage against his father, but he couldn't hear. After a moment, he dropped to the floor, sitting beside his mother as he waited for the turmoil to end.

There was a "whooshing" noise and a powerful gust of air as his father entered the spacecraft and took off, ascending into the sky with furious speed. Will watched as he flew higher and higher, drifting over the sea directly in front of them. Suddenly, the spacecraft halted and hovered, floating gently in mid-air. Will's heart leapt with hope for the possibility that his father had changed his mind, despite knowing how the story ended. His mother's sobs slowed beside him as her eyes too glimmered with the dream that Austin was about to return to her. With one, colossal "bang" that echoed terribly through the night, the spacecraft exploded into a spectacular ball of fire, illuminated the sky in a burst of orange and red.

Will got up and ran, covering his ears so he could not hear the horrible, broken screams that were coming from his mother. He could not bear to look at her, running until the water's edge had filled every corner of his vision. A glinting light in his peripherals caught his attention and he turned to see the mirror from Krecher's office materialising by the shore. He ran towards it at top speed, not caring if he smashed it to pieces, and threw his body against its surface. There was a moment of inky blackness before he fell, hitting the floor with a heavy thud. He lay still, refusing to open his eyes in case he should find himself still on the beach, trapped inside the terrible moment forever.

"Had a nice trip did you boy?" Krecher's gruff voice sounded from somewhere close by.

Will opened his eyes and saw, with great relief, that he was back in Krecher's office. Krecher himself was sat on his patchy, blue armchair, sipping coffee from a china mug and watching Will with concern.

"Come and sit down," he ordered him. Will stood up on shaking legs and did as he was told, moving to sit in the red armchair opposite Krecher.

"Cup of tea?" he asked and Will nodded, sitting in silence as Krecher rose and made his way over to the drinks machine in the corner, presenting Will with the piping hot beverage before sitting back down in his original position.

Will sipped the tea gratefully, the warm liquid soothing the numbness that had spread all over his body.

"So," said Krecher. "I see you found my Looking Glass."

"Y-your what?" Will stammered.

"The Looking Glass. That's what I call it," he motioned towards the mirror, standing perfectly in-tact in the corner.

"What is it?" Will asked, staring at its glass surface with terror.

"That's a good question," Krecher replied. "One I've spent many years trying to answer. The truth is, I don't know exactly what it is. I discovered it one day, a very long time ago when I was still a professor on Earth and I have been trying to understand it ever since. It's alien, of course, that much is clear. No human technology could ever match its capabilities. As to how it works though, I must confess it is still as much of a mystery to me as it was the first day I found it. All I know is that it shows you things, past, present and future, but only if they are relevant to you. Only if they mean something."

"I don't understand," Will shook his head. "How is that even possible? Just then... I was... It was like I was inside my mum's memories. How could that be?"

"It isn't memories," Krecher responded. "I thought so too at first but then I saw something from the future and realised it couldn't be so. It makes sense if you really think about it. Memories are unreliable. They are altered by time and perception. You can convince yourself of anything if you tell yourself its true enough times. No, this doesn't show memory. It shows you a point in time. It allows you to explore, to spectate, to journey about the moment to your heart's content, but it doesn't let you change anything. The people that you can see, they don't know you're there. Nothing you do has any effect on what happens. I've tried to change the past, to right a few wrongs, but it's impossible. You can't interact with anything. That is the mirror's curse."

"I think the curse is being able to see anything at all," Will swallowed and Krecher looked at him with worry.

"What did you see?" he questioned him. "If you don't mind me asking?"

"My dad," Will replied. "I saw my dad... die."

Krecher inhaled deeply.

"My boy, I'm so sorry," he sighed. "You shouldn't have been put through that."

He glared at the mirror with fury as though it could understand he was angry at it. Will said nothing, no words able to describe the way he felt about what he had witnessed.

"Well," Krecher continued. "You know my secret now Will. I trust you will keep it in exchange for me keeping yours."

"What's mine?" Will asked with confusion.

"Sneaking out after curfew," Krecher said with a smile. "Breaking into my office. I don't need to remind you how the Admiral would feel if he knew about all this. I think it's best for both of us that we keep this incident to ourselves."

"Yes, Mr. Krecher" Will said. "I understand if you're angry with me. I shouldn't have come here. It was wrong."

"I'm not angry," Krecher assured him. "Truth be told I feel I'm to blame for the whole thing. It was only natural that you'd come looking for answers after you saw a picture of your mother and father in here. I should have sat you down and spoken to you about it, but, I confess it's not a time in my life I enjoy discussing."

"How did you know them?" Will pressed, sensing that now may be the only chance he would get to ask the questions that had burned into his brain for the entire school term so far.

"I taught them at College," Krecher answered simply. "They joined my Alien Studies class, along with the Captain, in their final year. They were my best students. They showed a dedication to the subject that was unprecedented amongst their peers. I was terribly sad when I heard what happened to your father. He was a bright, young man full of promise, but his obsession with the Great Conspiracy got the better of him in the end. A real shame."

"Why didn't my mum tell me any of this?" Will wondered aloud.

"For the same reason that I didn't, I suspect," Krecher answered. "It can be incredibly painful to recall time spent with a loved one that you no longer have."

Will nodded, digesting this information slowly. He thought back to all the times he had questioned his mother about Austin as a boy and understood now why it put her in such a difficult position to answer. How could you tell a child about what he had just seen?

He finished his tea and put his cup down on the small, wooden coffee table beside his armchair, his eyes itching with tiredness. He let out a small yawn, his brain exhausted from all the revelations he had dealt with that evening. Krecher noticed this and got to his feet, Will doing the same.

"Probably time to get to bed now," he told Will. "Try not to get caught on the way back."

Will smiled and made to leave. He was a few centimetres from the door when Krecher called to him again.

"Oh, and Will... try not to get too lost in the past. There are things there that you may not want to discover."

Will left the office quickly, unescapable curiosity burning in his mind.

11.

The Creature In The Hallway

Lois flicked her perfectly coiffed blonde hair over her shoulder and sighed, examining the chipped pink nail varnish on her fingers. Despite her best attempts, contemplating which shade suited her best was not providing a sufficient distraction from Ms. Dido's lecture, which she had struggled greatly to concentrate on that day. Truthfully, she didn't think anyone enjoyed being confined to a classroom to learn about Resources, but the entire year group were forced to endure it once a week before their practical session started.

The effort not to look at the time on her Personal Device was strenuous and so she let her eyes wander around the class, taking in the mutual boredom of the Alderin, Armstrong and Grissom students alike. A pang of envy shot through her as she looked upon Penelope and Florence, her best friends from Floor One, sat beside each other and laughing silently at a whispered private joke. Ms. Dido insisted that her pupils were organised into alphabetical order, which unfortunately meant that Lois was stuck next to Kyan Smith, who spent most of his time smirking to himself and glaring at people in an off-putting manner. In all her time as his desk partner, she had never once heard him speak, his apparent mutism proving extremely problematic when they were set group work to do.

She glanced towards the window, hoping to amuse herself with the view of the lamplit school grounds, but was drawn instead to the sight of Will, sitting next to his friend Emily on the far side of the room. She watched as he bent down to rest his head on the desk, an expression of deep disinterest on his face. It reminded her of the first time she ever saw Will, standing awkwardly at her mother's funeral held in the Commiserations Hall on the Mayfly. Lois had only been five years old, but the memory of the day was still razor sharp in her head, available to replay in super high definition at any time.

"That's Will," her father had said, bending down to talk softly in her ear. "He's Elsie's little boy."

He pointed to Will's mother, who was standing beside him and doing her best to look the appropriate amount of sad. Her father's attempt to distract Lois from the fact her mother's coffin had just been launched into Space was feeble and she resented him for even trying.

"I've been hoping you two would meet properly," her father continued, "but Elsie and I are always so busy and you're always with the nanny..." he trailed off awkwardly, as was the custom for discussing the little amount of time he had for Lois.

She remained silent, watching Will as he took a small, toy rocket out of his pocket and began running it along the top of the benches, making "whooshing" noises as he did so.

"I think it might be good for you two to be friends," Alfie continued, "You know, what with you losing your mother and his father dying before he was born."

Lois remained silent. Earlier that morning, she had made a vow to herself that she wouldn't speak for the entire day. Her mother had been the only person who understood her, and if she couldn't talk to her, she decided that she would simply never speak to anyone again.

"Go and say hello," Alfie urged her, nudging Lois forwards.

She walked over to Will obligingly, if only to prevent further conversation with her father. Sitting on the bench that Will was playing on, she stared at him with her arms folded, scowling darkly to make sure he knew she wasn't happy to be there.

"Hello Lois," Elsie smiled at her sympathetically. Lois said nothing, continuing to regard Will with her fiery stare.

To her dismay, he was completely unaware of her anger. He continued playing with his toy happily, soaring the rocket above his head. Her desire to bait him into an argument and release some of her fury overwhelmed her, and before she could stop herself, she began to speak.

"Can I have a go?" she asked. She was almost certain that Will would say "no" given his obvious attachment to the old-fashioned toy and hoped that would be a valid excuse to start the quarrel she so desperately wanted. He paused for a moment, chewing his lip as he considered his answer.

"Okay," he shrugged, handing her the rocket.

Shocked by his positive response, she began to examine the toy, noticing the chipped, red paint on its body and the white scuffs on its wings that indicated how well-loved it was. In one swift movement, she threw the rocket to the ground and stamped on it as hard as she could, driving her shiny, black shoes into it repeatedly until it was completely obliterated. She looked up at Will, her nose scrunched up in rage and her eyes full of tears. His mouth was hanging open in shock as he gazed forlornly at the remains of the toy. His bottom lip trembled and he looked to his mother, who placed a firm hand on his shoulders.

"It's okay Will," she soothed him. "We'll go down to the lobby after this and get you a new one. There's no problem."

Will considered this for a moment then nodded, taking his mother's hand and squeezing it tightly.

"Thank you, mummy," he smiled and Lois felt as though her body was going to burst from hatred. She hated Will for being happy and she hated his mother for being alive and she hated her mother for being dead. Most of all, she hated her father for thinking that this cheerful little boy could possibly understand the magnitude of pain that had been weighing on her for every minute of every day since her mother had gone.

Ever since the funeral, Lois had tried her best to ignore Will, but it had become increasingly difficult after they joined the school, with him constantly seeming to draw attention to himself. She was sure, however, that she could have successfully continued pretending he didn't exist, had she not personally seen him exhibit a series of odd behaviours over the past few weeks that had begun to intrigue her.

The first strange occurrence had been on a night in half- term when some boys from the third-year had thrown a party in their dorms. Some of the older girls who had befriended Lois invited her and her friends to come along. They had been stood in the hallway, ready to leave, when Lois had caught sight of Will, decked head to foot in black clothing, ducking into the lift on his own. Thinking it strange, she had looked for him at the party but had failed to see him mingling amongst the guests. A few days later, she had found him standing alone in the corridor, staring transfixed at the school map. She had hung back and watched as he began tracing over pathways with his finger, as though planning a very elaborate journey around the school. Following this, she had watched him closely, observing him in the Dining Hall on several occasions, each time staring into space and looking uncharacteristically troubled. She had a distinct feeling that something strange was going on and was determined to find out what.

Her thoughts about Will had carried her successfully through Ms. Dido's lecture and she came back to reality just in time to start the practical segment of the lesson. She followed the other students out of the classroom and congregated with them around the entrance to the Resources Biodome, managing to find Florence and Penelope in the process.

"That was so boring," Florence complained with a sigh, the other girls murmuring in agreement.

"You two looked like you were laughing about something," Lois said to Florence and Penelope. They exchanged a knowing look and burst out into giggles.

"What was the joke?" Lois pressed them.

"Oh, you wouldn't understand, Lois," Florence said. "It was something that happened in our Rocket Control lesson but you're not in our class."

Lois sighed and turned her attention to Ms. Dido, who had begun booming her instructions.

"We will shortly be going to the Biodome to practise the skills we discussed in our lesson," she announced. "Your task will be to find a suitable drinking source in the Forest terrain within an hour. You will each take a flask from me and fill it with the water that you find. The group who finds the cleanest and freshest water will receive the highest grade. I must remind you as always, to abide by the rules of the Biodome, which means staying firmly in groups and not wandering off alone. No one is to leave until a proper headcount has been performed at the end of the class."

Following her address, she opened the doors to the Biodome and let the students into the simulated forest. Despite the fact Lois knew it wasn't real, she enjoyed the experience of being "outdoors" nonetheless. Often, she would ignore the tasks Ms. Dido had set, focussing instead on the feel of earth and leaves crunching beneath her feet as the birds sang overhead. She would sometimes imagine that she was walking through the forest on Earth, or some other planet, passing the time before she would go home to her family, which in her fantasies featured a mother who was still alive and a father who wasn't a celebrity.

As they roamed the Biodome that morning, searching for the damp ground and green vegetation that would signal a water source nearby, Lois found she couldn't focus. Even listening to Florence and Penelope as they gossiped and giggled was proving more of a challenge than usual. She hung back a few paces, trailing after them as they weaved around the trees in deep conversation. Suddenly, she was distracted by the sound of a familiar voice carrying from behind some bushes and shrubbery. Ducking under the cover of a nearby tree, she paused to eavesdrop.

"We won't get in trouble, I'm telling you," she heard Will insist from out of sight. "I've studied a route that can get us from our dorms to the Ivory Tower in a matter of five minutes. We're not going to get caught."

"I don't know," Emily replied. "I don't understand why we have to sneak out after curfew. What's in Krecher's office that's so important?"

"I can't explain it, I just need to show you. Both of you," Will answered.

"I'm in," she heard another boy say.

"Finley!" Emily exclaimed. "You don't even know what you're agreeing to. Will hasn't told us anything."

"I trust him," Finley replied.

"Thank you," Will said triumphantly.

"Fine," Emily hissed. "I'll come. But if we get caught- "

"Then I give you express permission to be angry at me for the rest of our natural lives," Will interrupted her. "Just meet me outside my room at half ten. I promise you won't regret it."

Lois lost her footing and slipped, snapping a twig loudly as her foot skidded across the ground. The noise seemed to startle Will and his friends and Lois heard them move off quickly into the clearing. Not wanting to be caught spying, she hastily ran to catch up with Florence and Penelope and joined in with their conversation enthusiastically, pretending she had been investigating a potential river.

111

Eventually, the girls found a freshwater stream, bending down on its bank to collect a sample in their flasks. Having completed their requirement for the lesson, they followed the trail back to the Biodome's entrance to hand their findings into Ms. Dido. Lois turned her face towards the roof on the way back, letting the UV light warm her skin. Overhearing Will's conversation had made her feel like she had been let in on a special secret and her mind was racing with all the possibilities of what to do with the information she had gained.

The thrill of the private knowledge carried her happily through the rest of the afternoon and into dinner, where she sat around the table with the Floor One gang, laughing at Spencer's jokes and listening to Alasdair explain his views on the corruption of the Roman Empire, which they were learning about in Civilisations. She couldn't help but indulge herself with daydreams of dinner the following night, where she would captivate them all with her tale of how she had followed Will and his two friends and uncovered whatever banned activity they were participating in after dark. She held back from telling any of them of her plans just yet, in case they went wrong or, worse still, in case any of them decided to turn up and share in her glory. She was determined that she alone would be responsible for the invaluable piece of gossip.

After dinner, she headed to her room to unwind, as was normal for her daily routine. She changed out of her school uniform, hanging the navy jumper in her wardrobe and folding the black trousers neatly over the back of her chair. Once she had changed and prepared her things for the following morning, she curled up on top of her bed and turned on the large television set her father had sent her from home. After browsing for several minutes, she finally settled upon the classic films channel, the 3D projection turning into a 2D picture before her eyes.

Watching old films reminded her greatly of her mother, who had spent many Sunday afternoons encouraging Lois to appreciate the century-old art form. She felt pulled under by the familiar stinging sadness she felt whenever her mother entered her mind. Deciding it was due, she allowed herself a passionate cry as an expression of her continuing grief. Once she had run out of tears, she got up from her bed and walked calmly into the bathroom, washing her face and taking a deep breath to bring herself back to normal. After looking in the mirror to examine how puffy her eyes were, she checked the time on her Personal Device, startling herself when she realised it was already twenty-past-ten.

Leaping across the room, she made the distance to her bedroom door in five seconds flat, opening it slowly and peering into the corridor to make sure Ms. Everly was nowhere to be seen. Seeing that the coast was clear, she moved into the hallway, immediately stopped in her tracks by the realisation that something wasn't right. All the lights in the corridor had been switched off, except for one at the end, which had been smashed and was flickering on and off intermittently. Lois' heart raced as she crept down the hallway, keeping her back close to the wall in case she encountered whoever was responsible for the damaged light. Her hands felt their way across the tile, bumping over the bedroom doors as she passed them. As she neared the elevator, her hand snagged on something sharp and she drew it back sharply, feeling the hot sting of blood trickle across her palm. She looked around to check where the injury had come from and saw through the flashing light that the door in question had been slashed in three places, causing it to splinter and break.

Fear closed around her throat and she began to run towards Will's room. She didn't know whether she intended to warn him or to accuse him, but she was certain that being in his company would be better than being alone in this terrifying scenario. As she got closer, she began to hear voices coming from outside Will's door and, losing her nerve, she dived into the shadows and waited, straining her ears to listen to the conversation.

"Seriously Will get out here," she heard Emily hiss, knocking persistently on his door. "Something really weird is going on!"

"I'm just coming!" came Will's muffled reply from inside.

"Do you think this has anything to do with what he wants to show us?" Finley asked Emily.

"I don't know," Emily answered. "But I'm starting to get scared. Why are all the lights off?"

"Maybe somebody knows we're out here," Finley swallowed.

"Don't say that!" Emily scolded him. "I've got the creeps as it is."

There was the sound of hinges creaking as Will opened his door and came outside, shining the torch on his Personal Device at his surroundings.

"Woah," he said. "What happened out here?"

"I was about to ask you the same question!" Emily replied. "Are you trying to play a trick on us or something? Because it's not funny!"

"Calm down, this isn't me," Will defended himself.

"Shine your light down there, see if you can see anything," Emily instructed him. Lois panicked, realising her hiding place was about to be discovered. Unsure what to do and unwilling to be caught standing silently in the hallway, she stepped forwards, revealing herself in the torchlight. Emily, Will and Finley screamed, jumping backwards and grabbing each other in fear.

"Lois?" Will said incredulously when he saw her. "What are you doing here?"

"I… er…" Lois trailed off, unable to come up with a convincing excuse for being outside Will's bedroom in the middle of the night.

"Are you spying on us?" Emily snapped.

"Well, not exactly," Lois replied.

"'Not exactly?'" Emily repeated. "What does that mean?"

"I overheard you talking in Resources," Lois confessed. "I knew you were planning to sneak out tonight and I wanted to find out what was going on."

"So, you were spying on us," Emily concluded.

"Why did you turn all the lights off though? Are you trying to scare us?" Will frowned.

"No, it wasn't me. I came out of my room and it was pitch dark. I thought you might know what was going on," she replied.

"Lois…" said Will, his body suddenly tense and stiffer than a statue. "Who else did you tell that you were coming?"

"No one," Lois replied with confusion. "I didn't tell anybody anything."

"Then," Will swallowed, raising a shaking hand to point to the corridor behind her, "who's that?"

Lois whipped her head around to see what he was talking about. Standing in the hallway, just a few feet away from them, was the silhouette of a man, so unnaturally tall that the top of his head was brushing the ceiling.

"Who's there?" Emily called towards the figure. He did not reply but continued to stand motionless. Lois began to back away carefully, able to see, as her eyes adjusted to the darkness, that the silhouette didn't belong to a man at all. The head was far too big and misshapen to be human, the body elongated and spindly.

"I hate to say this," Finley said as Lois reached the group, "but I don't think that's a person."

There was a hideous noise that sounded like a scream mixed with a high-pitched roar as the figure moved into the light of Will's torch. The four of them froze as their eyes fell upon its hideous appearance. Its skin was white and sallow and hung loosely from its bones as though it were too big for its skeleton. Its head was bulbous, the top half twice the width of the bottom. Its hands were made up entirely of claws, steely and sharp as knives. The most horrifying thing of all, though, was the creature's face. Its mouth was a huge pit, displaying six, pointed teeth within its depths, spittle dripping uncontrollably from each one. Its nose was an ugly slit in the centre of its head. Its eyes were awful, black, gaping holes. In all her life, Lois had never seen an alien like this. The thing resembled evil itself. All the while she looked at it, she could not move. She couldn't breathe. Time itself seemed to have been immobilised with fear. Feeling utterly powerless, she awaited her demise, certain that the creature would come for her at any moment. It was only when Will tugged on her arm and shouted in her ear that the numbness of her body subsided, causing her to spring back to life.

"Run!" Will yelled.

The four of them tore into his room as fast as their legs would carry them, Finley slamming the door shut behind them as they crashed into safety, throwing his weight against it to stop the alien creature from entering.

"Will, help me move the bed," Emily shouted and the two of them lifted the bedframe, placing it in front of the door as a barricade.

Once they had blocked the door, they stepped back, gasping as they desperately tried to catch their breath.

"What was that thing?" Emily cried.

"I don't know, I've never seen anything like it," Lois said with horror.

"What if it's still out there?" Will asked, his voice shaking.

The four of them stood in silence, listening for any sounds outside the doorway.

"I can't hear anything," Finley said.

"Did anyone see it move? Did it chase us?" Lois asked.

"I'm not sure," Finley swallowed.

"We can't just stand here!" Emily exclaimed. "We've got to check if it's gone."

"Who's going to do it?" Lois gulped.

They looked at one and other, each hoping that somebody else would volunteer.

"I'll do it," Finley declared.

"No," Will shook his head. "You don't know why it's out there. What if someone sent it to you?"

"Why would anyone do that?" Lois exclaimed, disgusted at the thought.

"Don't you remember our first Rocket Control lesson? Not everyone is happy about Finley being at the Space Academy," Will reminded her bluntly.

"What about your Floor One friends?" Emily scowled at her. "I know exactly what they think about Finley being here."

"No, they would never do that," Lois protested. "Will you know they're not capable of something that awful."

"Oh, come on," Emily said before Will could reply. "Don't you think it's a bit strange that Lois just happened to be outside your room at the same time as that horrible creature!"

"It is a bit of a co-incidence Lois," Will frowned.

"I had nothing to do with this!" Lois objected, her voice rising in panic. "I'm just as scared as you are!"

"Alright, everyone calm down," Finley interjected, raising his hands to quiet them. "Let's be reasonable. I don't think a thirteen-year-old student would be capable of controlling that thing. If Lois says she has nothing to do with this, then we should believe her. The longer we spend arguing, the longer that thing has to decide what it's going to do next."

"You're right," Will agreed. "I'm going to see if it's still there."

"Be careful," Emily fretted, watching with wide eyes as Will slid the bed away from the door, pausing for a moment before opening it just a fraction. Lois held her breath as he looked into the corridor, withdrawing and shutting the door after a few seconds.

"It's not there" he announced with relief.

"So, what do we do now?" Emily wondered aloud.

"Let's just try and figure this out," Will said, clapping his hands together and pacing the width of his bedroom. "Supposing it wasn't deliberate, is there any way that creature could have come here by accident?"

"What do you mean?" Emily asked him.

"Well, Krecher takes the aliens from the Ivory Tower out on the grounds at about this time of night. Maybe one of them escaped?" Will suggested.

"Krecher told us in class that all the aliens he takes out are completely under his control and act like pets. I wouldn't consider whatever that was to be "pet" material," Finley replied.

"My brother Charlie did tell me that other aliens sometimes visit the school," Emily said. "Apparently, only the older years get to learn about them because the younger pupils get frightened. Do you think it could be one of those?"

"I think the best thing to do is go to Krecher tomorrow and ask him directly," Will concluded.

"Won't we get in trouble?" Finley frowned. "We were out after curfew. I fought so hard to get into this school, I don't want to risk losing my place."

"I trust Krecher," Will assured him. "Besides we have to tell someone. In case, you know, something bad happens...."

They all shuddered.

"Can we stay here tonight?" Lois pleaded. "I can't go back to my room on my own, I'll be up all night terrified."

"Of course," Finley replied before anyone could argue. "After all, we're all in this together now." He looked pointedly at Emily, who crossed her arms and frowned.

Lois sunk down onto Will's bed, attempting to calm her heart rate as the shock began to settle in. Finley came to sit beside her, looking equally traumatised. They said nothing for a moment, the intensity of what they had witnessed rendering them speechless.

"Thank you," Lois said, once she had found the ability to speak.

"For what?" he asked her.

"For sticking up for me, just then."

"That's okay," Finley shrugged. "I know none of this has anything to do with you."

"How?" Lois asked him curiously. "You don't know me at all."

"I know you're not like the other Floor One students," he told her. "You're different... in a good way."

He smiled at her shyly and she grinned back, the two of them beaming at each other until they were interrupted by Will and Emily coming over and presenting them with a cup of tea. The four of them sat and sipped quietly, their eyes beginning to glaze and redden with tiredness.

"Maybe we should try and sleep," Will said with a yawn. "You three could take the sofas, they're quite comfortable."

Lois, Emily and Finley trudged over to the chairs, taking one each to settle on for the night. As she lay in the dark, Lois' eyelids began to grow heavy until she had no choice but to close them, losing her internal battle to stay awake in case the creature should return.

What felt like a few seconds later, she awoke to the sound of Will's alarm ringing out across the room. She rolled over and sat up groggily, trying to focus on her surroundings through the pain in her head.

"What time do you call this?" Emily grumbled, shoving the pillow over her ears to block out the noise.

"Sorry," Will croaked from the bed. "I set my alarm early so you could get back to your rooms before Ms. Everly does the morning rounds."

"Shall we go and find Krecher?" Finley asked as he got up, his hair sticking out on end after a night of tossing and turning. Before any of them could respond, their Personal Devices bleeped loudly to signal they had a message.

"Admiral Allance will be holding an emergency assembly before breakfast," Will read out loud. "All students must get dressed and report to the Gathering Hall immediately."

They stared at each other, completely perplexed.

"Do you think this has to do with last night?" Finley asked nervously.

"I don't know," Will grimaced. "We'd better just get dressed and go down."

Lois raced to her room and pulled her uniform on, dressing in record time before hurrying down to the foyer to meet the others. Side by side, they walked to the main school building and traipsed into the Gathering Hall, taking a seat in the front row. They waited impatiently as the rest of the students filed in, rubbing their eyes and ignoring the grumbling of their stomachs as they found their seats. Lois' heart sank when she saw Florence, Penelope, Alasdair and the rest of the Floor One clique striding in, staring at her with astonishment when they saw who she was sat beside.

"Lois?" Florence said as she approached her. "What are you doing? Come and sit with us."

"No, that's okay," Lois replied her face flushing beetroot.

"What's going on?" Alasdair asked, coming to stand beside Florence.

"Lois seems to have lost her mind," Florence told him.

"Don't tell me she's actually sitting there by choice," Alasdair said incredulously.

"Yes, I am," Lois told him calmly.

"Explain yourself," he demanded, looking from Will to Finley with disgust.

"I don't have to explain myself," she said firmly. "I just want to sit here."

For the first time since she had known them, Florence and Alasdair were completely speechless.

"I don't know what's happened to you and Will," Alasdair sniffed as he regained himself. "Mixing with such filth is beneath people like us."

119

"Give it a rest, Alasdair," Will sighed. "There's no law that says you can't be friends with anyone from a different floor."

"There should be," he replied.

"Goodbye, Florence and Alasdair," Lois said pointedly, and the two of them sauntered off, deeply offended.

"I'm so sorry about that," Lois said as soon as they were gone. "I don't know what to say."

"It's okay," Finley re-assured her. "It isn't your fault."

"Seems like you might have lost your friends though," Emily frowned.

"Don't worry about it Lois," Will grinned. "Between the Floor One gang and Rudy I've got more enemies than friends in this place."

"Quality over quantity," Emily smiled.

Their conversation was interrupted by a loud crash as the rear door in the hall bounced open and Admiral Allance strode in, taking his place on the stage with a series of heavy footsteps. He turned to address his audience with a sombre expression, his thick, silvery eyebrows knitted together with anger. His mouth was set into a deeper frown than usual and his body was stiff. Nobody in the hall dared to breathe as they awaited his speech.

"It has come to my attention," he boomed, "that there was a serious case of vandalism in the first-year dormitory last night."

Lois, Finley, Will and Emily gaped at each other in shock.

"This morning it was reported to me by Ms. Everly that there had been significant damage to one of the doors, as well as one of the light fixtures on the top floor. The power in the building had also been tampered with overnight. This is entirely unacceptable."

He paused to stare with fury at the faces of his pupils, his eyes seeming to accuse each one individually as being the perpetrator of the act.

"All students know that they must not leave their bedrooms after curfew, which is ten o'clock sharp. The fact that there are no surveillance cameras in any of your dormitories is a privilege, giving you the privacy and respect we here at the school thought you deserved. This trust and act of goodwill has been betrayed and in hindsight of the incident, myself and the school board will now be reviewing whether to install camera systems in the hallways.

"I am sorely disappointed that any student here at the Academy would be capable of disregarding our rules in such a manner and must emphasise that any student found to have been out of bed last night will be expelled immediately without trial."

Lois shifted uncomfortably in her seat, her heart racing at a million miles a minute. She tried her best to act normal, frightened that the look of guilt on her face would betray her.

"I would also urge my staff to report any information that they have to me immediately. Needless to say, it would be more than your job's worth to conceal any knowledge of students wandering the grounds after curfew from me."

Admiral Allance finished his speech and stormed from the stage, his fury lingering in the hall for several moments following his departure. After a minute, the students stood up and began to leave the hall, the chatter amongst them building from a whisper to a roar as they speculated the previous night's events amongst themselves.

Using the cover of the crowd, Lois, Will, Finley and Emily got up and exited the hall, speaking just loud enough for each other to hear.

"I suppose going to Krecher is no longer an option?" Finley asked Will once they had reached the Reception Hall.

"We can't go to him now," Will sighed. "I don't want to be responsible for him getting sacked."

"What are we going to do then?" Emily fretted. "That thing could still be out there."

"If they're adding more cameras across the grounds they might catch it themselves," Finley suggested hopefully. "We might never have to say anything to anyone."

"I've got an idea," Lois announced, struck by a sudden moment of inspiration.

"Go on..." Will urged her.

"Well it's Hallowed Eve soon isn't it?" she asked.

121

"Yeah…" Will replied uncertainly.

"My dad has a database in his office. It's got a list of every single alien that's ever been found by humans on it. If you all come over in the holidays, we can use it to find out what that thing is and whether it's dangerous. Once we know what we're dealing with, we can decide what to do," Lois suggested.

"It does make sense," Finley said.

"I don't see what other option we have," Lois replied. "As scary as that creature was, I don't want to be expelled."

"Me neither," Emily agreed. "My dad would kill me."

"Okay, it's a plan then. We'll all meet at Lois' the day after Hallowed Eve. The Captain should be back at work by then, right?" Will asked Lois.

"Yeah, he has to resume his duty immediately," Lois replied.

"Well then, it's agreed. In the meantime, we all need to watch our backs," Will added.

"And definitely stay in our bedrooms after curfew," Emily concurred.

"What if we see that thing again?" Finley expressed with concern. "What do we do then?"

"We run" Will said. "As fast as we can."

12.

The Dreaded Conversation

It was the first day of the school holidays and Elsie was waiting on the platform. Impatience bubbled inside her as she leant from side to side, desperate to catch a glimpse of her son. It had been several minutes since the Shuttle had docked, clanking loudly as it landed in the loading deck. She could hardly wait to see Will, who she was sure would have grown several inches since he left for school, and had spent the past few days making special preparations for his return. The fridge had been stocked with his favourite food, his bed had been stripped and freshly made and she had insisted that a reluctant Derek clean the entire apartment from top to bottom to ensure that everything was perfect when he came home. The anticipation of the moment had grown significantly with each passing day and knowing it was now only minutes away, she could hardly contain her excitement.

After what felt like an eternity, she caught sight of Will disembarking from the Shuttle with a pretty-looking brunette girl and a slightly dishevelled, mousy boy. They stood in a huddle a few centimetres from the door, talking intensely amongst themselves. After a moment, they were joined by Alfie's daughter Lois, who exchanged a few words with them before nodding her goodbyes. Elsie watched as Will patted the scruffy boy on the shoulder and gave the brown-haired girl an awkward hug, waving sadly to them as he strolled away, his eyes now searching the platform for his mother. She waved and rushed forwards, making her presence known to him and they came together in a warm hug, Elsie relishing the feeling of having her child in her arms once again.

"Hi Mum," he said once they had pulled away from each other, grinning nonchalantly as if they had only been apart for a few days.

"Hello darling," she replied. "Derek's bringing your luggage."

They walked side by side, manoeuvring their way through the crowd until they had safely made their way out of the platform, Derek trailing behind them with Will's bags.

"I've cleared my schedule for the day," Elsie told him. "I thought we could head into the lobby and get some lunch. You can tell me all about your first term."

"Will your clients be alright without you?" Will asked with concern. "I thought Hallowed Eve was a hard time for them."

"Yes, it can be," Elsie replied. "They've had a hard time adjusting after Earth, so naturally the celebration of The Split brings out some difficult emotions. It's been even harder for them since the Captain imposed a new law that Forgottens can no longer be mentioned by name. His intention was to try and stop people dwelling on the past, but it seems to have had the adverse effect. Still, I'm sure they'll be fine for one day. You're more important!"

Will smiled but said no more on the subject. They walked along in silence, travelling down the hallway outside the platform until they eventually reached the lift, squeezing themselves in amongst the other passengers. After zooming across the Mayfly to various locations at stomach-wrenching speed, they reached the lobby and disembarked, Elsie desperately trying to regain the feeling in her legs.

The lobby had been decorated for Hallowed Eve, with replicas of multicoloured planets and glittering paper rockets hanging from every available hook and high place. Luminous stars were stuck in shop windows, glowing invitingly from behind the glass as they passed by. Most disturbing of all the festive décor were the images of a dead Earth, traditionally handmade by the children of the Mayfly. They depicted the planet devastated by fire, with plumes of paper smoke stuck to poorly cut-out circles that had been clumsily coloured in shades of green and blue.

Without having to communicate, Elsie and Will made a simultaneous beeline for "Joe's", the coffee shop they habitually visited every time they came into the lobby. Will found them a table by the window and sat down while Elsie went over to the drinks machine and got them each a hot chocolate with extra cream. A familiar twinge of guilt knotted in her stomach as she paid for the drinks with a touch of her finger, electronically transferring a small amount of her unlimited credits to the business owner's account. She had tried to protest Alfie giving her access to such wealth but he had refused to hear it, insisting that she and Will should have everything they need.

 She returned to the table and sat opposite from Will, handing him his drink carefully and watching as he drank his first sips, the cream leaving a small moustache above his upper lip. She smiled as he hastily wiped it away on the back of his sleeve, suddenly able to see him as his younger self.

 "Would you like a slice of carrot cake?" she asked him, bringing up the interactive menu on the table top. "It was always your favourite."

"I'm okay, thank you, Mum," he replied.

 "So, tell me everything then," she beamed. "I want to hear every detail about what you've been up to at school."

 She listened intently as Will launched into an enthusiastic explanation of his first term, describing the school grounds, his dormitory and his lessons in vivid detail. When she probed him about his teachers he paused, his face clouding over as though suddenly remembering something unpleasant.

"I have Mr. Krecher for Alien Studies," he replied darkly. "He's my favourite teacher. Was he yours too? When you were at College?"

 For a second she was rendered speechless, the shock of being confronted by a past she had thought long buried blocking her ability to speak. Quickly, she regained control, fixing her face into a placid smile.

"Yes," she said. "He was my favourite. I didn't realise he was teaching at The Academy now. I had heard he was on the Mayfly but we never crossed paths."

Will nodded slowly. She could see from his expression that he knew there was more to the story than he was being told, but he didn't press her any further. She decided to seize the opportunity to change the subject.

"What about your friends?" she asked him. "I saw you getting off the train with a boy and a girl."

"Yeah that's Finley and Emily," he smiled. "Finley's the one I rescued at the start of term."

"You were very brave to go after him," Elsie praised him. "But also very foolish. That entire situation could have ended very differently if you hadn't been so lucky."

"If I hadn't have gone after him, he'd probably be dead. Anyone with any decency would have done the same," Will shrugged.

"What about Spencer and the others?" Elsie asked, taking a sip of her drink. "How are they doing?"

"I don't really speak to them anymore," Will mumbled. "We kind of drifted apart."

Elsie was sure Will expected her to admonish him for no longer talking to his former friends, but she didn't. In fact, she was secretly pleased that he had distanced himself from them. She had always known he wasn't much like them and was proud of the fact.

"And Lois?" Elsie continued. "I saw you with her on the platform too."

"I suppose we're friends now, yeah," Will confirmed, seeming surprised by his own revelation.

Satisfied with the information she had garnered from him, Elsie said no more and the two of them finished their drinks and left Joe's, wandering about the shops. They left the lobby with several new purchases under their belt and took the lift to Floor One, arriving home just as Derek was laying the table for dinner. She had insisted on preparing the meal herself that evening and had made macaroni cheese- Will's favourite- asking Derek to put it in the oven just in time for their return.

The two of them sat down to eat, Elsie sipping wine as she filled her stomach with the sumptuous meal. Will seemed to become more relaxed with each passing second, and was growing more animated, sharing tales about "Beaky", the pet alien he had been assigned to look after in Krecher's class and boasting about being the first person in his Resources lessons to successfully set a fire. She leant her head on her hand and listened as he described Finley's kindness and told her with laughter about Emily's fiery temper and quick wit. She knew by the fondness in his voice when he spoke of them that he was experiencing the same captivation she had felt at College upon finally discovering people she truly connected with.

After dinner, Will retreated to his room, talking to his friends on his Personal Device as he went. Unsure what to do with herself, Elsie went to her bedroom to change into the pair of silk pyjamas she had bought that afternoon and was somewhat surprised to find that Derek had already laid them out on the bed for her. In such moments, she felt a confusing sensation of gratitude mixed with the uncomfortable sense that her privacy was being invaded. She knew full well that Will resented Derek's presence in their home, seeing him as an intrusion rather than a help. She had never admitted it to him, but there had been several occasions where she had considered dismissing Derek, feeling guilty every time he performed a household task she could easily have done herself, but she was never able to bring herself to do it. Derek had been her assistant since her very first day on the Mayfly when she had been a struggling single mother weighed down by unimaginable grief. In those days, she had been completely useless at everything other than caring for Will, and Derek had made sure that she could focus on being a good mother to him without starving herself or the destroying the apartment in the process.

Once she had changed into her nightclothes, Elsie headed into the living room and sunk into the plush, white sofa, putting her feet on the coffee table and switching on the television. She was halfway through watching the traditional broadcast about the miracle of The Split when her Personal Device beeped to inform her she had an incoming call. She accepted, and Alfie's face appeared, projected in perfect definition into the air in front of her.

"Hi Els'," he greeted her. "Sorry to call you in the evening, I would have dropped by personally but I'm still stuck at work," he frowned, moving his head slightly to show the Mayfly's control room in the background. "I just wanted to check that you're coming to the Celebration Hall tomorrow for the traditional Hallowed Eve party,"

"Of course," Elsie responded. "As soon we've had our breakfast we'll come down. It'll be nice for Will to see Lois. They've recently become friends, you know."

"Have they?" Alfie asked with surprise.

"So I hear" Elsie replied.

"I haven't had a chance to see Lois yet," Alfie frowned. "I sent my mother to pick her up. I hope she didn't mind."

"I'm sure she didn't," Elsie said as convincingly as she could manage. "I'd better go and tell Will to get his best clothes ready for tomorrow. Try not to work all night!"

"I'll do my best," Alfie grinned, "Bye Els'".

He ended the call, his face vanishing as quickly as it had appeared. Elsie swung her legs off the sofa and padded barefoot down the corridor, reaching Will's room and knocking on the door.

"Come in," he said quietly.

Elsie walked in to find Will sat on his bed, his Personal Device discarded by his side.

"I was just coming to let you know we're going to Alfie's as usual tomorrow. Do you know where your smart trousers and jacket are?" she asked him.

"Yeah," he said dejectedly without making eye contact.

"Is everything alright, darling?" Elsie questioned him.

"I saw him," he replied.

"Saw who?" she asked with confusion.

"Dad."

The word pierced the air like a wailing siren.

"What do you mean, sweetheart?" Elsie asked, sitting down at his desk.

"In Mr. Krecher's office," he explained. "There was a photo."

"Oh," Elsie said, unsure how to respond. She waited for him to continue, bracing herself for the questions she knew were coming.

"Why have you never told me what really happened to him, Mum?" he demanded, his eyes bearing into her.

"He died in an accident, darling, I have told you that," she replied, straining to keep her voice even.

"There's more to it than that," he shook his head. "I know there is. I'm not a child anymore Mum. I want the truth."

128

There was a hardness to his expression that she had never seen before. She took a deep breath and swallowed, accepting that it was now time to engage in the conversation she had been dreading for the past thirteen years.

"After College, your father and I moved back to where he grew up. We had a small house in a little countryside village. His parents were extremely wealthy and so we managed to stay safe from the violence that was going on in most of the country. We lived in our own little world, his parents providing us security and food whenever we needed it. It almost felt like how it was before all the Wars started," she said wistfully.

"One day I came home from getting supplies to find your father in the strangest mood. He had received a message from an anonymous sender, asking him to go back to Snowdonia, where we went to College, to meet with them. Apparently, they had 'invaluable information' that he would find 'extremely useful'.

"In College, your father, Alfie and I joined this group called 'The Society of the Enlightened,'. Essentially, they were a club that believed in what we referred to as the "Great Conspiracy". The theory preached that The Split was evil and the Mayfly was unsafe. It's all very embarrassing now, I know, but we were young. Towards the end of our final year, we all agreed to put the whole thing behind us, each of us realising just how childish and naive we were. Or so I thought.

"The anonymous message had re-awoken your father's obsession with the conspiracy. He decided immediately he was going to meet the stranger who had contacted him. I begged him to stay. I was pregnant with you by then and the thought of him leaving terrified me. He wouldn't listen, though. He was adamant that he had to go. He went and gathered enough food and supplies for three days and told me to lock all the doors. He promised he'd only be gone for 72 hours and then he left."

Elsie paused, gathering herself together before she continued.

"After a week, I still hadn't heard from him. I was utterly beside myself. Just when I thought I was going to lose my mind, I got a message from your father begging me to come and find him. He said he had found out the truth and discovered a way to save us. I got in the car and drove to him there and then. It took me twelve hours to make the journey. I had to take

129

the scenic route to avoid hitting any cities or populated area where the gangs and looters had control. When I finally arrived, your father told me to meet him down on the beach we sometimes went to as students."

Will bowed his head, sensing what was coming next.

"I went down and found him, ranting and raving like a madman. He had stolen a ship and wanted us to go out into Space in it. I couldn't reason with him, no matter how hard I tried. When I wouldn't agree with his plan he gave me an ultimatum; either go with him or stay on Earth and die."

She swallowed hard to suppress the lump in her throat.

"I said no and he got in the spaceship anyway and flew away. He had no experience in piloting a craft like that. Something went wrong and it exploded. He was killed instantly."

She looked away, blinking furiously to stop her eyes betraying any tears. Will was silent but calm, his hard expression ebbed away by the sincerity of Elsie's story.

"Why did you never just tell me the truth, Mum?" Will said sadly.

"I was trying to protect you," Elsie replied. "I didn't want you to feel the hurt and betrayal that I did. I thought it would be easier for you to have a dead father than one who abandoned you by choice."

"I understand," he said after a long moment's pause. "But, I didn't know him. He's a stranger to me. It's you that was really hurt by it. It was you that he let down. I could have handled the truth. It would have been better than wondering all my life why I was never allowed to mention him."

A tear slipped from Elsie's eye as she was wracked with guilt.

"I'm sorry," she whispered.

"It's okay. You did what you thought was best," he replied.

"When did you get to be so wise?" she asked him with a smile.

"I always was," he grinned, "I just hid it well. There is one thing I don't understand, though."

"What's that, darling?"

"Dad's parents- my grandparents- you said they were wealthy. How come they're not on the Mayfly? I thought you said it was possible to buy your way on board," he frowned.

"That's a question I'm afraid I can't answer," Elsie said apologetically. "After your father died, we lost contact. They needed someone to blame and I was an easy target, considering I was the only person there when it happened. They were convinced I could have done more to stop him. I suppose it was easier to hate me than to accept what their son did in his last moments. When I came aboard the Mayfly, I looked for them but I couldn't find them."

"Looks like it's just you and me then," Will smiled.

"That's the way it's always been," she smiled back.

Drained from the heaviness of their conversation, Elsie made her excuses and left, retreating to her bedroom. She lay down on top of the covers, watching the ceiling vacantly. Thinking of Austin was never easy, and recounting the events of the worst day of her life had taken its toll. She longed for her mind to take her to one of her happy places, which often featured memories of her parents and childhood, but her brain seemed intent that she should dwell on the parts of her past she tried desperately not to think about. She fought against it but was pulled vividly into her memories, the scenes she had tried so hard to erase now playing graphically before her eyes.

13.

The Nature of Memory

It was September 21st, 2095 and Elsie was sat in the backseat of her Aunt Veronica's self-driving car. Veronica was sat beside her, legs crossed, scrolling through a fashion download on her I-Reader. Elsie was chewing gum, deliberately making her Aunt jump each time she popped a bubble between her teeth.

"Do you have to do that?" her Aunt snapped after the fifth or sixth time, hunching her bony, white shoulders in irritation.

"I'm bored," Elsie said. "I wish you had just let me drive."

"Oh, honestly Elsie nobody drives their own cars anymore unless they're poor," her Aunt retorted.

"Well then, I don't see the point of you coming with me," Elsie argued. "The car could have driven me there then driven itself home."

"Nonsense," her Aunt sniffed. "I made a promise to my brother that I would take care of you and I have no intention of breaking my word now. Unfortunately for you, that means seeing you safely to College."

"Don't pretend you're doing it for Dad," Elsie said with a roll of her eyes. "You just want to see me go so you know for certain I'm not coming back."

"Don't be so dramatic," her Aunt scolded her. "I know losing your parents has left you with a big chip on your shoulder but you'd do well to remember that I am the one who has provided for you for the past four years. Some gratitude wouldn't go amiss."

"Thank you," Elsie smiled with as much heavy sarcasm as she could muster, "for always making sure I knew how much of a burden I was."

"You could cheer up a bit you know," her Aunt sighed. "You're lucky to be going to College. Educational institutes are among the last truly safe places in this country. Plus, if you study hard enough, you might actually have a chance of being accepted for The Split."

"You mean you might have a chance," Elsie corrected her. "I know accepted applicants get to bring their immediate family on board. That's what this is really about, isn't it? Getting me skilled enough to get onto the Mayfly so you can escape Earth too. You'd probably miraculously stop recognising me the second your foot when through the Mayfly's door."

"Just try not to mess this up Elsie," she said with exasperation, returning to her article about which fur coats made their owners appear the wealthiest.

The rest of the journey passed in silence, her Aunt tutting every so often as she read or saw something online that she disapproved of. If there was anything Aunt Veronica loved to do, it was to disapprove. Her dad had once joked to Elsie that it was her favourite hobby. In fact, he had informed her with amusement, if Aunt Veronica didn't disapprove of you it was probably time to worry about your life choices.

Elsie was more than slightly relieved when they pulled up outside the old, decrepit building that was to be her accommodation for the academic year. An old University had existed long before College Snowdonia was built and those commissioning the project either didn't have enough money or enough care for the thing to replace the old structures. Thus, her home for the next ten months would be a dormitory that had existed for at least fifty years. Her Aunt sniffed when she saw it, but Elsie wasn't fazed by its run-down appearance. Anything this far away from home was beautiful to her.

"Isn't someone going to come and take your bags?" her Aunt complained after barely a minute of being out of the car.

"It doesn't look like it," Elsie replied, gesturing to the small cluster of other new arrivals, whose families were carrying their bags by hand.

"Ridiculous," Aunt Veronica muttered as she opened the boot with a snap of her fingers, revealing Elsie's suitcases inside. Between the two of them, they hauled the cases out of the car, through the open door, across the foyer and into the rusty lift, setting them down with a heavy thud and catching their breath as they ascended to the top floor, where Elsie's room was located.

They trundled along the corridor, cases in tow until they found the right room and pushed the unlocked door open to enter. The space was simple and plain, stripped of all decoration and technology to make it as impersonal as it could possibly be. The furniture was shabby and consisted only of the necessities; an unsteady looking single bed, a dented wooden wardrobe and an old, grey desk that was covered in the graffiti of previous occupants. The carpet was a discoloured brown, the mirror stained with streaks of black and the small, white hand basin had grown rust, the tap dripping steadily despite being switched off.

"It's awful," her Aunt breathed in horror.

Elsie gazed around, imagining all the different ways she could make the room her own.

"I love it," she grinned. Aunt Veronica stared at her like she was a madwoman but chose not to comment, the imminence of their separation suppressing her argumentative streak. They both knew, without having to say it, that this parting of ways would be a permanent one, and neither party were sure how to address the situation.

"Well..." Aunt Veronica said after a minute of uncomfortable silence, "I suppose I should leave you to unpack."

"Yes," Elsie replied.

Aunt Veronica cleared her throat.

"Good luck, then," she nodded and began to leave. Just before she reached the door, she turned back, wrestling with herself as she struggled to force her words out.

"They... would be proud," she said slowly. "Your parents that is."

"Thanks," Elsie said, trying not to smirk at the obvious distress her Aunt felt at having to be nice to her.

Veronica flashed a thin smile and left the room. Elsie imagined her punching the air and doing cartwheels in the corridor, unable to contain herself with the joy of knowing that her duty to her dead brother was over. Now she was free to return to whatever dreary, lonely life she had had before becoming Elsie's guardian.

The feeling of relief was mutual, and Elsie felt weightless as she began to unpack her things, placing her collection of framed photographs carefully on her desk and trying not to think about how many of the people in them were now dead. She gave the photographic version of her parents an affectionate smile. She knew Aunt Veronica had only been saying what she felt she had to, but Elsie couldn't help but think that her parents would be extremely proud if they knew she had gotten into College. She made a promise to herself that this would be a fresh start and a chance to finally shed the pain of her childhood. Everyone her age wanted to go to College and live as they would have, had there been no Wars and no tragedies, and for that reason, she was intent on making the most of the opportunity she had been given. She knew that's what her parents would have wanted.

A loud knocking disturbed her unpacking, and she leapt up from amongst a pile of clothes to answer, kicking socks and shoes across the room as she went. She opened the door to see two young men, not much older than her, standing with a cluster of leaflets in their hands.

"Welcome fresher!" exclaimed the one on the right, flicking his long fringe out of his face as he spoke. "My name is Dylan."

"And I'm Toby," his shorter-haired companion beamed.

"I'm Elsie," she replied with amusement, feeling like she was watching a badly rehearsed double-act on a children's television show.

"We are your student mentors," Dylan continued. "Which basically mean we're here to tell you about all the safest places to go drinking."

"As well as giving you essential tips for surviving your first year," Toby added.

"So, what are you studying here Elsie?" Dylan asked her.

"Psychology," she answered. They raised their eyebrows.

"Unusual choice these days," Toby noted.

"I want to be a counsellor," Elsie explained. "I want to help the people that have suffered. People who have lost someone they care about."

"So, everyone then?" Dylan joked. "At least you'd never be short of clients."

"What do you two study?" Elsie asked, desperate to take the spotlight off herself.

"Navigation," Dylan answered proudly, puffing out his chest. "I'm in my second year. I want to work in the control room on the Mayfly when it sets off. Maybe even apply for the Captaincy."

"You've got to dream big," Toby laughed. "I do Alien Studies. I'm in my third year. If you get a chance, take a module in the subject. You won't regret it."

"Professor Krecher is his hero," Dylan rolled his eyes. "He teaches the course. You'll probably see him around campus at some point. He does farming on the side of professing. He gives his students free apples when they get a good grade."

"He's got apples?" Elsie said with disbelief. She couldn't remember the last time she'd seen one.

"Oh yeah," Toby replied. "He's not one of your typical farmers either. Like Dylan said he gives all his stuff away, no charge. Even to the locals."

"Sounds like an interesting man," Elsie mused.

"He is. Anyway, believe it or not, we did come for a reason," Toby smiled.

"And what reason was that?" Elsie asked.

"To give you these," Dylan answered, handing her a few leaflets from his large collection. "You'll find everything you need to know on there. There's a map of the town and of the campus and then a few advertisements for places to drink and eat."

"Thank you," Elsie said, putting the flyers down on the desk next to her.

"We were going to do downloads for everyone's Personal Devices but we thought leaflets would be more impressive. They've still got a computer and printer on College campus from the old days. You should check it out if you get the chance- it's weird," Toby informed her.

"We also came to let you know there's a mixer this evening for the people living in this building," Dylan interjected. "There'll be free alcohol! It starts at seven pm in the foyer. It's a good opportunity to meet the people you'll be living with for the next year."

"I'll be there," Elsie smiled.

Toby and Dylan departed and Elsie was left alone once more to finish her unpacking. Once everything was in order, she inspected her handiwork and decided with satisfaction that her environment was beginning to look a lot more like a bedroom than a prison. As she made plans with herself to visit the market town in the morning to buy some new décor, she absentmindedly wandered over to the window, taking in her new view of high sycamore trees and far away mountain tops. In the gravel car park below, armed guards in full defensive uniform had started to patrol, their huge weapons cradled in their arms as if they were their precious children. Elsie raised her eyebrows. The Government were pulling out all the stops to protect education- one of the very few remaining aspects from the old culture that hadn't yet been destroyed. She wasn't sure whether it was out of compassion, or simply because skilled and intelligent workers would be needed to populate Novum once Earth was abandoned, but she certainly didn't feel any safer at the sight of the armed men.

Seven o'clock rolled around and before Elsie knew it, it was time to head down to the foyer to meet whichever lucky strangers had also made it to the Utopia that was College. She had dressed well for the event, choosing her best pair of black trousers with a matching black top and grey high heels. She had never had an occasion to dress up properly before but was sure she had read on one of her Aunt's fashion downloads that wearing all dark colours gave the most flattering impression. To add colour to the bleakness, she wore a gold chain necklace that she had stolen from Aunt Veronica's closet and painted a bright, red lipstick on her lips. She put her hair up, something she favoured to do ever since a boy once told her as a child that it suited her.

She made her way downstairs, her heels clacking on the stone steps as she descended. She reached the foyer and entered without hesitation, finding herself astonished by its transformation. The first thing that caught her eye was a huge, holographic banner projected in the centre of the room, reading "welcome freshers" in giant, multicoloured lettering. Machines had been attached to the faded, yellow walls, their functions varying from periodically spitting out confetti to blowing a constant stream of bubbles into the room. Between them, were several television screens displaying 3-D images of women dancing in time to the beat of loud music, which was blaring from an enormous sound system, currently operated by an ecstatic Toby.

The foyer floor was crowded with people mingling, already seeming to have formed exclusive friendship groups. Attracting the most attention was a sandy-haired boy who was stood in the middle of a gang of girls, hanging off his every word. Feeling intimidated by everybody's pre-existing relationships, Elsie headed over to the corner of the room, where a drinks

137

table had been set up. It was lined with dozens of plastic cups, filled with either a yellow or a red liquid. The cups were being handed out and refilled by a sleek, white robot, the letters "CS" standing for "College Snowdonia" emblazoned on its chest.

She approached the table with confidence. Drinking was something she had some experience in, mostly due to her Aunt's enthusiasm for the past-time, which had only seemed to grow more popular the worse things had gotten on Earth.

"What may I get you, Miss?" the robot asked her in a polite voice.

"What are these?" Elsie asked, looking dubiously at the plastic cups.

"I only know they are "red" and "yellow", Miss," the robot replied, its voice emitting from a speaker inside its spherical head.

"I'll have a yellow one then," Elsie said. The robot picked up a cup in its curved hand and passed it to her effortlessly.

"Thank you," she said.

"You are welcome," the robot answered.

"So, are you owned by the College?" Elsie questioned him, desperate to speak to someone, even if they were made of metal.

"I was programmed by the Interactive Tech company, commonly referred to as I-Tech" the robot replied, "I was purchased by the College in the year 2090. Tonight, I am in service of Mr. Toby Wyatt and Mr. Dylan Martinez. Does this answer your question, Miss?"

"Yes, thank you," Elsie confirmed and walked away, realising she couldn't make small talk with a robot.

She scanned the foyer, wondering if she'd be better off heading back to her bedroom rather than face the humiliation of standing there alone. She was just about to leave, when she saw a tall boy with dark hair, shrinking into a wall in the corner. Seeing this as her only chance to socialise, she made her way over to him, his timid posture suggesting he wouldn't be difficult to approach.

"Glad I'm not the only one that feels like hiding in the corner," she remarked with a smile when she reached him. "This is a bit overwhelming isn't it?"

"It is," the boy replied shyly. "Everyone else seems to know each other."

"I noticed that," Elsie frowned. "It's like they've all had a secret meeting without us. Maybe we missed the memo."

It was a phrase she'd heard on American television and she wasn't entirely sure what it meant but it seemed to resonate with the boy, who laughed musically.

"What are you drinking?" he asked her, pointing to her plastic cup.

"Honestly, I have no idea," she admitted.

"You chose yellow," the boy observed, peering over her shoulder. "I was too frightened by the smell. I've got what I think is supposed to be red wine but it just tastes like vinegar."

"I don't think much of the budget for this evening was spent on the drinks," Elsie noted, glancing again at all the garish decoration in the foyer.

"You might be right," the boy agreed. "I suppose people don't really have much to celebrate anymore. It looks like whoever organised this might have got a little bit carried away."

"You can say that again," Elsie asserted. Realising she hadn't introduced herself, she extended her hand.

"I'm Elsie by the way, Elsie James."

"Alfie," the boy grinned in response, taking her hand and shaking it.

"Just Alfie?" Elsie replied. "How diva of you."

"Alfie Sommers," he corrected himself with a blush.

"Nice to meet you, Alfie Sommers," Elsie smiled.

"You too," he grinned.

"It's a bit strange, really," Elsie noted, looking around her at all the happy faces. "You could almost pretend that nothing bad is happening to the world."

"My mother said it's the way of the British," Alfie smirked. "She said this country would fight Wars with tea and alcohol, given the chance."

The sound of approaching engines distracted them from their conversation and they looked outside to see a group of shiny, black cars adorned with the university logo pull up in the gravel car park. The patrolling guards rushed over to investigate, nodding their approval when they saw that the cars were College property.

"Are people going out?" Elsie asked Alfie. "Is it safe?"

"Must be," Alfie shrugged. "It is quite remote out here. I suppose all the real danger is in the cities."

"Who called the cars?" Toby shouted over the music.

"Guilty," the boy with sandy-blonde hair laughed from amongst his group of fans, holding his hands up in mock surrender. "A few of us thought we'd head out, see what the town's like. We've never been out at night before. Can't waste the opportunity."

Toby frowned, but even he could not argue with the boy's obvious charm.

"Be careful," Toby warned him.

"I always am," the boy grinned.

The gaggle of girls swanned their way into the cars first, but the boy hung back, looking around to double check he hadn't left anyone behind. It was at this moment that Elsie realised how attractive he was. There didn't seem to be a single flaw on his perfectly chiselled face. His eyes, noticeably green even from across the room, shone brilliantly, setting them apart from all his other features. He noticed Elsie looking at him and grinned impishly in her direction. Her heart began to race as he strolled towards her, his confidence seeming to fill every corner of the room. He stopped just in front of her, ignoring Alfie's presence to stare at Elsie with an intensity that made her blush.

"Hi," he said, extending his hand for her to shake. "I'm Austin."

Back in the present, Elsie sat bolt upright, cursing herself as a searing pain tugged across her chest. She had foolishly let her mind wander into such painful territory and now she would certainly suffer for it for the remainder of the night. It took every ounce of strength she had not to revisit the happy days of her relationship with Austin. She could not bear now, to think of the blissful five years she had experienced with him before he had so cruelly pulled the plug on everything she knew and loved.

Knowing she would not sleep otherwise, she retrieved a bottle of sleeping pills from her bedside drawer and took two, allowing them to calm her frantic mind and lull her into drowsiness. As she drifted off to sleep, her mind entering a state of numbness, she could not shake the unsettling feeling that her past was about to receive an incredibly rude awakening

14.

Hallowed Eve

On the morning of Hallowed Eve, Emily awoke early. She rushed out of bed and pulled on the purple, velvet dress her mother had selected for her to wear the night before. She dragged a brush through her thick hair, being sure to remove all the knots and kinks that had formed overnight. Once she had finished, she inspected her appearance in the mirror. Satisfied that she had made herself presentable, she took a deep breath.

"You can do this," she told her own reflection.

She walked from her bedroom and into the dining room, the smell of pancakes wafting out from the kitchen where Liza, the family assistant, was making their traditional Hallowed Eve breakfast. Emily's family were already gathered around the long, glass table that sat in the centre of the room. Her father was reading news stories from his tablet, grunting with disapproval every so often, while her brother, Charlie, tapped on his Personal Device furiously, sending messages to one of his many friends. Her mother was staring forwards, her eyes glazed and her face pale from working the night shift in the Medic Ward. Emily suspected she hadn't been to bed yet and was most likely exhausted, but missing the breakfast her father insisted on ordering every year would be more trouble than sleep was worth.

"Good morning," Emily said when she entered the room, announcing her presence.

"Morning sis'," Charlie grinned. "Happy Hallowed Eve."

"Morning sweetheart," her mother said, flashing a weak smile. "Come and sit down."

Emily did as she was told, sitting in the chair across from her mother and folding her hands in her lap as Liza brought in their food.

"Thank you," she smiled as her plate was placed in front of her, the food still steaming hot from the pan.

"You're welcome, Miss," Liza replied, continuing to serve the rest of the family. Emily's father sniffed as she put his meal in front of him, refusing to acknowledge her presence as he continued his engrossment with the news.

"Shouldn't you be at home, Liza?" Charlie asked her. "Nobody's supposed to work on Hallowed Eve."

"Mr. Pannell insisted I work today, Sir," she replied, her voice strained.

"Of course he did," Charlie grimaced, proceeding to attack the food on his plate with his fork.

"Stop talking to the help, Charlie," their father snapped. "You're distracting her from doing her job. Go and clear up in the kitchen now, Liza."

"Yes, Mr. Pannell," Liza nodded and disappeared.

"So, Emily," her father said, putting his tablet down and crossing his legs as he leant back to regard her. "I assume you've had a successful first term at The Academy?"

"Yes," she replied.

"Your examinations will begin when you return after the holidays," her father informed her. "I hope you will spend the rest of your time at home studying."

"I'm going to my friend Lois' tomorrow to revise with her," Emily told him.

"Lois Sommers?" he pressed her. "The Captain's daughter?"

"Yes," Emily answered.

"Excellent," her father nodded his approval. "The Captain is a fine man with excellent taste. That much became clear when he recently re-appointed me as Governor of Education for the fifth year running."

Charlie rolled his eyes in an exaggerated fashion, so that only Emily would see. It was the fourth time her father had mentioned his renewal of office since they had returned home for the holidays.

"I was wondering," her father cleared his throat, "has the curriculum at the Academy given you any ideas about what you would like to do when we reach Novum? Only Academy students are given the opportunity to take up important positions, you know."

"Yes, I know father you told me every day when I was studying for the entrance exams," Emily replied. "Anyway, I'd like to do something in technology, I always have."

There was a moment of silence as Charlie and her mother froze with surprise. Her father had voiced strong opinions about women working in such areas over the years, and up until this point, Emily had never been brave enough to reveal her true ambitions to him. He chewed over her words for a minute, calculating his response.

"Jarvis Holt, the CEO of I-Tech is an acquaintance of mine," he began. "He's a fine gentleman- an excellent businessman and very talented. He only takes the best of the best. If you wanted to work for him you'd better start working a lot harder than you do now. I'm not entirely sure you're cut out for it."

Emily looked down at the white, linen napkin she had folded on her lap, concentrating on the pattern of sewing across its hem as she tried to block out the noise of her father.

"Still," he continued, "at least you aren't following in your mother's footsteps. To be a nurse in this day and age is absolutely preposterous. The pay is laughable, there's no status in it and with all the medical science and technology we have, there's no need for human involvement at all. Perhaps you'll end up inventing something that will make your mother's 'job' completely obsolete, Emily. Wouldn't that be amusing."

"People need human contact," her mother said quietly. "They wouldn't recover without it."

"Oh, nonsense!" her father exclaimed, waving his hand in the air. "You tell yourself whatever you need to, dear. We both know if it wasn't for me, you'd be down on Floor Seven with the rest of the deprived population."

"My friend Finley is from Floor Seven," Emily said, setting her knife and fork down with a crash, "and he is probably the nicest person I've ever met, not to mention the most intelligent."

"What rubbish," her father replied. "I still can't believe Allance allowed him into the school. I was one of the Governors that voted against the motion you know. Such a pity I was overruled. Allance couldn't help but be swayed by the hefty sum of credits he was given by the board for taking a pupil from a disadvantaged background. A waste of a valuable school place if you ask me."

"Suddenly I'm not hungry," Emily said, pushing her plate away from her.

"Don't be dramatic, Emily," her father scolded her. "I'm only pointing out the truth. The boy can live out his little fantasy with the better half, but as soon as his education is over, it'll be off to the Bureau of Labour where he belongs. By the time we reach Novum, he'll be a faceless man in a crowd of builders, with no higher status than the dogs I used to own back on Earth."

Emily stood up, knocking the table with the force of the action and causing the glasses to wobble and clatter into each other.

"Sit down, Emily," her father ordered.

"No," she replied, turning to leave the table.

"Sit down," he repeated with force.

"I said 'no'!" she yelled back, her voice louder than she had ever heard it before. Her father recoiled in shock and she seized upon the moment, exiting the room as fast as she could.

"Go on, Emily!" Charlie called after her as she left.

She reached her bedroom and pulled out her suitcase, packing it with bundles of tangled clothes as she tried to see through the tears that were pricking her eyes. She was just about to leave when her mother walked in, stopping her in her tracks.

"Emily, sweetheart, you don't have to go," she pleaded, her eyes full of sadness.

"How can you let him speak to you like that, Mum? The things he says are awful. I don't understand why you just sit there and take it!" Emily exclaimed.

"Your father is very a complicated man," her mother replied.

"Complicated?!" Emily repeated. "He's not complicated, he's an awful human being. Why did you ever marry him?"

Her mother hung her head in shame and sat down slowly on the bed, sighing as she spoke in a cracked, tired voice.

"The Pannell family were very wealthy," she admitted. "When the Wars broke out on Earth, money was the only way to gain protection. I was young and I was scared. I met your dad when I was treating his father for war wounds he later died of. He left everything to his only son. Your father took a shine to me and I took the opportunity to provide my family with safety."

"Money!" Emily shook her head. "You married him for money!"

"You don't know what it was like on Earth," her mother defended herself. "In the last days it was just...awful. When The Split finally came around, I already had your brother to think of, and I was expecting you. If I hadn't have married your father, none of us would be here. Our family would have died out. I made the sacrifices that I had to make."

"Well you're here now," Emily pointed out. "We're on the Mayfly. Why don't you just leave him? I'd rather live on Floor Seven in poverty than live on Floor Two in misery."

"You don't know what you're talking about," her mother argued. "You're too young to understand."

Emily shook her head pitilessly and turned to leave, hauling her heavy bag onto her shoulder and making for the door.

"I had a brother, you know," her mother said suddenly, halting her. "He's a Forgotten. We're not supposed to talk about them anymore but, his name was Bernard. When your father got us a place on the Mayfly, there wasn't enough space for him. I had to choose. Let my children perish on Earth or leave him behind instead. Our parents were gone and I was all he had. Can you imagine having to make a decision like that?"

"You left him?" Emily said with horror. "You left your own brother alone to die?"

"I had to," her mother insisted. "I chose to protect my children, as any mother would. I still think about him every single day."

"So, you stay with Dad because you're worried he'll expose your horrible little secret?" Emily surmised.

"If I left your father now, then everything I did to secure us a decent life here would be for nothing. I'd never be able to forgive myself."

"You shouldn't be able to forgive yourself now!" Emily replied. "All along I thought Dad was the corrupt one, but you're both just as bad as each other! Wealth and status is more important to you than morals or decency."

"Just calm down, Emily. Come and sit back at the table," her mother soothed her.

"No. I'm going," she replied.

"Going where? It's Hallowed Eve!"

"It doesn't matter where, as long as it's far away from here," Emily snapped, storming out of the room and moving with purpose towards the front door. She opened it with force and slammed it behind her, causing the frame to shake and tremor.

Without looking back, she walked to the lift, riding it down to the lobby, which was devoid of all life. There was something extremely unsettling about being in a deserted place that was usually packed full of people, and so Emily moved quickly, her footsteps echoing across the marble floor. She glanced into shop windows as she passed them, taking in the sight of the frightening mannequins modelling the latest fashions and gadgets. Without the hustle and crowds to distract from the sight, she was able to fully appreciate the sheer size of the lobby floor, its epic proportions making her feel incredibly small in comparison as she passed under the gigantic screen that hung in the centre.

Veering to the left, she moved away from the central shopping area and headed towards the entertainment section, passing by doors that led to the Multiplex Cinema, the Holographic Room and the Water Park until she reached the large entranceway to the Celebration Hall. She could hear soft music playing from inside, broken up by the sound of glasses clinking together as people toasted one another and chattered in light tones. She knew she had successfully found the party Will and Lois attended every year on Hallowed Eve. The only obstacle standing between her and them was a surly looking Guard, stood in a military stance as she scoped the area for any signs of danger, her eyes fixating on Emily from under her black visor.

Trying her best not to look intimidated, Emily walked over to her, doing her utmost to convey the impression that she was supposed to be there.

147

She stuck her nose in the air and swanned forward, giving the Guard the same disapproving glower she had seen her father give Liza so many times in the past. The snivelling attitude seemed to work, and the Guard allowed her to pass into the Hall without querying her identity. Unable to believe her luck, she integrated herself into the party, for once grateful that her father insisted on formal attire at home allowing her to easily blend in with the other black-tie wearing guests.

She searched for Will and Lois, peering over the heads of the many adults that were mingling around the hall, talking with perfect expression and laughing loudly to show off their pearly, polished teeth. She recognised several faces, including Pax Madden, the stoutly, bald man in charge of Security and Wendy Weaver, the smiling, blonde who read the daily news bulletins on the big screen in the lobby. She couldn't help but feel smug at the thought of her father seething with jealousy when he found out that she had managed to find her way into such an exclusive event. She imagined all the things he might have given in exchange for a chance to schmooze with the elite class that she was currently surrounded with.

Spotting Will and Lois hovering by a buffet table at the back of the Hall, Emily weaved her way towards them, careful not to hit any of the prestigious guests with her overnight bag. They had their backs to her, turned to face out of the conspicuously large, gold-framed windows that lined the rear wall of the hall. She cleared her throat to alert them to her presence and they both jumped, spinning round to see who had interrupted their conversation.

"Emily!" Will exclaimed. "What are you doing here?"

"I'm sorry to grate crash," Emily replied. "I had to get away from home."

She gave Will a meaningful look, who nodded with understanding.

"What's in your bag?" he asked her, eyeing the bulging holdall with curiosity.

"My things. I was hoping I could stay with you until we go back to school," Emily answered, a look of pleading in her eyes.

"Oh…" Will stuttered, running his hand through the back of his sandy hair. "You know I'd love to have you Em', but I don't think my mum would let a girl stay over."

He blushed crimson, suddenly appearing much younger than his fourteen years.

"You can stay with me," Lois offered. "We've got plenty of room."

"Thank you," Emily replied.

"I'll get someone to take your bag," Lois said.

She shook her shiny blonde hair from her shoulders, so sleek it reflected the light from the silver chandeliers above their heads like a mirror, and raised her hand in the air, clicking to get the attention of one of the many staff that were serving the party. In seconds, a male attendant was upon them, balancing a tray of champagne glasses on his palm and nodding subserviently as Lois gave him his instructions.

With her bag safely out of the way, Emily felt less likely to attract attention as an intruder. Relaxing, she began to scan the party with interest, observing the peculiarly rehearsed manner with which the upper class interacted with each other. Her eyes were suddenly drawn to the face of Admiral Allance, his silvery hair and eyebrows unmistakeable in the crowd. Wearing the same navy-blue pressed suit he favoured at the school, he was deeply engaged in conversation with a dark-haired man in his mid-forties. In between the two of them was a small robot, whizzing in circles as its head spun wildly, its body bouncing from the legs of one man to the other. After further scrutinization, Emily noticed the words "I-Tech" inscribed on the robot's chest. With a surge of giddiness, she realised the dark-haired man was none other than Jarvis Holt, the CEO of I-Tech and her hero since she was a little girl. She nudged Will and pointed, unable to believe she was in proximity to such an exceptional human being.

"That's Jarvis Holt!" she exclaimed. "He's talking to Admiral Allance!"

"I know," Will replied. "He's here every year. He's very nice, actually. I could introduce you if you like?"

Emily was tongue-tied, the thought of conversing with her hero too much for her brain to comprehend. She stammered and stuttered, attempting to make some sort of refusal under the conviction that she would certainly embarrass herself beyond repair, but Will had already made his way over to Jarvis, interrupting his conversation with the slightly affronted Admiral. After a moment, Will beckoned Emily and Lois over to join them. Lois strode towards them with confidence, leaving Emily to drag herself on heavy legs, feeling as though she were wading through cement as she advanced towards the group.

"Mr. Holt, this is Emily," Will said, introducing her upon her arrival.

"Nice to meet you, Emily," Jarvis grinned, extending his hand, which she accepted into her own shaking one. "Are you a student at The Academy too?"

"Yes, I am," Emily replied, cursing herself for not being more eloquent or interesting.

"That's right," Admiral Allance interjected. "Emily is amongst some of our most gifted and talented pupils at the school."

Emily smiled at him, though she was positive he had no idea who she was.

"Excellent," Jarvis nodded. "I have just been discussing your fantastic curriculum with the Admiral. He has asked me to send him a sample of the projects I-Tech are currently working on so he can pick some to showcase in your Technology lessons."

"Emily's amazing at Technology," Will boasted. "She's easily the best in our class. There's nothing technical she doesn't understand."

"Is that so?" Jarvis raised his eyebrows.

"It's my favourite subject," she replied. "I hope to work in the field when I'm older."

"That is encouraging to hear. We're always looking for sharp, young minds to join our company. Perhaps we could arrange some work experience for you over your school holidays? If that's something you'd be interested in?" Jarvis offered.

Emily's ability to speak was momentarily lost as she struggled to stay upright, blown over by the proposition to fulfil her lifelong dream.

"I think Emily would be very interested, Mr. Holt," Will smirked.

"Great!" Jarvis replied. "I'll send the arrangements to your mother, Will. She can forward them to you and you can pass them on to Emily."

"Thanks, Mr. Holt," Will smiled.

"Well," the Admiral announced, "now that that's all been settled, why don't you children run along so Mr. Holt and I can get back to talking business."

Emily, Will and Lois excused themselves, retreating to the safety of the buffet table, which had been replenished with several new plates of food in their brief absence. Will helped himself to a selection of snacks, grumbling something about missing the school robots as he piled up his plate by hand.

"I can't believe that just happened!" Emily gushed. "Am I really going to do work experience at I-Tech?"

"Seems that way," Will replied through a mouthful of cheese cracker.

"It's amazing. Thank you, Will," she grinned, hugging him tightly.

"Don't mention it," he blushed.

"I'm happy for you Emily," Lois said with sincerity. "It'll be a great opportunity. My dad says there won't be a single piece of technology I-Tech won't provide when we get to Novum."

"When you work for them, you should tell them to make more serving robots," Will instructed her. "If they make them stupid enough, I'm sure they won't rebel this time."

"Thanks for your suggestion, Will," Emily laughed.

"That's okay," he replied. "See if they can make robot butlers too. I'd love for my mum to finally get rid of Derek."

"I don't think I-Tech is interested in making robot servants at the moment," Lois informed them. "I overheard my dad talking to the head of Security last night. Apparently, the company is in the process of developing experimental weaponry, in case we meet hostile forces when we reach Novum."

"Little do they know the hostile forces might already be here," Emily frowned, images of the creature from the hallway flashing into her mind.

"We don't know that yet," Will reminded her. "Let's wait and see what we find out from the Captain's database."

"About that," Lois frowned. "We're going to have to wait even longer for our answers. My dad has decided to take an extra day off work so we can have some 'quality family time'. We're going to have to put it off until the day after tomorrow."

"That's alright," Will replied. "At least we get another day of normality before we have to face finding out what that thing is."

"I know nothing is certain yet," Emily said darkly. "But I don't have a very good feeling about any of this, do you?"

15.

The Investigation

The day after Hallowed Eve came around fast and Finley found himself brimming with excitement. He checked his bag for the second time that morning, making sure he had packed everything he needed for his stay at Will's apartment. Certain that he had remembered everything, he swung the heavy bag onto his arm and left the bedroom he shared with his brother, Justin. He entered the living room, where his family were sat gathered around their electric fire.

"Have you got everything you need, love?" his mum asked, as soon as he walked in the room.

"Yes, Mum," he smiled.

"Now remember, I'll be upstairs on Floor One cleaning at the Bartholomew's apartment if you need me," she told him for the third time that day.

"I know, Mum. I'll be fine," he assured her.

"Be careful, won't you love?" his mum fretted, touching his cheek.

"Don't worry," he comforted her. "Will's a good friend. He'll look after me."

His mum nodded and attempted to smile, but Finley could see the worry and concern lingering in her eyes. He was about to comfort her further, when Justin snorted loudly from one of the armchairs, interrupting their conversation.

"Who would ever have thought it, eh?" he scoffed, addressing their sister Jess, who was sitting in the corner sewing. "Our little brother Finley off to Floor One. First the Space Academy and now this. He'll be one of them before we know it."

"Stop it, Justin," their mother scolded him. "You and Jess have been nothing but unkind to your brother since he came home from school. You should be happy for him making new friends."

"Oh, we are happy for him, Mum," Jess sneered. "We're so happy that he's off galivanting at a floating school in the middle of Space while we're stuck here going to the Textiles and Armed Services schools, slaving away for nothing. He'll probably end up our servant master when we reach Novum"

"That's enough, Jess," warned their mother.

"It is completely unfair though" Justin argued. "He gets to learn about Combat and Weaponry with all the most up to date technology and his teacher is a member of the McGowan family. They were heroes in the Wars on Earth. No one knows more about combat than they do. We don't have anything like that at the Bureau and we're the ones who are supposed to be learning how to protect people."

"It's not Finley's fault the way the system works," their mother sighed. "You should just be pleased that someone in the family has the opportunity to make something of themselves. Your father and I are very proud of Finley."

"I think it's amazing," Felicity piped up from the floor, where she was sat crossed legged, engrossed in her battered I-Reader. "I'd give anything to go to the Academy. You're so lucky, Finley. The Captain's daughter goes there too, you know."

"She's in my class," Finley replied and Felicity's mouth fell open.

"Have you spoken to her? What's she like? She always looks so glamorous. I want to be just like her when I'm bigger," Felicity gushed.

"She's lovely," Finley replied. "And even more glamorous in person."

"Oh, here we go," Justin laughed. "Don't tell me you're in love with the Captain's daughter, Fin"

"Now there's a 'Romeo and Juliet' story for the modern era," Jess remarked.

"I don't know her that well," Finley defended himself. "I was just saying she's nice."

Justin and Jess exchanged a look but said no more, the burning eyes of their mother forcing them into silence.

"You'd better go and catch the lift Finley," she said to him. "You don't want to keep your friend waiting."

She gave him a hug and said goodbye, Felicity wrapping herself around him the moment his mum had pulled away.

"Have fun!" she squealed.

"Yeah have fun Fin," Justin said. "Hopefully none of them will try and launch you into Space this time."

"Just ignore him, love," his mum said, walking him out the door and giving him one final kiss before returning to their small apartment.

Finally alone, Finley made his way along the corridor, nodding "hello" to his neighbours as he crossed their paths. After walking a few yards, he reached the steel lift and went inside, the doors snapping shut to seal him inside the metal box. He pressed the button for the lobby and the machine creaked into life, ascending slowly towards their destination.

The lift docked, grinding to a halt and sliding open to reveal the back end of the lobby. Finley made his way past the line of recycling bins that greeted him upon his entrance and headed through the small maze of cheap, convenience stores until he reached the main floor, in all its shiny marble glory. He knew the lifts from the higher floors came in near the entrance and so he picked his way through the crowds of shoppers until he found the right area.

He had only been waiting a few seconds when the glass elevator slid into position and released its passengers, among them an excited looking Will, who bounced over to Finley with great enthusiasm, smiling from ear to ear.

"Hey mate! You made it!" he greeted him.

"I did," Finley replied. "What's the plan then? Are we going straight up to your apartment?"

"Well..." Will began, an uncontrollable glint in his eye. "It turns out the Captain isn't going back to work until tomorrow, so we've had to put our investigation on hold until then."

"Which means?" Finley asked.

"Which means we've got a whole day to kill," Will explained, "and I thought we could have some fun doing it."

He pulled a pair of golden tickets from his pocket, each emblazoned with a red rocket in the top right-hand corner.

"Are those...?" Finley trailed off in disbelief.

"Rocket Racing tickets!" Will confirmed. "I know you've never been before, so I thought I'd take you."

"Wow, thanks Will," Finley beamed with gratitude, taking one of the tickets and placing it carefully in his pocket, as though handling a precious jewel.

"It's no problem," Will shrugged. "My mum gets me tickets every year for Hallowed Eve. I used to take Spencer but I'm sure you'll be much better company. Now come on or we'll miss the train!"

He led him away from the shops towards a gleaming set of gates, manned by a guard in smart, black uniform. He was standing with intimidating stillness, his expression unsettlingly vacant, and Finley tried his best not to look him in the eye. His brother, Justin, had often told him tales of how the human services had been taken over by robots on Earth, until they had rebelled and started one of the many Wars. As the guard checked their tickets, screwing his nose up as though trying to escape an unpleasant smell, Finley wondered whether a killer robot might have been friendlier.

They walked through the gates onto a small platform where a long, open-topped train was stationed waiting to ferry them to the Rocket Racing stadium. Will guided the pair of them over to the first carriage, sitting down in the front seats with the promise that they would have the best view. Finley sat beside him, waiting with apprehension and only half-listening to as Will explained in excessive detail about each Rocket Racer competing that day and their individual statistics.

Once the train had reached capacity, the Guard pressed a button on his control pad and the carriage gave a gentle lurch, sliding forwards on magnetic tracks towards a round, metal door, which opened as they approached it. Passing through the doorway, they entered an elongated tunnel with transparent walls, giving the impression that they were floating unaided through Space. Finley inhaled with amazement as they glided through the blanket of stars surrounding them. He could see the Rocket Racing stadium a few miles ahead, sealed inside its protective dome that the tunnel seemed to feed into directly. When they had reached the halfway point, Finley turned around, craning his neck to get a good view of the Mayfly. He had never seen it from the outside before and was awestruck by the ship's sheer magnitude. The colossal grey mass spread across his entire vision as he tried to take in its whole appearance, which proved to be impossible. The word "Mayfly" was adorned on the ship's side, each individual letter at least two-hundred feet tall. Captivated by the view, it took him a moment to realise that Will had been talking to him for several minutes and he hastily tuned in to listen.

"I can't wait to go back, though," Will mused.

"To where?" Finley asked.

"To the school," Will replied with confusion.

"Oh, right, yeah, sorry," Finley apologised for not paying attention.

"It's probably the most fun I've ever had in my life," Will continued. "You know, terrifying alien monsters aside."

"Yeah, that is a slight drawback," Finley laughed. "Still it could be worse. We almost had to have one-on-one counselling with Miss Fortem."

They both shuddered.

"That was a lucky escape," Will reflected.

"I seem to be good at those," Finley smiled.

Ten minutes later, they arrived at the stadium, riding an escalator up from the platform to the expansive seating area above. They found their seats and took them, Will pointing with excitement to a gigantic screen that was fixed along the stadium walls, currently displaying a countdown to the race. In the centre of the circular rows of seating was a vast, empty space where Finley assumed the main event would take place. With only five minutes to go, Will accessed the interactive refreshments menu imbedded in the armrest of their chairs and ordered them both fizzy drinks and a hot dog, promptly brought over to them by a glum steward, who Finley was sure he recognised from Floor Seven.

He was halfway through eating what must have been the best hot dog he'd ever tasted, when a loud announcement echoed over their heads, causing all the spectators to leap to their feet and begin cheering raucously.

"Ladies and gentleman, please rise and show your support as we introduce today's Rocket Racers!" the detached male voice shouted with animation.

Several hidden doors in the stadium centre slid open and the Rocket Racers flew out, parading around the arena in their spacecrafts and waving to their fans behind their heavy, protective gear.

"Let's hear a round of applause for our contenders; Amelia Monteiro, Zed Sinn, Symon Schoestein, Layla Atwater and Pablo Pianthus!" the announcer boomed.

Will clapped his hands together as hard as he could muster and whistled as the racers swept past them, pointing to one of the men in a glossy, red rocket with glee.

"That's Pablo Pianthus! He's the best by miles," he yelled over the crowd.

After the procession, the rockets and their riders lined up together in mid-air, next to a starting line that had been painted into the arena wall.

"On your marks, get set, go!"

The rockets zoomed into life, their engines thundering as they whizzed in circuits around the arena at breakneck speed. Finley's eyes could barely make sense of the blur of colours that rushed before him, his hair and clothes blowing backwards with the force of the speed as the racers zoomed past.

"How many laps are there?" he shouted to Will.

"Forty!" Will yelled back.

With each passing lap, Finley grew more exhilarated and by the time the race had reached its halfway point, he had found himself whooping and hollering along with the other spectators. As the event came to an end, he kept his eyes glued to the big screen, desperate to see who would come first. He watched, enthralled, as Pablo Pianthus crossed the finishing line, the stadium erupting into a gargantuan cheer as he was pronounced the winner.

"That was amazing!" Finley shouted, his cheeks flushed with delight.

"I knew Pablo would win!" Will rejoiced, continuing to clap his hands together with fury as a podium rose from the ground and the top three contenders stepped on to claim their prizes.

When Pablo Pianthus' name was announced, he removed his helmet, revealing a thick mane of chestnut, brown hair that swung around his shoulders. He was much older than Finley had expected, and far more good looking, his tanned skin and carved features making him the ideal poster boy for the Rocket Racing sport.

"Thank you!" he called to his fans in a thick accent. "Thank you so much!"

When the race was over, the two boys left the stadium, chattering with elation about the event for the entire duration of their journey back to the Mayfly.

"Did you see it when he overtook Amelia Monteiro?" Will asked Finley, without giving him a chance to reply. "Or when he made that impossibly tight corner! I thought for definite he was going to lose control."

"What about when he looped underneath Zed in the final lap?" Finley replied. "That was incredible!"

"There's no one else like him," Will continued as they disembarked the train and returned to the lobby. "He's a genius. You can count how many times he's ever lost a race on one hand."

They walked to the lifts and got inside, Will pressing buttons on a screen built into the glass before standing back and clasping on to one of the rails.

"You might want to brace yourself," he warned Finley.

"For what?"

Before Will could answer, the lift gave a stomach-wrenching lurch and they began hurtling towards the ceiling at an impossible speed, Finley barely managing to keep his balance as they shot all the way to Floor One in less than a minute.

"What just happened?" he asked, his head spinning in bewilderment.

"We're here," Will announced.

His dizziness subsiding, he followed Will across an impressive atrium, glancing up at an ostentatiously large chandelier hanging from the ceiling. Just before they reached Will's apartment, they passed by a set of double doors marked with the number "1". Finley's heart jolted as he realised that it must be where Lois and her father lived. He had never dreamed he'd be so close to the Captain's apartment, nor did he expect to feel such a rush of adrenaline at the thought of being near to Lois. Will pressed a finger to a touch sensor next to the doors marked "3", a clicking noise giving him the approval to enter. He grabbed the crystal doorknobs and twisted them, opening the doors in one synchronised motion.

Finley was stunned by the sight of the lavish apartment as they entered it. It was huge, the living room alone at least four times the size of Finley's. The furniture was colour co-ordinated and positioned perfectly, with not a single thing out of place. There was no clutter, no piles of washing on the sofa, no shoes strewn about the floor. The kitchen surfaces were gleaming, the dining table polished to a dazzling shine. A tall, dark-haired man wearing a white cotton shirt and black trousers was stood dusting by a large window that was flooding the whole apartment with soft UV light. As Finley gazed about himself with awe, one of the doors leading from the living room opened and Will's mother rushed in, attaching a bracelet to her wrist with her teeth as she balanced her Personal Device to her ear.

"Oh, let me call you back," she said when she saw the boys, hanging up and placing her Personal Device back onto its wrist strap.

"Hi boys," she smiled. Finley had never seen a mother like her. She was young and made-up, dressed like a businesswoman in fashionable, smart clothing. Her hair was shiny and sleek, like the models Finley saw in shampoo adverts, and her nails were long and painted. She made his own mother look like a grandma in comparison.

"Hi, Mum," said Will. "I didn't expect you to be home."

"I'm just rushing out darling, I've got another client," she replied, grabbing her handbag from a coat stand near the door.

"How was the race?" she asked, pausing for a minute to speak to them.

"It was good," Will nodded. "Pablo won again."

"Glad you had a good time," she smiled as she rooted through her bag, checking she had everything she needed, "Derek's made a lasagne for dinner. It's in the fridge when you're ready for it. Have fun darling. Oh, and make yourself at home Finley."

"Thank you, Ms. James, I will," Finley nodded. With a quick ruffle of Will's hair, she was out the door, leaving the smell of expensive perfume lingering behind her.

"You hungry?" Will asked, strolling over to the large fridge in the kitchen. Finley nodded and followed him in.

"Hello, I-Fridge," Will said and for a moment Finley had thought he had lost his mind.

"Hello, Mr. James, what can I do for you today?" the fridge replied.

"Reheat the lasagne please," Will answered.

"Yes, Mr. James, certainly," the fridge said.

"Your fridge talks?!" Finley asked. "And re-heats things?"

"Yeah, my mum's friends with Jarvis Holt, the guy who owns I-Tech, so we get all the best stuff," Will shrugged.

"Your mother forgot to tell you that your favourite soft drink is in the cupboard," the man with the duster interjected. "She got it especially for you so try to seem grateful. I know that might be difficult."

"Okay," Will replied.

"This is Derek by the way," he added for Finley's benefit. "He's the family 'assistant'. Derek this is my friend Finley."

"Hi," Finley waved awkwardly.

"A pleasure, I'm sure," Derek replied, his voice dripping with contempt.

"What's wrong with him?" Finley whispered to Will.

"Don't ask," Will sighed.

The rest of the evening passed pleasantly. Will was amazed that Finley had never seen most of the gadgets in the apartment before and wanted to show off his favourites. As a result, they ended up watching a horror film, using the 4-D system hooked up to Will's television. It was an experience unlike anything Finley had ever had before, with holographic ghosts popping up around the living room and the sound of wolves howling emitting from all directions. There was even a feature that sprayed the two of them in the face with water, supposed to represent the splattering of blood from an unfortunate character's gruesome death. After the film, they went to Will's room and played Earth Wars until it was time to sleep, their last moments of consciousness spent chatting keenly about their impending investigation.

The following morning, they woke early, dressing, eating breakfast and heading out as quickly as they could. With a rushed explanation to Will's mother about going to do homework, they dashed into the atrium, making it to Lois' apartment in ten seconds flat. Will pounded on the door and waited, the two of them twitching with anticipation as they strained their ears to listen for the sound of movement with in. The door swung open, causing Will and Finley to jump unpleasantly as an old, haggard, woman with a broad frame and cold, cruel eyes came to greet them.

"You're not Lois," Finley gawked, the words leaving his mouth before he had a chance to stop them.

"Well observed," the woman sneered.

"Hello, Ms. Sommers," Will greeted her. "Finley, this is Lois' grandmother," he explained.

"Oh, lovely to meet you," Finley gushed.

"Lois," the woman crowed into the apartment behind her shoulder. "Some rather unfortunate boys are at the door asking for you."

"Coming, Grandma," they heard Lois call from somewhere behind her grandmother's wide figure.

"Does your father know about this?" her Grandma snapped back, frowning at Will and Finley with as much disapproval as she could muster.

"Yes, he does, they're here to do a homework project for school," Lois replied from inside.

"Hmph," her grandmother sniffed but said no more. With a final look of loathing and disgust, she pushed past Will and Finley, hobbling with the aid of a walking stick to the set of double doors marked with the number "2", which she slammed behind her vehemently as she went inside.

"Nice woman," Finley joked. Will snorted loudly.

With her grandmother out the way, Lois, Emily and the apartment beyond became visible to the boys. Finley had been expecting to see extravagance, but the scale of grandeur was beyond anything he could have dreamed. The living room was the size of Finley's entire home and was filled with the most luxurious furnishings he had ever seen. There were soft, cream sofas, large enough to seat at least ten people apiece, centred around a gleaming, cut-glass coffee table, topped with golden and bronze statues of eagles that stood guard on every corner. There was a white, quartz fireplace with a paper thin tv screen fitted into the wall above it, the mantelpiece embellished with real gold candlesticks and vases that certainly would have cost more credits than Finley's father earnt in a year. Most wondrous to Finley, though, was the grand piano that stood majestically at the top of some carpeted steps, resting proudly on four silver lions that had been carved into its feet.

"Wow," was all Finley could say.

"I know," said Emily. "Wait until you see the bathrooms!"

"Come in then you two, don't have just stand there," Lois laughed, beckoning them into the apartment.

"Sorry, I think Finley's a bit mesmerised," Will grinned as they stepped inside.

"It is an amazing apartment, Lois," Finley nodded.

"Never mind that," Lois said, clapping her hands together. "Let's not waste any time. I told my dad we have to revise for our Alien Studies exam so he'd leave his office open and give us access to his database, otherwise we would have needed his fingerprints to get in."

"Good thinking," Finley smiled, "and not a lie either. Maybe we could actually do some revision after we've used the database for our plan."

"If this alien creature is known to humans, it'll be on there," Lois continued. "Along with everything else that's known about it."

"It's important we find out whatever we can, no matter how scary the information is," Will urged them.

"Let's just hope it turns out the thing is harmless," Finley said. "Although if its appearance is anything to go by, I'm not holding my breath."

"This way then," Lois pointed and the three of them followed her out of the room. She led them down a short hallway, decorated with several unnerving paintings that featured images of the dying Earth. They reached a large, crimson door that had been left ajar and walked into the Captain's office, Lois sitting down at a grand, pewter desk and pressing a concealed button underneath it. A moment later, a wide computer screen appeared from a hidden compartment in the wall, an accompanying keyboard springing up from nowhere. Lois began typing rapidly, indiscernible images and text flashing up on the screen.

"Here we go," Lois said. "I've found the alien files."

"So, where do we start?" Finley asked.

"There's a video file here, it seems to be the only one," she observed, pressing the "enter" key so that the clip started playing. Grainy images of Earth appeared on screen, featuring narration from a loud, male voice.

"In the year 1985, humans first made contact with aliens," the voice began. Will rolled his eyes and scoffed.

"Can we skip the history lesson?" he complained. "We already know all of this."

"Sorry," Lois said, shutting down the video. She scrolled through the database, revealing hundreds of individual files on screen.

"How are we going to know if that thing's on there?" Will said with despair. "There's thousands of files."

"There should be a way to search by characteristics," Emily interjected.

"In English?" Will sighed.

"It's a database," Emily explained. "There will be a way to search through it, hopefully by typing in what the alien looked like."

"Go ahead," Lois said, vacating her seat so that Emily could sit down.

While Emily was absorbed in typing, Will began to wander off, nosing through the shelves of dusty old books that were sat beside the Captain's desk.

"Why does your dad have books, Lois?" Will asked her. "Shouldn't they be in the Museum or something?"

"I don't know," Lois sighed. "He likes to collect things from Earth."

"Maybe you shouldn't touch them," Finley frowned, but Will ignored him, choosing books at random and flicking through them to examine their contents.

"Any luck, Emily?" Lois asked her, after she had been at work for ten minutes or so.

"I don't think so," she frowned. "There doesn't appear to be any aliens on here that match the description of what we saw."

"Are you sure?" Lois pressed her. "Maybe you missed something."

"I can't be certain, no, not without opening every single file individually and reading through them, but that could take days," she replied. "It says here there are 300,000 entries in total."

Finley's shoulders slumped with defeat. He looked at the others in desperation, hoping one of them would suggest an alternative idea, but their faces appeared just as blank as his own.

"Guys…" Will said slowly from behind them. "I think I've found something."

"What is it?" Emily asked him, jumping up from her chair. Will rushed forwards, a cluster of tattered notebook pages clutched in his hands.

"Look at this," he demanded and the three of them gathered around him.

"Where did you get those?" Lois asked him.

"They fell out of one the books," Will replied.

Finley looked down at the pages and was bewildered to see a drawing of the creature from the hallway, every feature perfectly recaptured in pencil. Its various atrocities had been labelled in an untidy scrawl, with everything from 'claw-like hands' to 'empty eyes' included in the illustration. Next to the drawing was an almost illegible sentence, which after scrunching his eyes up tightly, Finley read as 'drawn to human emotion'.

"Look there," Finley said, gesturing to some scribble at the top of the page. "This person's given the alien a name; 'The Vacuous'"

"Whose notes are these?" Lois wondered out loud, her face contorted with confusion.

"They're your dad's aren't they?" Emily replied.

"That's not his handwriting," she said. "I don't recognise it."

"Hang on," Finley added, pointing to the top of one of the pages, "what are those numbers?"

"2098," Emily said out loud. "That must be the date these notes were taken on."

165

"Wait a minute," Will mused, his eyes darting back and forth as something began formulating in his brain. "I've seen that date written before, in Krecher's office."

Finley, Emily and Lois looked at him with bewilderment.

"Krecher was a teacher at the College that my mum, dad and the Captain went to back on Earth. He had a photo hanging in his office with them all in it. It had the date '2098' written underneath," he explained.

"So... these notes belong to Mr. Krecher?" Emily asked.

"I think so," Will replied. "He had a journal in his desk with a padlock on it. Some of the pages were missing. I'm betting this is them."

"What were you doing in Krecher's desk?" Finley frowned. Will ignored the question.

"More to the point, why does my dad have Krecher's notes about the aliens?" Lois asked. "Do you think he knows about them too?"

"I think they might have all known," Will nodded. "Your dad, Krecher and my parents. They must have come across them when they were all at College."

"So, what you're saying is, these "Vacuous" creatures were on Earth?" Emily clarified, "and your parents, the Captain and Krecher all saw them."

"I think that's possible," Will nodded.

"But how can we ask them about it without admitting everything? If anyone tells Allance we were out of bed that night, we could end up being blamed for the vandalism," Lois fretted. "After all, we haven't got any proof that the Vacuous was there."

"Forget Allance" Will replied. "My mum wouldn't let me set foot at the Academy ever again if she knew there were aliens roaming in the dormitories at night."

"Mine either," Finley realised with deflation.

"If we can't tell our teachers and we can't tell our parents, then what are we going to do?" Emily frowned.

The four of them stood in silence, each attempting to conjure an impossible solution in their minds.

"There is a way we can find out what our parents saw… without having to ask them anything," Will announced.

"How is that possible?" Lois asked.

"The Looking Glass," Will replied cryptically. "The answers are in the Looking Glass."

16.

Return To The Past

The new term at the Space Academy began with a flurry of exams, putting the plans that Will had made on hold until the chaos of the first few weeks died down. In truth, the four of them had been so absorbed in their scheming that they had hardly managed to prepare for any of the rigorous tests they were now facing in every subject. So far, they had endured a practical Combat and Weaponry exam, which involved fighting off a horde of holographic aliens in a simulated war zone using the laser weapons they had been studying that term. A written assignment for the subject had demanded they write a gruelling two-thousand-word essay on the War of the Classes, which Will was certain he would have failed had he not paid attention to a few of his mum's stories about Earth.

For their Alien Studies exam, Krecher had brought out an array of species for the class to identify, which, thanks to Finley's insistence that they use Alfie's database for revision, hadn't been too difficult. Emily had prepped them all the night before their Technology exam in which Mr. Mayhem asked them to evaluate a piece of existing tech. Finley had chosen the I-Fridge, seemingly have a lot to say about the device. For Resources, they had spent an entire day in the forest and were marked by their ability to forage food, find water, build shelters and make a fire. The most important exam of all, however, was their Rocket Control test. Mr. Zeppler had taken the class out into Space to fly personal rockets around a suspended obstacle course and had informed them that passing the test meant that they would receive their first licence, allowing them to fly small rockets unsupervised. Will had found the obstacles exceptionally easy to navigate, but Finley, still scarred from the incident at the beginning of the year, had lost his nerve several times and had to retake the test twice before he was able to complete it successfully.

The last day of the exam period rolled around and a heavy essay on the Ancient Egyptians for Civilisations was the only thing now standing in the way of their freedom. Having spent the last four weeks on guard for any signs of the Vacuous, it hadn't taken much for Will to convince Finley, Emily and Lois to sneak out with him to the Looking Glass at the first opportunity. He had recounted his first experience with the mirror in vivid detail, igniting their curiosity and convincing them that the answers they sought would be found inside. With Admiral Allance's threats still looming over their heads, Will had studied their designated route several times, until he was certain that it was the best path to take to avoid detection.

That night at dinner, they established Will's room as their meeting point, agreeing to arrive there as soon as Ms. Everly's evening rounds were finished. Having settled this, they spent the rest of the meal eagerly speculating about what the Looking Glass might show them and what secrets they could unearth. Despite the ominous nature of the Vacuous, they couldn't help but be excited by the prospect of solving the mystery that had been presented to them.

When the hour arrived, Will left his bedroom door unlocked, allowing Lois, Emily and Finley to enter discreetly, each of them wearing black clothing at his request. Once they had regrouped, they snuck out of the dormitories, which were now deserted after curfew thanks to the "vandalism" incident, and into the dark grounds beyond.

"Did Allance ever say whether they decided to put cameras in the dorms or not?" Finley whispered with worry as they set off.

"Well if they did, we'll soon know about it," Will replied ominously.

They navigated their way across the school campus, using the shadowy pathways that Will had meticulously picked out for them, and reached the Ivory Tower in ten minutes flat.

"Can you hear any aliens out in the grounds?" Emily asked the others as they loaded into Jeff's shuttle. "What if Krecher's still up there?"

"We've come this far," said Will as he started up the engine. "No use turning back now."

Emily's fears however, luckily turned out to be unfounded. Upon arriving at the top of the tower, they found Krecher's classroom quiet and empty. Satisfied that there were no discernible signs of life in the building, the four of them headed into the office, closing the door behind them with care.

"Over there," Will instructed, pointing to the hilted mirror in the corner.

"This is it?" Emily asked, staring with scepticism at the ordinary looking piece of furniture, which was innocently displaying their curious reflections.

"Yes," Will confirmed. "That's it."

"How do you know it's going to take us to the right place?" Finley questioned him.

"I don't know for sure" Will admitted. "But it showed me what I needed to see last time."

They stood and waited, Emily, Lois and Finley shuffling on their feet and exchanging sideways glances as the mirror continued to reflect only the room around them. Will stared at the mirror patiently, holding absolute faith that it would allow them to see what they desired.

"How will we know when it's working?" Lois whispered.

"Maybe it only works for one person," Finley frowned.

"Maybe Krecher put some kind of block on it after you broke in last time," Emily sighed.

"Do you think we should go back?".

"Just wait," he told them. "It'll happen."

As though the mirror had heard him, a shiny handle suddenly materialised on its surface, rewarding Will for his faithfulness and stifling the other's doubts.

"Woah," Finley said. "That was impressive. How does it work?"

"It's alien," Will replied shortly. "That's all I know. Are you all ready?"

The three of them nodded and Will gripped the handle and took a deep breath before twisting it to the side.

"Follow me!" he shouted, pulling the mirror open with force and running at full pelt into the blackness beyond.

This time, he was ready for the gut-pulling disorientation that followed entry into the Looking Glass, staggering only slightly as he let his lungs fill with the cool, clean air that only Earth could provide. He was busy studying the street around him when a series of heavy footsteps indicated the arrival of Finley, Lois and Emily.

"Are we in the right place, Will?" Finley asked, gawking at their surroundings.

"Yeah, this is it," Will nodded, noting the snow-peaked mountains in the distance. "This is where my parents went to College. If the Vacuous were here, we'll find them."

"So, where do we start?" Emily inquired.

Will scoped the area, scanning for clues that might suggest which path they should take. His eye was caught by an old, stone building, looming upon a hill top a few miles from where they stood. There was something drawing about its presence and gut instinct told Will it would be a good place to start their search.

"Over there," he pointed, marching towards the building with the others in close pursuit. They navigated their way through the winding streets of sleepy houses, startling at any sign of movement and checking over their shoulders in case a Vacuous suddenly appeared behind them. As they drew closer to their destination, Will's nose was overpowered with the unpleasant stench of rotting food, causing him to stop dead and recoil.

"What is that smell?!" Emily exclaimed when she caught up with him, pinching her nose between her finger and thumb.

"I don't know, but brace yourselves, we're about to find out," Will grimaced.

He pulled the collar of his black, cotton jumper up to the ridge of his nose and continued forwards, breathing through his mouth to keep the powerful odour at bay. Keeping in step with one and other, Will, Emily, Finley and Lois rounded the next corner, finding themselves on a residential street, almost identical to the others in the area. As soon as they stepped onto the smooth tarmac of the road, it immediately became clear that something was very wrong. Every single one of the large rubbish bins positioned outside of the houses had been knocked over, causing litter and debris to fill the street. Flies swarmed in their hundreds, descending upon old, discarded food in packs of dark, vibrating, clouds. Metal drink cans scraped across the floor and plastic wrappers rustled with every gust of wind, interrupting the silence that hung over the street. Upon further inspection, Will noticed that one of the cars parked next to the pavement had been bashed out of place, its wide, silver rear sticking out

171

diagonally into the road. Etched into the paint work on the side of its body were three, deep claw marks, their impact so powerful a small dent had been left in one of the doors.

"I've seen marks like that before," Lois swallowed, fear rising in her voice. "In our dormitories the night we saw the Vacuous."

"There's one here," Will concluded.

"It won't be able to see us, will it?" Emily fretted.

"No, we can't be seen or heard in the Looking Glass. It's like being a ghost," Will reassured her.

"Can we move anything?" Emily queried, walking over to one of the discarded bins and attempting to pick it up.

"No, you can't touch anything either. Technically, you'd be changing the past which the Looking Glass doesn't allow" Will explained. "Come on, we'd better keep going."

Hugging themselves against the bitter cold, they trudged through the streets, following every fork and bend in the road that led them closer to the ancient building. Eventually, they came to an old high street, the shop windows gathering with dust after being abandoned by their owners, with only a few appearing to still be in business. They crossed the town centre, passing under an imposing, grey clock tower that chimed urgently to inform them it was midnight, before meandering through the backstreets, finally reaching the foot of the hill they had been searching for. Carved into the grassy slope was a set of sturdy, stone steps which they ascended hastily, clambering to the peak of the hill within minutes.

Once they had reached the top, they were met with a set of wrought iron gates, with two eagles carved into the flanks. Across the top, the words "College Snowdonia" were inscribed above a motto that read "Prudentia Salvi Erimus". Will realised with a giddy surge of adrenaline that they had found his parent's College, his belief in its significance growing stronger by the second. By some miracle, one of the gates had been left slightly ajar, allowing the four of them to enter without being stopped by their inability to touch anything. A short, gravel path took them to the entranceway of the stone dwelling, which comprised of a set of mahogany doors under a stone archway. The doors had also been left open by whoever had proceeded them, revealing the dim glow of artificial light from inside the

College. The four of them took one last glimpse at the building, which rose from the ground imposingly above them, its twisted turrets and domed windows giving it the stately appearance of a stern church rather than a place of education. Despite its threatening exterior, Will confidently led the others over the building's threshold, relieved to find that the inside was much friendlier than the outer shell would suggest.

They had walked into the main entrance, made apparent by the large reception desk in the centre of the room, covered in various I-Tech gadgets that provided a small amount of comfort and familiarity. The walls were covered in art work created by the students, hung amongst an excess of posters and flyers advertising for various sports teams and clubs, including football, lacrosse and 'The Society of the Enlightened'. To the right of the doors was a coffee shop and small seating area, discarded paper cups scattered across the round metal tables. On the right-hand side was a green door which had been left ajar, a sign reading "Lecture Rooms" attached to the front. With a glance at the others to confirm they were all in agreement, Will walked through the doorway, finding himself in a long, musty hallway. The walls in this part of the building were bare and painted in a faded magnolia, giving an eerie feel to their surroundings. They reached a corner and turned it, entering a second identical hallway. Suddenly, the lights began to flicker and fade, plunging them into pungent, impenetrable darkness.

"Someone get the torch on their Personal Device!" Finley called out from somewhere in the blackness.

"Mines not working," Emily replied from Will's right.

"I don't think Personal Devices work in the Looking Glass," Will frowned.

"Great, so we're just stuck in the dark then," Lois complained.

"Wait, ssh!" Finley hissed. "What's that noise?"

The four of them stood in deathly silence and listened attentively. The sound of voices echoed down the hallway towards them, distant at first but growing louder as each second passed.

"It's getting away!" a male voice cried. Heavy footsteps thundered towards them, reverberating loudly from the walls. Will froze, his heart thumping loudly in his ears. He narrowed his eyes as they began to adjust to the gloom and was sure he could make out a shadowy figure, standing just a few feet in front of them.

"Where did it go?" a second voice spoke from around the corner.

"That's my dad," Lois whispered.

Suddenly, bright torchlight burst into the hallway, forcing Will to shield himself from its glare. He blinked rapidly, waiting for the coloured spots to fade from his vision so he could see again. After a few seconds, his sight returned to normal and his blood ran cold. Directly in front of him was a Vacuous, identical to the one they had encountered in their dormitory. Its misshapen head was cocked slightly to the side as it emitted hissing noises, twitching it's sharp claws as it stared through hollow eyes. A chill ran down Will's spine as he was overcome by a strange feeling that the Vacuous could see him.

"There it is!" Elsie shouted as two more beams of torchlight flooded into the hall. Will peered around the Vacuous to see younger versions of Alfie and his mother, accompanied by his father, Austin.

"What's it doing?" Austin asked, unable to see Will and the others standing petrified in the creature's wake.

"It's looking at something," Alfie frowned.

"But there's nothing there?" Elsie said with confusion, waving her torch in different directions to investigate the corridor.

The Vacuous, startled by the sudden movement of light, turned away and let out a bloodcurdling screech. It spun around and began to run on all fours, moving exceptionally fast on powerful limbs. Will, Finley, Lois and Emily jumped out the way as it passed them, the force of its weight thudding deafeningly through the corridor each time it hit the ground.

"Let's go!" Austin shouted, sprinting after the creature at full speed with Alfie and Elsie close on his tail. Will followed them, running as fast as he could to keep up as they darted out of the building and back into the night. The cold air hit Will's face like needles in a painful contrast to the warmth of the building inside, but he continued pursuing Alfie and his parents nonetheless. He pounded down the stone steps with Emily, Lois and Finley a few paces behind him and raced through the backstreets of the town, passing invisibly through a small crowd of people who were emptying from a high-street bar, wrapping themselves in coats and scarves to keep out the cold.

Mercifully, Alfie, Elsie and Austin had ground to a halt in front of the clock tower and doubled over to catch their breath. Will copied, gasping as he desperately tried to fill his lungs with air, his stomach knotting uncomfortably as his chest burned with exhaustion. Finley, Lois and Emily thundered to a stop alongside him, wheezing and panting with the exertion of running long distance, which none of them had ever had cause to do before. Feeling dizzy, Will sat on the ground to listen as Alfie and his parents began to speak.

"Did you see where it went?" Austin puffed, leaning against the clock tower, his face dewy with sweat.

"No," Elsie replied with deflation.

"Damn it!" Austin cursed, banging his fist against the tower's stone base. "I can't believe we let one get away again."

"They'll be other chances," Elsie soothed him.

"I've been thinking," Alfie interrupted them, his tone sombre. "I don't think us hunting the Vacuous is such a good idea anymore."

"What?" said Austin and Elsie in unison, exchanging a look of bewilderment.

"I think we're wasting our time," Alfie re-iterated.

"How can you say that?" Austin demanded. "Nothing is known about these creatures. Not even Professor Krecher can figure out what they are. We need to find out why they're here. It could be the difference between human extinction and survival!"

"Yes, that's what we keep telling ourselves," said Alfie bluntly. "But aliens have been visiting Earth for over a hundred years. Just because we've never seen this species before, doesn't mean they're harmful. I mean, look at the facts. Every time we see the Vacuous they run away from us and we've never seen anyone be hurt by one."

"Not yet, but look at them! Their clawed hands, their sharp teeth, the way they can move… They're built for killing." Austin argued.

"We can't base all of our assumptions on their physical appearance," Alfie replied. "It's not enough evidence to justify what we're doing."

"We've been following the Vacuous for nearly a year. You've been convinced we were right up until this point," Austin countered.

"Look, I'm just trying to be realistic," Alfie sighed. "We stumbled upon these aliens and started tracking them down, convinced we were saving the world in the process, but the truth is we have no idea what we're doing."

"Then we ask for help. We need to contact the Government again," Austin insisted. "Something needs to be done! We need answers!"

"I told you, there's nothing the Government can do. We haven't been able to provide any evidence that the Vacuous pose any kind of threat. Think how many fanatics must have come out of the woodwork since The Split was made public," Alfie answered. "They're bombarded daily with false reports from people who are trying to stop it from happening. They're not going to take us seriously."

"Elsie, tell me you don't agree with this!" Austin pleaded with her.

"I don't know," Elsie said uncertainly. "Maybe we should talk to Krecher again."

"Krecher doesn't know anything, he's just as confused by this whole thing as we are. I supported going to him at first, but it hasn't helped. Showing him the Vacuous only seems to have terrified him. He hasn't been the same since," Alfie replied.

Elsie frowned, contemplating his words carefully.

"Look, I know I'm right about this," he pushed. "If we carry on doing what we're doing, we're going to mess up our Graduation and we won't get places on the Mayfly. It's not going to matter what the Vacuous are if they're here on Earth and we're up in Space. They can't follow us to Novum," Alfie declared.

"How do you know for certain? The Split could be part of their plan," Austin pointed out. "The Great Conspiracy predicts that the Mayfly isn't safe. Maybe it's referring to the Vacuous. Maybe they want the Mayfly for themselves so they can get to Novum."

"That seems a little bit far- fetched, Austin," Alfie frowned.

"Why does it?" Austin demanded, his eyes wild, his breath coming thick and fast. "Do you think we're the only species that have wrecked our home planet? I'm betting we're not. If the Vacuous somehow found out about Novum, they could see it as a second chance for their own kind. It doesn't seem that impossible to me. Why else would they be skulking around a College? They must know educational institutes are working with the Mayfly project to create skilled workers. They're trying to find out how to get on board! I'm telling you... I can feel it in my gut."

Elsie and Alfie exchanged a look of concern.

"Perhaps this has all gone too far," Elsie said after a moment. "It's turning into an obsession. I think it's time to let it go, Austin. All we're doing is chasing shadows."

Austin slumped to the ground in defeat, resting his head between his knees for a moment as his breathing slowed back to normal.

"Of course you would side with him," Austin said darkly.

"I'm not siding with anyone," Elsie insisted, "and it's only because I care so much about you that I'm saying this. The Vacuous have ruled our lives for long enough. Imagine how good it would feel to be normal again. To go back to how things were before we knew they existed. Regardless of what happens, there isn't much time left on Earth. I'd rather spend it being happy than chasing aliens who may or may not be dangerous."

"Fine," Austin conceded. "I'm not doing any of this without you, Elsie. If you tell me to stop then I will."

"I think it's for the best," Elsie smiled, going to sit beside him and placing an arm around his shoulder. "We can save the world another day."

"So, we're all in agreement then?" Alfie clarified. "No more Vacuous and no more Great Conspiracy. It all ends tonight."

"Alright," Austin nodded reluctantly. "It ends here." Elsie squeezed his hand, looking up at him with shiny adoration.

Will got to his feet. A mirrored door had materialised next to the clock tower, informing him that they'd seen all the Looking Glass wished to show them.

"Time to go," he told Finley, Emily and Lois, who silently trailed behind him as he opened the door and stepped through, returning to the present day in Krecher's office.

 As soon as they arrived, Will made his way out of the door, through the desolate classroom and into the shuttle, flying it to the ground without speaking a single word. Sensing his dark mood, Finley, Lois and Emily said nothing, waiting until they had retreated across the school grounds and reached the safety of Will's bedroom before they dared speak.

"Are you okay?" Emily asked him, swinging herself up to sit on his desk as he hunched over the end of his bed, twiddling his thumbs together with agitation.

"Yeah, it's just weird seeing my mum and dad together," Will frowned. "Especially knowing that he abandoned her so soon afterwards."

"It was weird seeing my dad, too," Lois agreed, curling her legs up on one of the armchairs. "Back then he almost seemed like an actual human being."

"At least we got some answers though," Emily pointed out. "We know the Vacuous were around on Earth."

"Yeah, but that's all we know," Finley disagreed. "We still don't know whether they're dangerous or not, or what one was doing hanging around our dorms in the middle of the night."

"And I don't think we should try and find out either," Will stated bluntly. "Lois' dad said they'd never seen a Vacuous hurt anyone and that all they ever seemed to do was run away. We might not know why there's one at the school but I think if we try and find out, we're going to put ourselves at risk."

"At risk for what?" Emily asked, folding her arms.

"For being expelled, for getting hurt," he paused. "For seeing things that we might not want to see."

"I understand why you'd say that," Emily replied, "but the Vacuous were hunted by your parents and now they've turned up at our school. Don't you think it's a bit of a strange co-incidence?"

"Co-incidence or not, it's not worth the trouble to find out," Will insisted. "If the Vacuous are dangerous and they're wandering around the school,

Allance and the teachers will deal with it. In the meantime, I think we should follow Alfie's advice and leave alone what we don't understand."

"But your dad-" Emily began.

"My dad's dead," Will interrupted. "His obsession with the Vacuous drove him to make some horrible decisions that eventually killed him. If that isn't a clear enough sign that we should leave this entire thing alone, then I don't know what is."

There was an awkward silence. Finley and Lois shifted uncomfortably in their chairs as the words from Will's outburst lingered for a moment in the air.

"If you're sure that's what's best..." Lois said uncertainly.

"I am," Will replied with force. "If my dad had done the same then he might still be alive."

"Okay," Finley smiled weakly. "We can drop it."

Will stared at Emily who was chewing her lip, her arms still folded around her chest.

"Fine," she huffed. "We'll forget about it."

With their new decision in place, Emily, Finley and Lois traipsed off to bed, leaving Will to stew in the fresh feelings of anger the Looking Glass had brought to the surface of his mind. If he was being honest with himself, he knew that Emily was right. His parents hunting the Vacuous in College and then one turning up outside his room fifteen years later had to mean something, but his desire to honour the promise his father had broken was stronger than any need to unravel the truth. In his mind it was very simple. Vacuous or no Vacuous, he would never be the same as Austin. Of that he was determined.

17.

The Happy Interlude

Lois sat in the Dining Hall, drumming her fingers against the table and staring unwaveringly at the blank screen on her Student Planner, ignoring the delicious smell of French pastries that was wafting over from the breakfast buffet. Any minute now, her planner would beep, delivering the dreaded message that contained her grades for every subject. After a few minutes of sitting alone in abject terror, Lois was joined by Finley, Will and Emily, whose appearances reflected the tired dishevelment that Lois felt. They bleated "good morning" half-heartedly, each producing their own planners and resting them delicately on the table, eyeing them fearfully as though they were bombs about to explode.

"I'm guessing you guys didn't get much sleep either, then," Lois observed.

"Not a wink," Will replied.

"How could we?" Emily stressed. "If we don't get good grades in these exams, we won't be able to come back to school next year."

"We have our final projects too, remember," Finley reminded her. "They count towards our overall marks."

"Yes, but we hardly revised for our exams at all!" Emily continued to fret. "We were so distracted."

There was an awkward pause as they were all reminded of their promise to Will not to mention the Vacuous or anything associated with their previous ordeal. It had been difficult at first, with Lois, Emily and Finley forced to discuss the situation in secret whenever Will wasn't around. Over time, however, their inclination to talk about the subject had faded naturally. These days, Lois found that the Vacuous only entered her mind when she was alone at night and vulnerable to the chain of unsettling thoughts her brain liked to present her with in order to make sleep difficult.

"Remind me one more time how the grading system works," Emily said to Finley, running her hands through her already unkempt hair.

"You get a score from one to five," Finley explained calmly. "One is the best and five is the worst. Three and above is classed as a 'pass' whereas four and five are 'fails'."

"And how many subjects do we need to pass to get back in next year?" Emily asked him, despite knowing the answer to the question full well.

"All of them," Finley replied morbidly. Will groaned and sunk his head into the table, Emily sighed in an exaggerated fashion and Lois began massaging her temples, pulling the skin around her eyes a little too aggressively for the act to be relaxing.

"Don't worry," Finley laughed in response to their reaction. "You won't have done that badly!"

"Easy for you to say, Fin," Will grumbled. "You're top of nearly every class."

"Well, I still messed up in my Rocket Control exam," Finley reminded him.

"At least Mr. Zeppler let you retake it," Lois pointed out.

"He only did that because we're supposed to go out in Space this term. If I don't get my licence, I'll have to stay behind every lesson while you all go off flying," Finley said.

"What time is it?" Will complained, not wanting to take his eyes away from his Planner.

"7:59," Finley told him.

"One minute to go!" Emily squealed.

Lois' heart began to beat heavily in her chest. Despite all her dad's excessive funding into her education, she had never been the brightest in her tutor group and always struggled to apply herself properly in her lessons. The curriculum at the Academy, however, fascinated her beyond belief and she could only hope she would be allowed to continue studying it.

The sickening sound of beeping erupted around the hall and the entire student population seemed to draw in breath as one. Lois, Will, Finley and Emily looked at each other, their eyes wide as saucers as they realised the message of their fate had been delivered.

181

"All together?" Will suggested and they nodded, picking up their Student Planners in unison.

"One, two, three...."

Lois winced, opening the message and turning her face away from it slightly, as though reading it would blind her. She skimmed down the page quickly and was immensely relieved to see there were no fours or fives in any of her subjects. Her fear subsiding, she read through the page carefully, making sure not to miss any details. The page stated:

"Lois Sommers,

Mid-Year Examination Results:

Alien Studies ~ 1

Arithmetic ~ 2

Civilisations ~ 2

Combat and Weaponry ~ 2

Rocket Control ~ 2

Resources ~ 3"

"How did you do Lois?" Finley asked her.

"I got a 'one' in Alien Studies!" she gushed. "I got 'two's in everything else, except Resources which I got a 'three' in."

"Well done!" he congratulated her. "I knew you'd pass."

"What did you get?" she asked him.

"I got a 'one' for everything but a 'three' in Rocket Control," he replied happily. "I was convinced I'd failed that exam."

"I got four 'ones'," Emily interjected. "In Alien Studies, Technology, Combat and Weaponry and Arithmetic! The rest were 'twos'."

"Nice," Finley smiled. The three of them looked at Will who was staring down at his Student Planner in disbelief, his face frozen in an expression of shock.

"Everything okay?" Emily asked him.

"I got a 'three' in Civilisations," he replied flatly.

Lois looked at Finley and Emily, unsure how to react.

"I can't believe Miss Fortem passed me!" Will laughed with euphoria.

"Did you get any 'ones'?" Finley asked him.

"Yeah, in Alien Studies, Rocket Control and Combat and Weaponry," he answered merrily.

"Seems like Mr. Krecher was very generous this year," Finley noted.

"I know. It makes me feel a bit guilty, considering we broke into his office," Lois admitted.

"I'm so excited we all passed," Will beamed, changing the subject. "All we have to do now is not mess up on our final projects and we'll be coming back in September."

Just as Will spoke, Rudy and his followers passed by the table, overhearing his announcement.

"Isn't that nice?" Rudy said to his posse, his voice heavy with sarcasm. "Emily and her boyfriend together for another year."

"He isn't my boyfriend," Emily blushed.

"It's a shame we won't be partners for our final projects, isn't it Emily?" Rudy continued to taunt, ignoring her completely. "You and I made a great team looking after that Beakin thing."

"You hardly did anything, Rudy. Monster would have starved if it wasn't for me," Emily snapped back.

"Well, if you find yourself missing me, you know where I am," he winked, before sauntering away.

"He really isn't very bright, is he?" Finley mused after him.

"At least I didn't have to fight him this time," Will smirked.

"Now that's all over, let's eat!" Emily exclaimed and the four of them strolled over to the serving station together, asking the robots to pile their plates high with celebration food.

Back at the table, they sipped merrily on sweet, cold orange juice and chewed on buttery, warm croissants, their conversation flowing as they basked in the glory of their success. Half-way through their breakfast,

Emily's older brother, Charlie, strode over to their table, sitting down assertively between Finley and Lois and squashing them to the end of the row.

"Guess what?" he grinned, not bothering with greetings or introductions.

"You passed your exams?" Emily ventured.

"Well, yeah, obviously," he waved his hand dismissively. "I got 'ones' in everything. But no that isn't what I meant. What I was going to say is, we're passing by a Sun."

"What do you mean, Charlie?" Emily sighed.

"The school!" he exclaimed with frustration. "We're passing by a nearby Sun in whatever solar system we're travelling through."

"So?"

"So, it means we get real sunlight!"

"What do you mean?" Will asked him, his brows furrowed in confusion.

"Oh my goodness," Charlie rolled his eyes in exasperation. "We are flying past a Sun in a see-through dome. Therefore, we will experience real, genuine sunlight for a few days," he explained, enunciating every word carefully as though speaking to very young children.

"That's never happened before on the Mayfly," Finley frowned.

"Well, of course not, there aren't any real windows on the Mayfly. It only happens here at the school," Charlie replied. "There's nothing else like it. You can even swim in the lake and sunbathe. Trust me, once you feel proper sunlight you'll never forget it. That fake UV stuff has got nothing on the real thing."

"How do you even know about this, Charlie?" Emily asked him with suspicion. "None of the teachers have announced anything."

"I have contacts in all the right places," he winked.

Just as he spoke, a pinging noise rang out across their heads, travelling over the Dining Hall and provoking an instant reaction of silence from the students inside. The noise seemed to be coming from an intercom that Lois had never realised was there.

"Here we go," Charlie whispered.

"Good morning, Space Academy," Admiral Allance's voice boomed through the speakers.

"First, allow me to congratulate you all on your excellent exam results. I am sending this message to the school through every television screen and sound system to make absolutely certain that every student knows how truly proud I am of their achievements this year so far."

Lois couldn't see the Admiral's face, but his flat tone of voice greatly contradicted the expression of pride he was trying to convey. Had she headed out into the school and found a T.V screen, she wouldn't have been surprised to find him reading his speech from a piece of paper.

"Secondly, I would like to inform you that we will shortly be bypassing a Sun on our way through the Irodonius solar system. If you would like to make your way outside in an orderly fashion, you will be able to witness the magical moment that we are bathed in natural light!"

The Admiral's announcement ended and the hall erupted with the noise of benches scraping against the floor as everyone rushed to their feet to observe the spectacle. Lois, Finley, Emily and Will joined in amongst the herd, converging with dozens of students in the Reception Hall as they pushed towards the school grounds.

Searching for a decent spot within the gathering crowds outside, Lois and the others planted themselves on the lawn opposite the school's main entrance, turning their faces towards the black sky where an orange glow had already begun to form. In the far distance, thousands of miles above their heads, the planets of the Irodonius system were visible. They ranged in colour from deep magnificent blue to rich emerald green and floated enigmatically in perfect orbit around their Sun. Rings of dust could be seen swirling around one of the celestial bodies, forming a hazy layer of cloud around the planet's burnt yellow surface.

Captivated by the fascinating sight of the solar system, Lois almost missed the moment the grounds were flooded with brilliant, bright light. She felt the warmth spread across her body and closed her eyes, basking in the pleasant heat. She was amazed at how it was possible for the light of a single, burning star to carry instantaneous feelings of happiness in its rays. She remembered something her mother had once told her about all humans being made from stardust and wondered if that was the explanation for the wonderful sensation that was spreading through her bones.

Opening her eyes again, she looked about the grounds with a new, sharp focus as though seeing them clearly for the first time. In the new light, she could make out the exact shade of grey concrete that had been used to build the main school, which appeared far less imposing now it was out of the shadows. The golden logo of Novum above the navy, blue doors glinted as the Sun reflected off its large, spherical surface, blinding the beholder who gazed at it for too long. The glass windows shimmered, the Resources Biodome sparkled and the smooth, metal roof of the school Observatory swam hazily in the distance, visible waves of heat rising from its metal shell. The grass they stood upon was suddenly a bright shade of green, looking far more realistic than it did under the black sky. Even the asphalt paths that provided passage around the school looked beautiful in the Sun's illumination, glittering in hues of charcoal and silver.

With the arrival of the Sun came several days of bliss, in which many of the teachers decided to move their lessons outside to make the most of the rare show of natural light. Mr. Krecher took the opportunity to showcase one of his favourite alien specimens; a beautiful, four-winged creature with crystal skin that refracted the sunlight, casting rainbows onto the floor as it flew above them.

In between lessons, Lois, Finley, Emily and Will spent their time by the lake, sunbathing and dipping their toes into the cool, clear water to ease the effects of the intense heat. When they weren't relaxing outside, they confined themselves to the library, where they found their good spirits had even managed to make Mr. Mayhem's uncharacteristically boring final project about "How the early intervention of aliens in the 1980's greatly advanced the space travelling capabilities of humankind" a relatively bearable task.

In the wake of her new positive attitude, Lois had been persuaded by Emily to accompany her to the Book Club she attended every Friday evening, insisting, despite Will and Finley's teasing, that her membership had nothing to do with the librarian, Martyn, or his charm and good looks. Lois went along obligingly and discovered a great joy in reading the famous works of antique literature, never having realised what true pleasure could be found by holding a real book in her hands. As a result, she had taken to spending the evenings curled up on her bed, reading novels as the strong sunlight poured through the window, turning their crinkled pages in her hands and inhaling their musty aroma, until the shutters in her bedroom closed at ten p.m., forcing her into sleep.

It was as though they had left reality and entered Utopia, where there were no troubles and no negative feelings at all. So wonderful were the days of sunshine that Lois was filled by a genuine depression when Admiral Allance announced they were soon to pass through the solar system, leaving the warmth of the Sun's presence behind. To temper the sting, she invited Will, Finley and Emily to her room after dinner, under the premise that they would start work on the lengthy project Mr. Krecher had set them, which entailed picking five different species of alien and explaining how humankind had discovered them. In truth, she didn't want to be alone when the darkness resumed and was even willing to pretend to be enthralled as Finley explained in great length about the trade deals humans had made with aliens, resulting in the acquisition of many different specimens.

When the light finally faded, they began to rub their eyes, putting their tablets down wearily as the darkness enveloped the school once more. Will yawned and stretched, complaining of a dead leg and mumbling something about homework being bad for his health. Emily got up from her crossed-legged position on the floor and cricked her neck, heading to the drinks machine to pour herself an icy drink. Finley rose from the bed next to Lois and strolled absent-mindedly to the window, staring out at the inky blackness that had returned outside. Lois was in the middle of tidying the blankets that had been strewn across her floor, when Finley suddenly let out a cry of horror, causing her to drop everything she was holding and rush to the window, Will and Emily hot on her tail.

They stood for a moment, united in confusion as they scanned the grounds for the source of Finley's distress. All at once they saw it, letting out simultaneous gasps of horror as they reeled from the terrible sight. Standing clear as day by the lake was a Vacuous, its bone, white skin shining like a beacon in the gloom. Its long, spindly arm was outstretched, its clawed hand grasping thin air as though it were frozen in some sort of strange, dramatic tableau.

"It's back," Will whispered, his pupils wide with terror.

"What's it doing?" Lois whispered back, hardly daring to breathe. "It looks like its holding something invisible."

"It's not invisible," Finley said darkly. Lois scrutinised the scene once more, straining her eyes to distinguish the shapes amongst the shadows. It was then that she saw it. Letting out a scream, she covered her mouth and staggered backwards, her stomach heaving at the realisation of what she had witnessed. The Vacuous's gnarled claws were not clutching the air at all, but were clasped around the throat of a man, dressed all in dark clothing. As she watched, the terrible creature released its grasp, letting the lifeless body of its victim slump horribly to the ground. Lois fell backwards, fear overpowering her as she lost control of her legs. Will and Emily ducked beneath the window, crouching on all fours to avoid being seen. Finley, however, remained standing, his face ghostly white as he stared paralysed at the awful scene before him. Will tugged firmly on his clothes, knocking him off balance and dragging him to the ground and out of sight. He sunk to the floor, shaking uncontrollably as he looked to his friends in terror.

"It saw me," he swallowed. "It looked right at me."

"Are you sure?" Lois asked him desperately.

"I'm sure," he replied with harrowing certainty.

Will leapt to his feet, locking the door and barricading it with Lois' bed. Emily pressed a button beside the window so that the shutters drew shut, concealing them from anyone watching outside. Lois went and sat beside Finley, putting her arm around him to comfort him as he continued to tremor, his skin freezing cold to the touch.

"Okay," Will said, struggling to level his tone. "What do we do?"

"We have to tell," Emily replied with resignation. "We don't have a choice."

There was a long pause as the statement resounded across the room. They were each afraid of the consequences they would face from telling the truth, but knew they had no other option. Will began to pace, walking back and forth with such a fury that Lois was surprised he didn't wear a hole in her carpet.

"Did anyone recognise that man?" he asked. "The one the Vacuous..."

He trailed off, unable to bring himself to say the word "killed" out loud. The three of them shook their heads in response.

"We haven't got any evidence," he frowned, "and we can't name the victim. Who are we going to tell that's actually going to believe our story?"

"Someone just got murdered on school grounds, Will," Emily reminded him, flinching as the words left her mouth. "There'll be a missing person's investigation, there'll be a body. We have to go and tell someone what we've seen, right now!"

"You want to go now?" Will said with disbelief.

"The longer we sit on it, the more trouble we risk getting in," she replied. "This goes way beyond expulsion. People found guilty of a crime get thrown off the Mayfly. Failing to come forward as witnesses to somebody dying would definitely constitute that."

"Lois' dad is the Captain," Will protested. "Do you really think he'd let his own daughter get thrown into Space?"

"He might not spare the rest of, though," Finley fretted.

"We've got to go to the Admiral," Emily pressed. "We need to tell someone who can do something fast."

"Where will he be?" Will wondered, frantically gathering his things up as he prepared to depart.

"I know where the teacher's live," Emily replied, putting her shoes on and tying a knot in her laces. "Charlie's pointed it out to me before. It's not too far from here."

Lois jumped to her feet and rushed to her wardrobe, pulling a hoody on over her uniform and following Will and Emily towards the door. It was only when they were about to leave that they realised that Finley hadn't moved from the floor. They turned back to see him getting unsteadily to his feet, his complexion now a shade of green as he balled his fists up tightly.

"You can't go out there," he warned them. "It's too dangerous."

"We have to," Emily insisted.

"That thing saw me!" Finley exclaimed. "It knows I know what it did. It could be waiting out there in case I try and tell someone."

"We can't just sit in here doing nothing," Will argued. "And besides, it saw you in this room. If it was coming after you, it would come here. It still might. The best thing to do is find Allance. We'll be safe with him."

Finley shook his head profusely.

"Lois," he pleaded with her, knowing she was his last hope. "You can't go."

She hesitated, his emotional display setting her in a dilemma. As much as she wanted to comfort him, the thought of the Vacuous coming for them while they were trapped in her bedroom was far more terrifying than the possibility of encountering it out in the open, where they would at least be able to run or hide.

"Come on Finley," she encouraged him. "We're all in this together now."

He took in a deep breath and then let it out again, nodding slowly as he acknowledged her words. He stepped forward, placing his hand firmly into hers so that she could feel the sweat that was moistening his palm. With a meaningful look at Will, he gave his silent consent for them to leave and the four of them began to run, hurtling towards the dark of night and towards whatever fate was awaiting them.

18.

The Admiral's Confession

Finley sprinted as fast as his legs would allow, the noise of his blood pounding in his ears and mingling with the sound of thundering footsteps as he, Lois, Emily and Will raced to find Admiral Allance. He dared not look around, petrified that he would see the Vacuous lurking in the dark and waiting pitilessly to kill him. Instead, he kept his eyes forwards, focusing on Emily's back as she ran ahead, leading them to the building where the teachers slept.

"It's just up ahead," she called, without turning around to address them in case doing so slowed her down. She pointed to a bland, high-rise block a few yards in front of them that had almost no distinguishable features, save for a small replica of the school logo attached to the very top. Finley had passed the building many times before but had always assumed it contained classrooms. He had expected the place where the teachers resided to be more luxurious and was surprised that they would value their privacy more than their taste in the finer things.

As they approached the block, his heart began to soar with hope. He could see the front door beginning to take shape. If they could just figure out a way in, he was convinced that the Admiral would be able to help them stop the Vacuous before it hurt somebody else.

His joy turned to terror as something large and pale white caught the corner of his eye, causing the air in his lungs to turn to ice. With sickening fear, he looked towards the silvery figure, everything around him turning to slow motion. The Vacuous cocked its head to the side as it regarded the running group of children a few metres in its wake. As soon as it realised it had been seen, its empty, black eyes connecting with Finley's wide brown ones, it began to run towards them, its muscular limbs carrying it at a pace Finley knew none of them could match.

191

Finding his voice, he yelled out in panic to alert the others, who had continued dashing forwards with no idea of the imminent danger that was approaching them. In unison, they turned their heads towards the Vacuous and screamed, chaos descending as they all ran in different directions, scattering like pieces of shattered glass. Finley knew what he had to do. Instead of fleeing with the others, he set his sights firmly on the building ahead of him and dashed towards it as fast as he could. Given how quick and agile the Vacuous was, he was almost certain it would intercept his path before he reached Admiral Allance, and he braced himself, flinching with every step as he anticipated the pain of its sharp claws on his skin.

Somehow, he reached the building unscathed and was surprised to find the front door had been left slightly ajar, meaning no fingerprint identification was needed for him to enter. He paused briefly before going in, scanning his surroundings wildly for any sign of the Vacuous or of the others. Seeing nothing, he called out in hopes that someone would hear him.

"Lois! Emily! Will!" he yelled, cupping his hands around his mouth to project his voice.

"Finley!" Lois' voice echoed from out of sight.

"Get to safety!" he called back. "I'm going to get Allance!"

Without awaiting a reply, he hurried inside, painfully aware that he had just alerted the Vacuous to both his location and his intentions. He found himself in a small lounge, furnished only by two white armchairs, a coffee table and a large plant. At the back of the room was the lift, and Finley made his way over to it, reading from an inscription of names and numbers on the wall beside it. He scanned down the page, noting the names of "Miss Veronica Fortem, Mr. Albert Mayheim, Ms. Helen Dido and Mr. Kurt Krecher" until eventually, he found the Headmaster's address, written simply as "Admiral Allance- 6A". He jumped inside the lift and pressed the button for the sixth floor, riding it to the very top of the building while strange elevator music played eerily through the speakers.

He arrived on the correct floor and exited, finding Admiral Allance's door within seconds, since it was the only one on the entire floor. He hammered on the steel surface, battering his fist red raw in the process. After a few minutes, there was a clicking noise and the door swung open, revealing a confused Admiral Allance on the other side. Despite the late hour, he was dressed in his usual attire, his midnight-blue suit perfectly pressed and his silk, silver tie knotted around his neck.

"Sir," Finley began before the Admiral could say anything. "I'm sorry. I know it's late and I'm not supposed to be here, but I really need to speak with you. It's an emergency."

"Yes, yes of course," the Admiral replied, eyeing Finley with concern. "Come in then boy. Finley, is it?"

"Yes, Sir," Finley nodded, following him inside.

He stepped into Admiral Allance's lounge, which was shockingly simple and bare. Most of the room had been left empty, with only one reclining black, leather chair and matching footstall breaking up the view of the cream coloured carpet. Shelves had been installed on the walls but had been left empty, save for a dead plant in a chipped, magenta vase. There was a desk in the corner with a tablet and various other gadgets slung carelessly upon it, but other than that the room was exceptionally underwhelming. The only part of the entire set-up that mildly resembled what Finley had expected for the Headmaster was the large window on the back wall, which allowed for a spectacular view of almost the entire school and the stars beyond.

"Sit down," the Admiral instructed him, gesturing towards the leather chair. Finley obeyed and the Admiral locked the door behind them.

"So, Finley, would you like to explain to me what you're doing knocking on my door in the middle of the night after curfew?" he asked, raising a thick, silvery eyebrow as he stood in front of Finley, his arms folded behind his back in a military stance.

"Yes, Sir," Finley replied calmly. "I'm here because I've witnessed a murder."

The Admiral blinked, his authoritarian demeanour slipping for a moment as he regarded Finley in shock.

"I'm sorry," he said gruffly. "Did you just say that you had seen a murder?"

"Yes, Sir," Finley nodded. "I saw a murder, and so did my friends, Emily, Will and Lois. We all saw it. It happened on school grounds. It was done by..." he paused for a moment, knowing he was about to share the most

193

unbelievable part of the story. "It was done by an alien, Sir. The most horrific and terrifying alien I've ever seen."

The Admiral rubbed the bridge of his nose and began to pace as he processed what Finley had told him. An expression of acute stress pulled at the edges of his mouth, causing him to frown deeply.

"You saw an alien kill someone?" he repeated.

"Yes," Finley confirmed.

"And when did this happen?" he asked.

"About thirty minutes ago."

"And you say your friends also saw the attack?"

"Yes, Sir."

"And where are your friends now?" the Admiral pressed him, standing still to watch Finley closely for his answer.

"They ran off. When we were on our way to find you, we saw the alien again. It's still out there. It chased the others away," Finley explained, hoping the wealth of questions he was being asked meant that the Admiral was taking him seriously.

"I see," the Admiral replied bluntly. "And the victim of this crime... was it a student?"

"I don't know, we couldn't see properly. It didn't look like a student, though. It looked like it was an adult man," Finley answered, a lump growing in his throat as he recalled the horrific moment.

"Well, naturally this is very concerning," the Admiral replied. "If one of Mr. Krecher's aliens has escaped confinement and committed such an atrocity, then there will be severe consequences for both himself and the specimen involved. I'll contact him now to discuss the matter. Perhaps he can help us track down the creature before it hurts anyone else."

"I don't think it's one of Mr. Krecher's aliens, Sir," Finley interjected, stopping the Admiral from tapping on his Personal Device.

"What makes you say that?"

Finley hesitated. He desperately wanted to explain everything but feared confessing he had witnessed the Vacuous on Earth through a magic mirror would earn him a one-way trip to the Psychiatric Ward on the Mayfly.

Besides this, the full version of the truth was lengthy and launching into it would be a waste of precious time when Lois, Will and Emily were potentially still in danger.

"It doesn't look like a creature anyone would want a study or one that would allow itself to be kept in confinement. It's intelligent and it knows what it's doing. I don't think Mr. Krecher has anything to do with it. What I do know, though, is that it's still out there and something needs to be done immediately to stop it," he said firmly.

"Yes, of course," the Admiral concurred, beginning to sound flustered. "I will alert the other teachers immediately and we'll form a search party. I'll make sure you're escorted safely back to your dormitory in the meantime. I'll send a group out to the lake as well to see if we can retrieve any evidence. Does that satisfy you?"

"Yes, Sir. Thank you, I-". Finley stopped dead mid-sentence, an unsettling realisation coming over him.

"What is it?" the Admiral asked impatiently.

"I didn't mention the lake, Sir," Finley replied slowly, his legs beginning to lose their feeling.

"What?" the Admiral responded, waving his hand dismissively. "You must have done. How else would I know that's where the crime took place? And anyway, all the bedrooms on the top floor of first-year dormitories have a view of the lake- it's part of their design."

"But, my bedroom isn't on the top floor, Sir. Lois' is. It was her room I was in tonight when I saw the murder happen. But how could you know that? Unless... you were there," Finley looked up at him darkly. The Admiral sighed.

"Oh, foolish boy, if only you had just left it alone," he replied, strolling over to his desk and removing a thick rope from the inside.

"I don't understand," Finley jumped to his feet in panic. "How could you have been there? There was nobody else around."

The Admiral laughed mirthlessly, positioning himself between Finley and the door to block any chance of escape.

"You still haven't worked it out?" he mocked. "Oh dear, child, and to think, I went to all the trouble of holding a special assembly to deter you after you saw me in the dormitories that night. I needn't have bothered. You and your little friends aren't as clever as I gave you credit for."

"Saw you in the hallway? You mean... you're the ..." Finley trailed off, the end of the sentence too horrific to utter out loud.

"I'm the terrifying alien, yes," the Admiral replied bluntly. "At least, that is my true form in all its glory."

"But...how?" Finley said pathetically, completely lost for words.

"How? You really want me to detail the extremely complicated process my species undertook to be able to emulate the DNA of human beings? Because I can assure you, it's extremely boring, and in any case, I need to be getting on with your disposal," the Admiral answered, approaching him with the rope in hand.

"I think perhaps the question you meant to ask me was "why" not "how". Why am I here? What do I want? Why was I in your dormitories in the middle of the night and who did I kill beside the lake? These are all fascinating questions with equally enthralling answers," he continued as he began to wind the rope around a petrified Finley's limbs. "The fact you're wrapped up in this – both the situation and the rope- is a terrible mistake. It's my fault, really. After that idiot Mayheim knocked the cameras out with his failed experiment, I couldn't resist taking the opportunity to roam the grounds as my real self, free from the limitations of this human disguise. The first few times were glorious. I remained completely undiscovered, but alas, the night you saw me I was drawn to your dormitories by a big surge of pathetic human emotion. I forgot you see, about all the raging hormones and complicated feelings adolescent humans have. I was like a moth to a flame. Your feelings, particularly despair and sadness, they are like a sort of drug to our kind."

The Admiral paused, tying the ropes around Finley's legs and arms and pushing him back down onto the leather sofa.

"It's a shame that I have to do this, Finley. I don't like to kill unless it's necessary. Killing a student will be particularly messy. I'll have to do well to cover this one up. Taking you to a nearby planet and leaving you there is out of the question, considering our current position in the galaxy. I'm sure I can come up with a believable story, though. Maybe one of your peers took revenge on you being at the Academy, despite your low status and finished the job Josie Jones tried to start at the beginning of the year. Or maybe the condescending looks and harsh judgements finally got too much for you and you flung yourself into the abyss of Space, unable to bear the pain any longer," the Admiral smiled. "Did you know I have my own private launch bay? It leads straight from my apartment into Space. I think you and I should go on a little rocket trip, don't you?"

"It won't work," Finley challenged him, the prospect of impending death inspiring him with a new courage. "Lois, Will and Emily know I'm here. They've seen everything I've seen. If I go missing now, they'll know it was you. They'll figure it out. Would you really risk murdering the Captain's daughter? You'd be found out in seconds."

The Admiral faltered, his face falling slightly as he digested this information.

"Very well," he said after a moment. "In that case, there will be a different narrative."

He began twitching his hand, Finley watching with horror as it transformed from the human hand of Admiral Allance into the gnarled claw of the Vacuous. Allance strolled over to the window and smashed it, shattering the glass into hundreds of razor-sharp pieces without flinching. He then took the claw and tore at his own clothes, slashing his suit and undershirt and grazing the skin underneath just enough that it drew blood. After that, he morphed his hand back to normal and returned to his position above Finley.

"The vicious alien burst in attacked me and then snatched you, fleeing into Space before I could do anything to stop it. It must have known you had witnessed its crimes and kidnapped you as a result. How unfortunate it will be for your family knowing you are lost forever but never truly understanding why" he feigned a sad expression. "How does that work for you?"

Finley fell silent, his body slumping with defeat. The cover-up was perfect, all angles had been considered. Even Lois, Emily and Will would believe it. It was over. This was how it would end.

Admiral Allance grabbed the rope that was tied around Finley and pulled it so that he fell off the chair, hitting the ground with a sickening thump. He began dragging him across the floor, painfully bumping his head on the doorway as they moved from lounge to a long hallway that ran through his apartment. The light was dingy, but Finley could still make out the strong muscles of the Admiral's back as he hauled his body forwards. Even in his human form, there was no way Finley would be able to fight him off.

They reached a metal door at the end of the hall with a 'caution' sign drilled into its front. Finley knew without having to look that this was the entrance to the launch bay. The Admiral used his fingerprint to access the room and bumped Finley across the threshold, wincing as the cold steel of the floor rubbed against the carpet burn that had spread across his back. From his position on the ground, he could see several small spacecrafts - each only big enough to carry two or three people - all parked in a steel hangar. At the end of the room was a tunnel, not dissimilar to the one he had flown down during his eventful first Rocket Control lesson.

It pained him now to think of that day. He had been strangely grateful to Josie for doing what she had done, for it had indirectly brought him to Will, Emily and eventually Lois, who were the only real friends he'd ever had. His heart hurt as he imagined them grieving for him after his disappearance with no idea what had really happened. They'd continue their life at the school, completely unaware of the danger they faced daily simply by being there, under the rule of a murderous alien disguised as the Headmaster.

As Admiral Allance loaded him into a small red rocket, a single tear slid down his face. He longed to reach his Personal Device so he could send a message to his mother, telling her that he loved her and that he was sorry. He wished now more than ever that he had listened to his brother and not insisted on taking the entrance exams for the Academy. He should have stayed at home and gone to one of the training bureaus on the Mayfly like the rest of his family. If he had, he wouldn't now be on the brink of death and his mother wouldn't have to experience the agony of losing a child, which he was certain would destroy her.

"Stop!"

The voice echoed across the launch bay, resounding from every wall. At first, Finley thought he had imagined it. Surely, it couldn't be real. From his current position, all he could see was the interior of the rocket, but he held his breath nonetheless, praying for the voice to speak again and prove that its owner was really there.

"What are you doing to him?!"

"Let him go!"

Finley's whole body lit up with euphoria. It was Will, Lois and Emily. They had come to save him.

"He's the Vacuous!" Finley called out to warn them. "It's him! It's Allance!"

There was a loud crashing sound, followed by the loud purr of an engine starting up as the Admiral made his escape.

"He's getting away!"

Finley watched as a pair of feet, which turned out to belong to Will, swung into the rocket he was lying in. He began tapping his fingers on the control panel at expert pace, Finley once again feeling exceedingly grateful for the amount of attention Will paid in Rocket Control. Seconds later, Emily and Lois jumped in, Lois rushing to untie Finley the moment she entered. The engine hummed into life and they began ascending slowly into the air, heading towards the tunnel that would carry them into Space.

"Wait!" Finley called to Will. "We haven't got gear on!"

"Emergency seal, remember?" Will said with a wink, pressing the button that caused a glass dome to protectively seal over the top of their heads.

"How many minutes of oxygen did Mr. Zeppler say this would give us?" Finley asked dubiously as they raced through the tunnel.

"About fifteen! No time to lose," Will replied.

They flew through the tunnel in seconds, Will guiding them with expert precision into Space. Their rocket soared through the stars at breakneck speed as they pursed Allance, who was only a few metres ahead of them

"How are we going to stop him?" Finley shouted to Will. "We haven't got much time!"

"Leave it to me!" Will shouted.

"Finley," Lois addressed him, her voice thick with worry. "Are you alright? What happened in there?"

"Allance told me he's the Vacuous," he replied darkly. "I saw him transform his hand into a claw right in front of my eyes. Once he knew his secret was out, he tried to kill me. He was going to take me into Space and make it look like an accident- or suicide."

"Thank the Universe we showed up," Lois gasped.

"I didn't think anyone was coming," Finley admitted. "I thought I was dead."

"Don't be ridiculous, there's no way we would have left you on your own out there!" she exclaimed.

Finley smiled at her thankfully and she smiled back, the two of them forgetting for a moment that they were currently wrapped up in a rocket chase, pursuing an incredibly dangerous alien.

"I don't mean to spoil your moment, guys, but I think you might want to see this," Will shouted from behind the steering wheel.

Finley scrambled to his feet, hurrying to the front of the rocket with Lois and Emily by his side. Looking out, they watched curiously as Allance stopped his spacecraft mid-flight, turning it around slowly to face their own.

"What's he doing?" Will muttered to himself, bringing their own rocket to a halt.

They waited in silence, holding their breath collectively as the Admiral smiled at them through his front window. Suddenly, a pair of bulky cannons sprung from each side of his rocket, making his deadly intentions painfully apparent.

"He's going to shoot!" Finley yelled.

Two pale blue balls of fire sprung from the canons, hurtling towards them at top speed. Will grabbed the steering wheel, veering sharply to the left. The rocket tipped and the four of them smashed hard into the steel wall, Finley winded by the sheer impact of the fall. As they rotated through the air, one of Allance's fireballs clipped their wing, sending them into a sickening spin. They tumbled over one and other, hitting against each other's bodies as the rocket lost control, rolling chaotically through the depths of Space.

"Somebody get the wheel!" Will shouted as Finley felt the vomit beginning to rise in his throat. He was so dizzy, he could no longer make sense of what was Space, what was rocket and what was human. Just when he thought he would certainly lose consciousness, they were unexpectedly pulled level and out of their spin. He collapsed against the wall, breathing deeply to steady his stomach as he waited for his giddiness to subside. His vision came back to him and he saw Lois, clasping the steering wheel in her shaking hands.

"Lois, you saved us," Emily said with surprise.

"Allance is getting away, though," Lois panicked, pointing to his rocket now several miles into the distance.

Will rushed over and took the wheel from her, putting the spacecraft into the highest gear it could take and setting off at full speed.

"Will, maybe we should go back," Emily said with worry. "We don't know how much oxygen we've got left."

"We have to catch him," Will shook his head. "We need proof."

"Is there some way we can communicate between the two rockets?" Lois asked, struck by sudden inspiration.

"There's a radio system somewhere in the control panel, but I'm not sure how to work it. What good would it do, though?" Will replied.

"Get hold of the Admiral and get him to confess," Lois commanded, tapping on her Personal Device with fury.

"What? Why?" Will asked with confusion.

"Just do it," she asserted. "Emily, can you work the radio?"

"Bottom right of the control pad," Will instructed Emily as she hastened forwards. "There's a button that controls the frequencies."

Emily set to work, twisting and turning the button as she navigated through the static white noise on the radio.

"I've got him!" she cried victoriously.

"Allance!" Will called through the frequency. "Can you hear me?"

There was a brief crackling noise, followed by the sound of the Admiral's voice projecting into the rocket.

201

"It's no use, boy, I'm not going to stop" he hissed.

"Why are you running? There's nowhere for you to go," Will responded. "It doesn't matter where you are, the Captain will find you."

There was a moment of silence where it seemed the Admiral was contemplating Will's words. Capitalising on the opportunity, he continued.

"Just turn yourself in," Will pressed. "The Captain is a decent man. I'm sure he'll show you mercy if you do the right thing. Surely anything's better than dying out in here in Space."

The Admiral laughed, the cold hollow sound sending chills down Finley's back.

"If I turn myself in, I'll be executed," he snapped back. "Perhaps I should just kill you all and then continue with my plan."

"Plan? What plan?" Will demanded.

"Only a little agenda myself and my kind have to take over the Mayfly," the Admiral snickered.

"Take over the Mayfly?!" Will scoffed. "Do you really think you could manage that? Do you know how many Guards there are, how much security you'd have to face just to even get close to the control room?"

"But that's the most brilliant part," the Admiral continued. "Mr. Holt and his partners at I-Tech have been developing a very interesting piece of technology. The computerized weaponry allows you to control the minds of any living organism of your choice. Imagine it. An army full of Academy students storming the Mayfly! Do you really think the Captain and his high-ranking friends would give the orders to shoot and kill their own children? We would be unstoppable!"

"You can't do that!" Finley cried. "It's sick."

"Don't you worry my boy," Allance laughed. "Your peasant family will be safely down on Floor Seven. They'll do nicely as slaves when the Vacuous are in charge."

"Why now?" Will asked him. "You've had thirteen years to take over the Mayfly. Why wait this long?"

"We had to blend in," the Admiral answered. "Wait for an opportunity. Jarvis Holt's technology provides just that."

"You won't get away with it," Will warned him.

"How cliché," the Admiral taunted. "Are you sure about that, child? Who do you propose is going to stop me? So long as nobody knows my plan, I will succeed. After I've killed you, no one else is going to find out what's happening until it's too late."

"It's already too late," Lois spoke suddenly.

"Stupid girl, what are you talking about?" the Admiral guffawed.

"I've been recording this entire conversation on my Personal Device," Lois replied. "It's being sent in a live stream to my father as we speak. I should imagine his forces will be here in, what, five minutes?"

Suddenly, the Admiral's rocket stopped ahead of them, suspended statue-still in the star-strewn sky. The protective seal across the roof came down and the Admiral stood up, his foot poised on the edge of the spacecraft as he prepared to fling himself overboard.

"Wait!" Will shouted, but it was no use. With one final look of contempt in their direction, the Admiral jumped out, floating at an almost comically slow speed as he drifted into the never-ending abyss of Space. The four of them watched as he floated away, his human form fading as he transformed into the dreadful creature he truly was. His slender, white body heaved as it gasped for air it would never find and his terrible empty face twisted into an expression of anguish. After a moment, his elongated arms fell to his side and he became still, drifting into the distance and out of sight.

"Why would he do that?" Finley asked Will breathlessly after the shock of what he had just witnessed subsided.

"I suppose he knew it was over for him anyway," Will shrugged, turning their rocket around and speeding back towards the safety of the school, just as the first of the Captain's fleet began to appear as tiny silver dots in the distance.

19.

Homecoming

The days after Admiral Allance's death were a chaotic blur. The Space Academy grounds had become swamped with Security from the Mayfly within hours and a full investigation into Allance's crimes had been ordered by the Captain. Will, Emily, Finley and Lois were subjected to extensive interviews with various high-ranking Guards, who probed them on what they had witnessed until they were completely exhausted and sick of repeating their story. By the time their part in the proceedings was declared over, they were deeply relieved to be sent back to their lessons and return to normality, concentrating on their final projects and end of year results.

In the final week of term, rumours that a body had been pulled from the lake began to circulate amongst the students, with the identity of the victim being heavily speculated upon. Fortunately, Will's classmates had enough sense not to question him or the others on the matter, despite their involvement in the saga being incredibly well-documented. Even Rudy maintained a respectful silence, giving Will the occasional dirty look but otherwise keeping his distance. The teachers also seemed to have been given instructions not to discuss the incident, conducting their lessons without a single mention of Allance or the murder that had taken place on school grounds. On several occasions, however, Will caught some of them staring at him with concern, as though expecting him to break down at any moment. Indeed, the only person who was brave enough to mention the situation at all was Mr. Krecher, who pulled Will into his office after Alien Studies one day and forced him into an armchair, thrusting a hastily made cup of tea into his hands.

"Are you alright, my boy?" he asked, as soon as the first sip had slid down Will's throat.

"I'm okay Sir," he replied with a weary smile for added conviction.

"No use starting that 'Sir' business with me now," Krecher told him. "'Mr. Krecher' will do fine."

"Sorry," Will said with embarrassment. "Force of habit from all the interviews with the Guards."

"Ah yes, of course," Krecher frowned, beginning to pace around his office. "I don't suppose you mentioned anything about the Looking Glass in those interviews, did you?"

"No, I didn't," Will replied honestly. "I'm not sure how I'd explain something like that when I don't fully understand it myself."

"I see," Krecher's face filled with relief. "That is good news. I've been beside myself with worry. If the Guards find out I've got an unregistered alien artefact, I'd be in all kinds of serious trouble. Not to mention the fact it would be confiscated from me. Such a device could do a great deal of damage if it fell into the wrong hands."

"Don't worry, we won't tell anyone," Will promised.

"We?" he repeated. "You mean there are others who know about the Looking Glass?"

Will's cheeks flushed crimson.

"Yes. My friends Lois, Emily and Finley do," he confessed. "I brought them back here one night and we all went in together. It was after we had seen the Vacuous and we thought we could find some answers in the past. I'm sorry."

"Lois is the Captain's daughter," Krecher fretted. "What if she tells her father?"

"She won't," Will shook his head vigorously. "I trust her."

"If you're certain..." Mr. Krecher replied.

"I am," Will assured him, then seizing upon the opportunity to speak to him alone, added, "there is something I wanted to ask you, Mr. Krecher."

"Yes, what is it?"

"When we were in the Looking Glass, we saw Alfie and my parents talking. They said they'd gone to you for help about the Vacuous and that you'd seen them too. Is that true?"

Krecher sighed.

"Yes, I must confess they did rope me into it all. They joined my Alien Studies class, you see, shortly after they encountered the Vacuous for the first time. Once they had decided they could trust me, they showed me images they'd caught of it, asking if I recognised the species. I told them that I didn't and that these aliens were unknown to humankind. Afterwards, I became intrigued by the entire thing, hunting the Vacuous by myself in secret. They were terrible creatures, horrifying beyond anything I'd ever seen. It drove me a bit mad after a while, trying to work out what they were and what they wanted. I gave up my research when we left Earth. I never dreamed there'd be a Vacuous here at the school," he frowned.

"You didn't know about Allance then?" Will confirmed.

"No, no, of course not," he denied. "If I had I would have contacted the Captain straight away. They don't like to speak to me anymore, he and your mother. I suppose I remind them of things they'd rather forget, but had I known what was going on, I wouldn't have hesitated to involve them."

"There's something else that's bothering me," Will frowned. "All of this happening… it means that my dad was right about everything."

"Forgive me, I don't follow?" Krecher replied.

"My dad's belief in the "Great Conspiracy", Will explained. "He knew the Mayfly was unsafe and he suspected the Vacuous had something to do with it. He was right all along and no one believed him."

"Your father was a very passionate man," Krecher reflected. "Once he got something into his head, there wasn't much that could make him let it go. At least you have the comfort of knowing that you succeeded in exposing the Vacuous. The Captain won't rest until he's certain he's stopped them all. Your father's work to uncover the truth has been continued through you."

"The Great Conspiracy might have been real, but I still can't forgive my dad for what he did," Will said slowly. "He abandoned me and my mum, not knowing whether we'd live or die. Nothing can ever change that."

Will stared at the Looking Glass standing innocently in the corner and began to relive the horrific scene of his father's death that it had shown him.

"Visiting the Looking Glass can be incredibly difficult" Krecher sighed. "You've seen much more than a boy your age should. My advice to you now is that you move on from all this. You've done your part. Leave the rest to the Captain and his forces."

"Trust me, Mr. Krecher, after the year I've had I'll be happy to spend the holidays as a normal teenager. No more Vacuous and no more trips into mirrors," Will replied sincerely. Krecher smiled to himself and then dismissed him, bidding him to take care until they met again.

With the announcement of final results came a much welcome distraction for Will, and he was both shocked and delighted to find that he had passed the year, receiving an overall "2" grade along with a formal invitation to return the following September. Despite facing two separate attempts on his life, Finley had managed to obtain a "1" for his results, an achievement which was celebrated by an evening of playing Earth Wars in Will's room at Finley's request.

All too soon, the morning of their final day at the Academy was upon them and they found themselves trailing their suitcases across the grounds gloomily, their hearts heavy with the prospect of leaving their new home for ten whole weeks. Waiting in line with the other deflated first years, Will studied his surroundings with precision, his eyes drinking in every detail of the main school building and the grounds as if he would never see them again. Even the fake grass that covered the floor suddenly felt like a novelty that he would deeply miss. He only hoped that come next year he would be able to truly appreciate studying in such a unique and wonderful place, with no distractions from murderous aliens or, indeed, dead fathers.

The Shuttle journey back to the Mayfly seemed to pass twice as quickly as it usually did and in the blink of an eye, they had reached the platform, unloading en-masse into the waiting crowds of parents, who were even more anxious to see their children's safe return than usual. Will was surprised to see his mother standing with Finley's family and Emily's parents. They were all huddled together in a stance of mutual concern, except for Emily's father, who stood haughtily in the background, appearing deeply embarrassed to be present. When they saw their children, the mothers rushed forwards, pulling them into bone-crushing hugs as they babbled incoherently about how worried they'd been. After a few minutes of being suffocated, Will was released by his mother, who kept her grip firmly on his arms as she bent down to address him.

"Will, my darling," she said frantically. "I'm so sorry for what you've been through. Alfie told me what the Headteacher looked like when they found his body in Space. He's an alien that we've seen back on Earth, but we had no idea how dangerous they really were! If only you had told me what was going on, I could have helped you. I feel so terrible you had to do all this alone!"

"I wasn't alone," Will smiled, looking towards the others.

"We didn't know the aliens could take human form!" she cried. "It's awful. Derek's been arrested. Apparently, he was one of them."

"I knew there was something wrong with that man!" Will exclaimed.

"Alfie's going to make a speech in a moment about everything they know so far," Elsie continued. "Is Lois with you? He asked me to pick her up and bring her with us."

Will pointed to where Lois was standing, holding her arm awkwardly as she watched the intimate embraces of the parents and children around her. He called her over and she looked relieved to have been noticed, accompanying Will and Elsie as they manoeuvred towards the exit, Finley and Emily's families following close behind.

They walked briskly down the corridor and loaded into the lift, riding it all the way down to the lobby where a colossal crowd had gathered around the exceptionally huge screen that hung there. A Guard escorted them to near the front of the ensemble, standing protectively nearby as Alfie's face appeared in gigantic proportions on the screen in front of them.

"Good morning, citizens of the Mayfly," his voice boomed over their heads. "I am making this important address in light of the recent events that occurred at the Space Academy, of which I am sure you are all aware. I know that many of you have questions and I hope to provide you with as many answers as I can by sharing what we have found so far through our investigation.

"As you may have heard, Admiral Allance, the school's renowned Headmaster, was discovered to be a rare species of alien in disguise. His body was retrieved from Space and examined in its true form, the results of which have been studied. When I saw his appearance, I realised that he belonged to a species that I had, in fact, encountered personally on Earth. Back then, we referred to the specimens as "Vacuous", a name which describes the empty features that are characteristic of their breed. This name has now been officially registered and the Vacuous have been added to our database of known alien creatures.

"We have discovered that the Vacuous are capable of taking human form, something which has been unprecedented amongst alien beings until this point. A specially trained team have been assigned to try and work out how their transformation may be possible. A full-scale enquiry has also been launched across the Mayfly, and several Vacuous have been caught already. Through special means of interrogation, we have managed to determine their motive. They had plotted to take control of the Mayfly and follow that, Novum itself. Their false identities were so elaborate that many of them could be traced back for years on Earth, attending Colleges and working in high-profile jobs in order to gain places on our ship. "Most shocking of all our discoveries is that two adolescents, going by the human aliases of 'Kyan Smith' and 'Josie Jones' turned out to be Vacuous'. These young aliens were students at The Space Academy, positioned there, we believe, to help Admiral Allance with his plot until Josie attacked a fellow student and forced him to expel her to cover their tracks."

Will exchanged a wild look of surprise with Lois, Emily and Finley.

"We believe this indicates that the younger Vacuous are less able to control their murderous urges, making them easier to identify," Alfie continued. "The Captains of the other spacecrafts have also been informed of everything we know so far, and we will be taking a number of steps to ensure the safety of their citizens. Our priority is to maintain the integrity of humanity's mission to Novum and to ensure our safe passage to the planet remains guaranteed.

"Unfortunately, before Allance could be stopped he claimed the life of one victim, whose body was retrieved from the lake at The Space Academy about a week ago. I can now reveal the identity of this victim as Mr. Jarvis Holt, a dear friend of mine and the CEO of the Interactive-Tech company. Mr. Holt was an incredibly intelligent man and a deeply valued passenger on the Mayfly. His death comes as a severe blow to both his friends and family and to the innovation of our future technology. A memorial will be held for him in the Commiserations Hall next Monday to celebrate his life's achievements and to give his body a safe and dignified send-off.

"For those who are wondering what Allance's motives were for Mr Holt's murder, I can inform you that an extensive search of his office revealed plans to gain access to some experimental technology I-Tech had been developing. He intended to use the technology on the children at the school, essentially turning them into robots he could use to take over the Mayfly. He knew the higher officials on board would not shoot at their own children and had he not been discovered, his plan may well have been unstoppable."

A gasp of horror rang around the lobby as parents clasped their children tightly.

"It is thought that he lured Mr. Holt to the school with the objective of offering him a significant amount of credits taken from the school budget in exchange for use of the technology. When Mr. Holt refused, he was murdered. It is therefore paramount that Jarvis is remembered as the hero that he truly was, protecting that which we find most precious even at the cost of his own life.

"Now, despite the dark circumstances that have surrounded the school this year, the board of Governors and I have decided that The Academy should remain open and that term will resume as normal in September. We feel it would be unjust to allow the actions of one twisted individual to ruin the chance the more- able children to experience the excellent education the school provides. I have appointed Miss. Fortem as Headmistress, a position which she will formally accept following a thorough check on her person, and have set up regular inspections at the school to guarantee its pupil's safety in the future.

"Continuing on a positive note, it is now that I would like to give a special thanks to my daughter, Lois Sommers and her friends, William James, Emilia Pannell and Finley Campbell. In case you were not aware, it was these four students who unravelled Allance's true identity, and it was only through their bravery and initiative that he was stopped before he could put his terrible plan into action. It is remarkable that these young teenagers could face down such an incredible adversary and win at their tender age. More impressive than this is that they all managed to pass their academic year, with Mr. Campbell achieving one of the highest grades in the entire year group. As special congratulations and as a show of our gratitude, I have decided to elevate the Campbell family to Floor Two, offering Finley's father the prestigious position of Governor of Maintenance."

Will looked over with jubilance at Finley, who was staring open-mouthed at the screen, unable to believe what he was hearing. His mother and father were crying with happiness, while his younger sister shrieked and hugged her stunned older siblings.

"I conclude my address today by making a promise to you all that we will go above and beyond to ensure the safety of every innocent passenger aboard this ship. Any and all Vacuous found hiding amongst our population will be punished with the severest consequences and we will not rest until we are certain they have all been discovered. In the meantime, I urge my citizens to be vigilant and to immediately report anything suspicious to a member of Security, no matter how small it may seem. We are only powerful when we work together. Thank you for your time."

The screen turned to black and the lobby erupted into a roar of loud discussion about the announcement. Passers-by stopped on their way towards the lifts to point and stare at Will and his friends, causing a number of Guards to rush over and form a wall around them, urging the spectators to move on. The four of them converged into a huddle, congratulating a shell-shocked Finley on his promising new status.

"I don't feel like I deserve it," he said, shaking his head in disbelief. "Lois, please thank your father for me. I don't know how I can ever repay him."

"You don't need to repay him, you earnt it!" Lois replied. "You're the one who went to see Allance and worked the whole thing out."

"Well, only because he basically told me he was an alien. If you hadn't all shown up, I'd be dead. Besides, Will's really the one who stopped him," Finley blushed.

"Me? No way!" Will argued. "All I did was chase him through Space and shout at him a bit. I wouldn't have been able to do anything without all your help, especially Emily fixing that radio."

"It wasn't that hard," Emily said bashfully, though she looked extremely pleased to have been complimented.

"You all did brilliantly," Lois told them sincerely. "Who knows what would have happened if Allance wasn't stopped."

"You were brilliant too, Lois," Finley reminded her. "Streaming Allance's confession to your dad was a fantastic idea."

"We make a good team," Will concluded and the four of them smiled warmly at each other, lost in a moment of silent comradery.

"I can't believe Holt is dead..." Emily said, turning the tone of the conversation sour.

"I know," Lois said sadly. "He was such a kind man."

The four of them bowed their heads as they reflected on the hideous crime Allance had committed.

"Do you think I'll still get my work experience at I-Tech?" Emily wondered.

"Emily!" Will scolded her.

"What?" she replied indignantly. "I was just asking..."

"We'll still see each other over the holidays, won't we?" Lois implored. "No matter what happens?"

"Of course," Finley beamed.

"Promise?" Lois pressed them.

"Promise," they all agreed in unison.

"Now Finley," Will said, placing an arm around his shoulders. "Let's go and have a look at your new apartment. I have to tell you though if it's nicer than mine I'll have no choice but to hate you for the rest of my life."

"I understand," Finley laughed and the four of them walked off together, united in a bond they felt absolutely certain would last forever.

11000775R00125

Printed in Great Britain
by Amazon